# THE
# RAVENOUS
# DEAD

## Darcy Coates

Poisoned Pen
PRESS

Published by Poisoned Pen Press, an imprint of Sourcebooks
P.O. Box 4410, Naperville, Illinois 60567-4410
(630) 961-3900
sourcebooks.com

Library of Congress Cataloging-in-Publication Data

Names: Coates, Darcy, author.
Title: The ravenous dead / Darcy Coates.
Description: Naperville, Illinois : Poisoned Pen Press, [2022] | Series:
  Gravekeeper ; 2
Identifiers: LCCN 2021049980 | (trade paperback)
Subjects: GSAFD: Horror fiction.
Classification: LCC PR9619.4.C628 R38 2022 | DDC 823/.92--dc23
LC record available at https://lccn.loc.gov/2021049980

Printed and bound in the United States of America.
VP 10 9 8 7 6 5 4

# CHAPTER 1

"YOU'VE BEEN DEAD FOR a long time."

Keira's hair stuck to her face, drenched by the thick fog that rolled through the barely lit landscape. Each word came out as a cloud of condensation as she breathed in the near-freezing air. It was before dawn, and Keira struggled to see the ground ahead of her feet.

Gravestones surrounded her. Some were less than a decade old, but others had been there for centuries, giving them time to crack and tilt and sink into the earth. They were all neglected. Weeds and long grass choked the ground between them. Lichen grew across the slabs, blotting out names and dates.

An immense figure lingered to Keira's left, half-hidden by the heavy mist: a stone-carved angel, its wings sagging and its hands clasped under its chin in supplication. Age had stained it. Lines ran over its draped gown, showing where decades of water had flowed. They created tracks running from its eyes to its chin, as though it wept.

Keira shivered, drawing further into her jacket, her numb fingers clenched in her pockets. She faced a small, square grave marker. The inscription read *Marianne Cobb, 1801–1835*.

"Nearly two hundred years. It's a long time to linger after death," Keira said. Each breath of condensation merged into the mist, swallowed into the mass within seconds.

A shape swayed at the edge of her vision. Keira strained to see it more clearly, but she only caught glimpses. Curling, frayed hair, pinned into a messy arrangement underneath some kind of shawl. Bony hands wringing together. The woman hunched, keeping the gravestone between herself and Keira, her eyes averted.

She was a ghost. A faint one. Gone for more than a hundred and eighty years but still present. Still waiting. For what, Keira didn't know. That was her job now: to find out.

"I hope it's not rude to point that out." Keira tried for a smile and an easy shrug, even as a drop of condensation ran down to her chin and dripped onto her jacket. "I'm still new to this. Sorry."

She thought the spirit tilted toward her a fraction, but it was hard to be sure through the mist. The ghosts seemed to be made up of the same fog that permanently lingered in the graveyard. They were a see-through, vacant white, their eyes turned a heavy, inky black. Every movement was slowed, as though they were trapped underwater. As the spirit's head moved, so did stray strands of hair—floating behind it, tugged by an invisible current.

She didn't think it was her imagination that the spirits of Blighty Cemetery were avoiding her. They watched from a distance sometimes, but almost all vanished when she turned toward them.

Condensed mist trickled down Keira's back like an other-worldly finger tracing her spine. She shuddered, hunching her shoulders further. She thought she must be nearing the grounds-keeper's cottage. Some of the markers looked familiar.

Keira circled a tree, running her hand across the damp, cracked bark as she passed it. Her view ahead momentarily cleared and she glimpsed an elderly woman in elaborate Victorian dress. Keira dipped her head politely as she approached. "Hello!"

Unlike Marianne, this spirit was crisp and bright. She seemed to glow like a light through the fog. Her wrinkled, angular face didn't even turn toward Keira, but her eyes narrowed as she lifted her cane and strode through a magnificent headstone. She didn't come out the other side.

"All right, cool, we'll catch up another time." Keira rubbed wet palms on her jeans. *Am I imagining it, or are these ghosts being kind of…picky? I mean, I know I'm new at this, but it's not like spirit mediums come through here every week.*

Then, ahead, she caught a flash of motion. A spirit's hand waved at her. Keira's heart lifted and a smile grew as she length-ened her gait. "Good morning—"

A beaming man emerged from between two headstones. He was plump, middle-aged, mostly bald, and completely naked.

"Oh. Okay." Keira cleared her throat and held up a hand to block her view of his lower half. "Well, hi, it's nice to meet you?"

Dimples puckered his cheeks as he waved both hands. Unlike Keira, he had no compunction about his state of undress. He was friendly at least, so Keira kept her eyes fixed on his face as she moved nearer. "Which grave's yours?"

He patted the top of a waist-high slab. Flakes of frost spread over the stone where he touched it. Keira leaned forward to read the epigraph. "Tony Lobell, huh? Nice to meet you."

The stone said he'd passed away in 1998, age fifty-two, making him the most recent ghost she'd met. Even though he was recent, his grave was untended, with weeds growing over the mound. A small metal holder had been attached to the headstone, but if it had ever held flowers, they'd long since decayed. That struck Keira as deeply melancholy, but the grave's state wasn't unusual. Only a handful showed any sign of human care.

Keira tried to keep the sadness out of her voice. "Do you have unfinished business keeping you here?"

Tony shrugged. The motion jiggled his belly, revealing more than Keira would have liked. She quickly repositioned her hand. "You're not sure?"

He tapped the side of his head and gave her a what-can-you-do kind of smile.

"Oh, you can't remember?"

A shake.

"Nothing at all? No…important messages you want passed on or anything?"

Another helpless shrug.

"Right. I'll see if there's anything I can do to help anyway. I'm staying in the cottage, and you'll probably see me around a fair bit, so you know how to find me if you remember something. I'd better keep moving, but thanks for talking with me, Tony."

He beamed and waved, and Keira couldn't help but match his infectious smile as she shuffled past him.

The strain of keeping the ghosts in sight created a throbbing headache that radiated through her skull. The skill seemed to get easier with practice, but she didn't think she could hold on to the second sight for much longer.

*One more introduction, then I'll call it a day.*

A pale spirit stood near the forest's edge, not far from her cottage. His old, well-mended traveling coat moved in a breeze Keira couldn't feel. He faced away from her, staring into the trees.

"Hi," she said as she neared him. "I don't know if you heard me earlier, but my name's Keira."

The specter didn't respond. His arms hung limp at his sides. He seemed to sway lightly, but it was hard to be sure when his form was so heavily disguised by the flowing fog. He stood on a grave—*his* grave, Keira guessed—with a small, discreet headstone at his side.

Keira kept her distance as she circled him. "How long have you been—?"

Her words died as she stopped ahead of the man. He wore old, tattered clothes that looked at least a hundred years old. Weeds grew high around his legs, their tips white with frost. And his face…

He didn't *have* a face. The space between his temples and his chin had been carved away, hollowed out, as though it had been hacked at with an ax. No eyes, no mouth, just a gaping hole that extended deep into his head. Keira swallowed and abruptly looked away. She felt as though if she stared into that pit of flesh for too long, she would be in danger of falling into the chasm.

"Okay. Sorry, I didn't expect…" She swallowed again and hazarded another look. "Um, can you hear me? Can you raise your hand if you understand me?"

The faceless spirit didn't move except to sway, his patched coat twisting around his ankles, his hair, overdue for a cut, floating as though weightless. His ears were still intact, Keira saw. He should be able to hear her. He just wasn't responding.

She looked at the stone at his side. There was no name, only a date: *November 15, 1891.* Keira frowned. "That's strange. I've never seen a stone without a name before."

The spirit seemed to shiver, then his form melted away like an illusion, leaving Keira standing alone beside the grave site.

Heavy steps crackled through the frost. Keira turned. A dark figure wove toward her. She recognized the silhouette: Adage, the church's pastor. Keira tried to shake free from the unease the faceless spirit had created and jogged to meet the pastor halfway.

Adage was swaddled in a greatcoat that bunched around his chin, with hints of his favored cardigan visible underneath. He removed his condensation-glazed spectacles and wiped them on his sleeve. "What a morning. How are you feeling today, child?"

"Pretty good, everything considered." Keira shrugged, and a twinge of pain in her arm reminded her she still had stitches holding a gash together. It had been barely thirty-six hours since she'd had to defend herself again Gavin Kelsey in the nearby stream, but it felt much longer than that, even though she'd slept through most of the previous day.

The pastor replaced his glasses, blinking rapidly as the lenses began to fog again. "Your overly cautious would-be doctor says you're supposed to be resting."

"I'll have to apologize to Mason later. I'm too excited to do nothing."

"I had wondered if you'd made a start already." Adage nodded at the stones surrounding them. "Have you been able to…make contact? Is that the correct term?"

Adage alone knew about Keira's ability to see the dead. He'd offered her a home in Blighty, occupying the abandoned grounds-keeper's cottage and with a small weekly wage in return for her helping the ghosts move over to the next life.

"You probably know the lingo better than I do. But yeah, I've been able to talk to a few of the ghosts here. There's not much I can do right now when they can't talk back, but I want to at least meet everyone and learn their names." Keira turned to the stone behind them. "On that subject, I don't suppose you'd know who this is? His grave doesn't say."

"I'm afraid I don't. We have a map of the graveyard in the church; I'm sure that would have the name marked. Which is convenient, since I have something else I'd like to discuss with you, and I'd prefer to do it somewhere a little less humid."

Adage had retained his sense of direction better than Keira

and led them toward the parsonage. Keira reached for the aching muscle behind her eyes and opened her second sight a final time. The spirits blinked into view: vague, swirling shapes interspersed between the darker headstones.

Adage thrust his hands into his pockets. "It's early days, I know, but have you learned anything about our resident spirits?"

They were passing Tony Lobell. He pretended to sit on his headstone, legs crossed and hands resting on the top knee as he hovered half an inch above the stone. He gave her an overly formal nod as she passed, then broke into a broad grin.

Keira cleared her throat. "Well, it looks like spirits wear whatever clothing they died in. Including no clothing at all."

"Remarkable." Adage's look of curiosity morphed into one of concern. "Perhaps I should start wearing bathing suits into the shower. Just in case."

Keira laughed. They passed through a gap in the hedge that divided the graveyard from the parsonage. The air seemed a degree warmer and the mist a fraction lighter. Adage set a brisk pace, and Keira matched it as he led her past his house and toward the modest stone church near the main road. He unbolted the main doors and stepped back to let Keira through.

She hadn't been inside the church before. A series of large stained-glass windows were positioned above the wooden pews, each one depicting a biblical story.

"You should see it on a sunny day," Adage said, shedding his coat and hanging it on a hook beside the door. "It rains color. This way."

She followed him to the front of the room, past the lectern, and through the door hidden behind a curtain. Unlike the classic charm of the main hall, the back rooms were small, cozy, and arranged like offices. Desks and filing cabinets cluttered all available space, and corkboards were overflowing with timetables and lists. Adage wove through the mess with practiced ease, and Keira followed, pressing her arms to her sides in an effort to avoid bumping anything important.

He stopped in the last room and opened a filling cabinet, riffling through the papers and muttering under his breath until he pulled out a thick, yellowed sheet. "Here we are. It's nothing fancy, but it's been maintained by every pastor since the church was built." He unfolded the paper onto a desk.

Keira bent close. The shapes and words were hand-drawn with what looked like many decades of ink.

"Here's the parsonage." Adage indicated a faded shape. "The groundskeeper's cottage." A smaller square near the paper's edge. "And all the graves." Hundreds of tiny rectangles and equally tiny names and dates were scattered over the map.

Keira brushed her hair out of her face as she leaned over the markings. The smell of dust and old parchment filled her nose. She mentally followed the path to the nameless stone and traced it along the map, eventually arriving at an old ink rectangle. It had the right date—November 15, 1891—but instead of a name, all it said was *Unknown*.

"Huh."

Adage frowned as he bent closer to the map. "That *is* strange.

Perhaps it belongs to an infant that passed before it could be named? But then why isn't the family name listed—"

"It's a man," Keira said. "In his thirties or forties, if I had to guess. He's missing his face."

Adage exhaled heavily and his shoulders sagged. "I'm afraid I can't be much help, then. I don't spend very much time among the graves."

"Well, that's my job now. I'll figure something out."

"Talking about jobs…" Adage lifted the map, tucked it under his arm, and beckoned for Keira to follow him. "I've been giving it some thought. People in town will want to know why you're staying here, and there's no easy way to explain that I hired you to speak to the ghosts."

Keira pulled a face. She'd been in Blighty for less than a week, but it had already impressed her as one of the world's nosiest towns. She'd need to come up with an explanation for her presence if she was going to stay for any length of time.

"I have a bit of a plan." Adage stopped beside an ancient photocopy machine. The map was too large to fit on the glass, so he positioned the top corner and fiddled with the settings. A clattering, clunking noise filled the room. Adage had to raise his voice to be heard over it. "We'll tell people you're my niece. You wanted to spend some time in the country, so I hired you to tend the graveyard. No one could say that it's not needed."

Keira nodded. "That's perfect. It also gives me an excuse to spend time in the cemetery."

Adage adjusted the map to print another corner. The racket

resumed. "It also allows you to leave on short notice if you ever need to—we can just say your family wanted you home. The only issue will be whether that conflicts with what you've told others in town. How many people know your actual circumstances?"

"Not many. It's more than a little awkward to tell people you woke up in a forest with no memories. The only ones who know are Mason and Zoe."

"Good." Another page shot into the tray, and Adage adjusted the map a final time. "Mason's a good boy. And as unlikely as this sounds, Zoe is actually quite good at keeping secrets when she needs to."

The machine finally powered down. Adage took the yellowed map out and folded it carefully, then handed the four printed pages to Keira. "I can't give you the original, I'm afraid, but hopefully these will help."

"Definitely. Thank you."

Adage indicated to the hallway that led back to the hall. "Anytime, Keira. I hope you'll join me for dinner tonight. I'm cooking pork, and my fridge is too full for leftovers."

"I'd love to." That left Keira with most of the day free, and she already had an idea of how to spend it. Blighty was the kind of town that held on to records of its history. She might not have a name for the faceless ghost, but she did have one clue to pursue: his date of death.

# CHAPTER 2

KEIRA BLINKED AS SHE stepped out of the church. The day was overcast, but the sun had risen enough to add a layer of glare. The light that came through the clouds seemed to reflect off the mist.

She held the maps to her chest as she followed the path back to the groundskeeper's cottage. The papers would make her job infinitely easier; she could highlight the graves that had spirits attached and keep notes.

Except for her new John Doe. She chewed on the inside of her cheek. *It can't be pleasant to be trapped like that, but there's not much I can do if I don't know anything about him. How can I get a name? His death was so long ago that I doubt many people would remember it. I could ask Zoe…*

Zoe, urban legend fanatic and conspiracy theorist, might be able to help. An unnamed grave would appeal to her curious nature. But Keira was also wary of relying on Zoe too much.

There were limits to the questions she could ask about the town's dead without making Zoe suspicious. Only Adage knew about her unnatural ability to see the dead, and she doubted many other people could take the news in stride like he had.

Faint chatter floated through the fog, and Keira squinted toward her cottage. Two shapes waited by the low stone fence that circled the dead garden. Even through the veiling effects of the haze, she recognized them. The taller figure's long coat and dark-brown hair couldn't belong to anyone except Mason, and Zoe's voice was unmistakable.

They seemed to be arguing. Zoe waved her arms in exaggerated arcs. As Keira drew closer, she saw Mason's face held the grim, helpless expression of a man who had explained a simple concept five times and couldn't endure much more. Keira quickened her pace to a jog.

"Well, *obviously* that's what they want you to think," Zoe cried. "If they did it through more conventional means, people would start to suspect them!"

Mason clasped his hands together. "I'm just saying—if people are having their minds erased, why have we never noticed?"

"Because you've been brainwashed to think you're not brainwashed!"

"Hey!" Keira called as she neared them.

Relief flooded Mason's face. "Oh, thank goodness. I don't think I could have taken much more."

"Just because you can't handle the truth—"

Mason pinched the bridge of his nose, his eyes closed in a

grimace. "She thinks the government is putting subliminal messaging in contrails. It's like she took two normal conspiracies and smashed them together into one awful, mutated frankenspiracy."

"You can't win this argument with wordplay." Zoe threaded an arm through Keira's and began leading her toward the cottage. "Come on, Keira. You and I can discuss theories later, once we're away from the guy who thinks facts are more important than dramatic flair."

Keira matched Zoe's pace as they wove through the dead yard. "Sorry for making you wait. I was just with Adage."

"No problem." Mason's expression relaxed. "How are you doing today? Other than ignoring my recommendation to rest?"

As Keira pushed the cottage's door open, Daisy shot between her legs and frisked toward the fireplace. Keira hadn't even seen her hiding in the garden; she could swear the cat was more shadow than feline.

"I slept for an entire day," she said, laughing. "That's too much rest for me. What can I get you to drink? Tea? Coffee?"

"Tea, thanks," Mason said, followed by Zoe's, "Anything, as long as it doesn't have chemicals in it."

"I'm pretty sure *everything* is chemicals technically." Keira waved her friends toward the seats by the fire. "But I think I saw some organic tea in the cupboards. Can we compromise with that?"

Zoe ignored the chair she'd been offered and moseyed into the kitchen area. She began opening cabinets and examining their contents. "No word from Dane, by the way. No police reports. No gossip about people trespassing on his yard. I guess that's the benefit of harassing a hermit; they don't have any friends to complain to."

Keira cringed. Two days before, she'd ventured onto the sprawling estate owned by the town's wealthiest family in an attempt to help a spirit with unfinished business. Only, her intrusion hadn't gone unnoticed. The memory of being chased through the woods by the reclusive Crispin heir was still fresh in her mind. "Sorry about what happened. I never wanted to put either of you in danger. I didn't realize he'd go...*feral* like that."

"Eh." Zoe peered into the cupboards beneath the sink. "Blighty's options for fun are limited. I'll take what I can get. Hey, where's your toaster?"

"I don't have one yet." Keira had inherited the cottage and all its furnishings from the previous groundskeeper, who had left her a working stove and kettle but apparently hadn't seen the need for certain other appliances, including a fridge.

Zoe looked more concerned than Keira thought the situation warranted. "Seriously? You've gotta fix that. I can bring you one from the general store."

"Don't worry about that. I'll buy one later."

"All right." Zoe sounded skeptical but retrieved a box of Danish pastries from her pocket, popped it open, and shook it out for Keira to take one. "You know I'd never judge you, but I'm worried about what *other* people will think if they find out you don't have a toaster."

Keira snorted to disguise her laughter as she chewed. The kettle was close to boiling, so she began setting out mugs. Mason motioned her toward the fireplace and patted one of the seats. "Can I borrow you for a moment? I'd like to check your arm. Zoe can make the drinks."

"Zoe *can* make the drinks," Zoe muttered under her breath. "But *will* Zoe make the drinks?"

Keira obediently sat. Daisy appeared out of the shadows and leaped onto her lap and curled into a softly purring ball as Mason pulled up his own chair. He opened his medical case and began sifting through the contents. "No fever? Dizzy spells? Stiffness or swelling?"

"I bet she's experiencing a pain in the neck," Zoe called from the kitchen.

Mason ignored her.

"No problems at all. I don't really feel it unless I try to lift things." Keira watched as the bandages came away. She had two stitched cuts. The first had come from the night she arrived in Blighty: she'd woken in the forest with no memories but a cut on her head and a gash on her arm. Those—along with her clothes, a small amount of money, and an old photograph—were the only clues she had of her past life. Those, and a glimpse of shadowy men hunting her through the forest.

The more recent injury had come from Gavin Kelsey, the local doctor's son. She'd made the mistake of rubbing him the wrong way shortly after her arrival, and he'd turned out to be trouble. She was fairly sure she'd frightened him enough that he wouldn't bother her again…but that didn't mean she was rid of him. She'd caught a glimpse inside his mind when they'd fought. He'd killed a man years before. There was a good chance he'd try it again someday. And Keira still wasn't sure how she could bring the town's notice to their secret killer when his first murder had, from all perspectives, seemed like an accident.

Despite that, she figured she was lucky, all things considered.

Mason's eyebrows knit together as he examined the mark. Then he turned back to his kit and began hunting through the equipment. "Could be worse. I'll just clean it and redress it. The stitches will need to stay in for another few days."

The kettle clicked off, and Zoe began splashing water into mugs with a little more enthusiasm than Keira thought it warranted. "On the subject of recluses and stitches…you wanna tell us what happened?"

"Oh. Yeah, of course." Memories resurfaced: escaping from Dane Crispin, hiding in the mill, discovering the room where Emma Carthage's child had perished, calling the constable, getting jumped by Gavin, and finally releasing Emma's spirit. It had been a chaotic night, and all of it needed to stay a secret. "Sorry for disappearing. My phone died. I led Dane into the woods a little way, then hid for the rest of the night before coming home."

"And the new scar?" Zoe waved the kettle toward Keira, inadvertently spilling water over the wooden floor. "I bet there's a story behind that."

She'd already lied to Mason about the cut's origin. It was a terrible excuse, but she was committed. "You know how people tell you not to run with scissors? Well, there are no scissors in this story, but I *was* running with a knife."

"Please don't try to tell me you tripped." Zoe's deadpan glare warned that the excuse wouldn't fly, but there was no turning back.

"Bingo." She returned Zoe's eye roll with a smile. "Pure bad luck. All the wrong stars aligned, etc. By the way—"

"Don't change the subject."

She stubbornly forged ahead. "*By the way*, I have some good news. Adage is letting me stay here."

"He is?" Mason looked up from bandaging her arm. Some of the tension he seemed to carry in his shoulders melted away. "That's good. That's really good."

Zoe brought the mugs over and put them on the small table between the seats. Her owlish eyes narrowed suspiciously as she glared back and forth between Keira and Mason. "Why's that good news? I thought it was a given."

*Oh. Crap.* Keira had forgotten that Zoe didn't know. She licked her lips. "Well, uh, Adage had found me a job in another town. I was supposed to leave for it yesterday."

"Yesterday?" Zoe's eyes reduced to slits. "And you were planning to tell me *when*?"

"I tried to. But it came up so suddenly, and then there was that incident with Gavin in the store, and—"

"Uh-huh." Zoe folded her arms. "Just so you know, you're the worst best friend I've ever had."

"Worst… Hang on." Keira grinned. "We're best friends now?"

Zoe collapsed into a chair, flipping her dark hair out of her face. "We've got to be, right? I know you don't have any other friends except the plaguemonger here"—she poked at Mason's knee with her sneaker—"and honestly, there's no way anyone would pick him over me. Ergo, best friends. *Forever.*"

Keira's laughter shook Daisy awake. The cat stretched, arching her back, and rolled too close to the edge of her lap. Keira grabbed for her but, with one arm held still by Mason, was too slow to stop Daisy from tumbling to the floor. The cat lay in an awkward pile at Keira's feet, opened her mouth in a brief, silent meow, then stretched and went back to sleep.

"Don't take this personally." Zoe scratched her chin. "But I think your cat might be broken."

Keira gave her pet a tight-lipped smile. "I like to imagine she's a genius, but just…really good at hiding it." Faint purrs rumbled from the floppy black feline, and it was impossible to keep the fondness out of her voice.

Zoe reached down to scratch the creature's belly. "Sweet Daisy. Good little Daze."

"No." Keira filled her voice with mock indignation. "Don't you dare call my cat that."

Mason hid his face, but his voice was full of laughter. "It *does* suit her. And Daisy doesn't have many other options for abbreviations…"

"We are *not* calling my cat Daze." Keira bit her lip as she watched the rumpled, undersize feline twist itself into a new configuration. "But I am glad I get to keep her."

"You're staying permanently, then?" Mason finished his work and closed his kit.

"Sort of. I mean, if those people are still looking for me, I might have to move on again. But I haven't heard any whispers about them since that night I woke up. What about you, Zoe?"

"Nothing." Zoe leaned back and kicked her feet toward the fire. "And literally every juicy bit of gossip filters past me in that convenience store. If there were strangers in town, I'd know about it."

"That's good. Adage came up with an alibi for me too. I'm his niece from out of town. I'll be the new groundskeeper for the graveyard." She rubbed at the back of her neck. "It's probably best not to tell anyone about the lost memories or the shady origin. Not yet anyway."

"Of course," Mason said. Zoe mimed zipping her lips. Keira felt a rush of fondness for the pair of them.

The clock on the mantel chimed ten. Zoe blinked at it, then swore and bolted out of her chair. "I shouldn't have sat so long. I'm supposed to be on shift at the store."

Keira stood and retrieved her discarded jacket. "Can I walk with you? I wanted to go into town today anyway."

"It's going to be less of a walk and more of a crazy run." Zoe was already halfway to the door, drinks forgotten. "But you're welcome to get gross and sweaty with me."

Keira glanced at Mason to check whether her stitches could stand up to some exercise, and he nodded. "Gross and sweaty sounds fun. Let's go."

# CHAPTER 3

ZOE SET THE PACE. She'd promised a mad run, but they quickly settled into a steady jog. Keira tied her jacket around her waist and matched the speed easily. After spending the previous day in bed, it felt good to stretch her legs.

Mason flanked her other side, breathing deeply but not gasping like Zoe. Keira was just getting comfortable with the pace when Zoe stumbled to a halt. "Sorry." She spoke between wheezing breaths. "So unfit. Gym membership doesn't work…if you never attend…"

Keira patted her back. "Take it easy. We can walk from here."

They were close to the junction where the church's driveway joined the main road leading into Blighty. The sign advertising the cemetery was barely visible between the trees.

"Oh boy." Zoe straightened and ran her fingers through her hair to get it out of her face. "My boss said she was going to fire me if I was late again. I mean, she's been saying that for years, but she might actually go through with it one of these days."

"I can be your alibi if you need one," Keira offered. "Tell her I saw a flying saucer and needed your professional opinion or something."

Mason added, "I'm not qualified, but I can forge a pretty convincing doctor's note."

Zoe snickered. "Thanks. If I'm lucky, she'll have slept in and won't even notice I was missing."

The rest of the walk was surprisingly relaxing. Keira and Mason chatted while Zoe focused on breathing. They followed the bend onto the main cobble road and approached the fountain in the center of the small cluster of shops. Blighty had struck Keira as a sleepy kind of town. True to form, there was barely anyone on the roads, except for a crowd gathered outside the convenience store.

Zoe whooped. "She overslept! Today's my lucky day. Catch you two later." With a wave, she resumed her jog while pulling a ring of keys out of her bag. The shoppers set up an irate murmur as Zoe forced her way between them to reach the doors.

Keira waited until her friend was indoors, then turned to Mason. "What're your plans for today?"

"Nothing exciting." He shrugged. "I promised a neighbor I'd help her with her garden. Arthritis makes it hard for her to kneel."

An idea struck Keira. "Since I'm going to be staying in the cottage for a while, I was thinking I could fix up my own garden a bit. Or make it a little less dead at least. If you see some nice plants, could you get me some clippings?"

"Absolutely. Any preferences?"

Keira opened her mouth to answer, but her mind hit a wall. If she'd had a favorite type of plant before arriving at Blighty, that knowledge had been lost with the rest of her memories. She cleared her throat. "Dealer's choice."

"All right." He glanced along the main street. The sun had finally broken through the persistent clouds and glinted off the shingled roofs. "What are your plans in town, if you don't mind me asking?"

"I was hoping Blighty had a library."

"Oh!" Mason looked happy. "That's a good idea actually. Reading could help jog some of the lost memories. And you're in luck—we do have a library. It's just past the café. Can I walk you?"

"Thanks, but I've been distracting you long enough. Your neighbor's garden won't weed itself."

He laughed and turned to the crossroad that led into the residential areas. "All right. Let's catch up for a coffee later."

"I'd like that."

Keira watched him until he disappeared down one of the side roads, then turned toward the café. Her motives for finding a library were a little different from what Mason had assumed, and she couldn't answer any of the awkward questions her task might prompt.

She found the stone library down the road from the café. Based on the large display windows, Keira guessed it might have been some kind of retail store before being converted. Now, though, the windows showcased an assortment of well-loved, dog-eared books, plus a handful of fresher offerings that she assumed were new releases.

Rusty hinges creaked as she pushed on the door. The atmosphere was cool and dusty, and the lighting was muted despite the massive window. The area didn't seem large, but what space there was had been crammed with ceiling-height bookcases. The shelves were pressed so closely together that they bordered on claustrophobic. Keira liked it. It felt like the kind of place you could lose yourself in for hours.

She made for the reception desk, where a middle-aged woman was working on a book of crosswords. She looked up as Keira neared and a gentle smile grew over her face. "Morning. Haven't seen you before."

"Uh, no, I'm new here." Keira rubbed sweaty palms on her jeans. Lying never sat well with her, despite how often she found herself resorting to it. "I'm Adage's niece. Keira. I'll be staying with him for a while."

"Hmm. Didn't think he had a niece."

Keira dreaded follow-up questions, but the librarian only closed her book of puzzles and stretched.

"I suppose you'd like a library card, love?"

Her voice was slow and deep and smooth, as though soothing anxious patrons was a part of her job description. Keira figured she'd look suspicious if she declined, so she said, "Sure."

"I'm Hanna, by the way." She took a clipboard out of the drawer and passed it to Keira. "Fill that out. I make the cards myself. You can pick yours up tomorrow if you like."

Keira chewed her lip as she struggled with the form. She didn't have a proper address, so she wrote, *Groundskeeper Cottage, Blighty Cemetery.* Her phone was a loan from Zoe, and Keira didn't feel comfortable putting her friend's number down. Her date of birth was a mystery. She didn't have a surname either, so she hoped Adage wouldn't mind her borrowing his. Hanna didn't bat an eyelid as she took the form back.

"Go ahead and check out some books, if you like. I'll remember you."

"Um, actually, I was hoping to learn some history about Blighty."

Hanna shifted out of her chair, the unflappable, gentle smile still in place. "We do have some history books. I'll show you."

"Do you have any newspapers?" She prayed it wouldn't sound like an odd request. "Old newspapers, I mean?"

Hanna blinked slowly. "Of course, yes, we had our archives scanned a few years ago. This way."

Keira cheered silently. She waited as Hanna set up the machine and showed her how to use it, then pretended to sort through random dates until the librarian returned to the front desk and reopened her book of crosswords.

She didn't have a name for the hollow-faced man in the cemetery, but she did have two clues: a death date and the way his faced seemed to have been carved away. Keira was almost certain he'd been murdered, and in a town as sleepy as Blighty, that would make him extremely newsworthy.

The papers were weekly, so Keira went for the edition

following the faceless man's death. The paper was discolored and the scanning process had left it grainy, but a thrill of triumph coursed through her at the headline: **MAN MURDERED**.

A photograph showed policemen in late-nineteenth-century uniforms clustered around the base of a small tree. Keira squinted through the distortion and enlarged the image. She thought she could see a flash of pale skin between the policemen's legs.

She skimmed the article quickly, then reread it at a slower pace to make sure she hadn't missed anything. The phrase "unknown man" was repeated through the story multiple times.

*At least this confirms why his grave marker doesn't have a name. He wasn't from town and no one knew who he was.*

The man had been found early in the morning by a farmer. He had been strangled and stabbed multiple times and left under a tree near the outskirts of town. Police were asking for witnesses to come forward. No arrests had been made yet.

Keira moved to the following week's paper. John Doe was no longer the top story, but Keira found an article about him on the third page. The killer still hadn't been located. The police complained about the crime scene being contaminated; because it was just off a main road, it was apparently hard to know if pieces of evidence came from the man's death or from casual passersby in the days before. Keira read the story carefully, but there was very little new information. The coroner had concluded that the man had died at the scene—rather than his body being dumped there—sometime between three and five in the morning. His body was being stored for viewing in case anyone could recognize him, but there were still no leads to his identity or that of his killer.

"Come on." Keira blew out a breath and moved to the following newspaper. It only had a small, token article. No leads. More requests for witnesses. She kept moving, hoping the mystery might have been solved sometime later—perhaps the man's name had been uncovered, but no one bothered to carve it on the gravestone—but the last update was to announce the man's funeral after two months of no leads. Keira scanned through nearly a year's worth of papers following that, but nothing significant occurred.

Keira stretched. As the day neared lunchtime, more visitors had joined her in the library. The quiet creaks of shifting chairs and the shuffle of books being pulled off shelves created a gentle background hum. It was making her sleepy.

She glanced over her shoulder just in time to catch Hanna watching her. The librarian quickly looked back at her crosswords. *I've been here too long. She's getting curious.*

Keira went back to the first newspaper, the one announcing the body's discovery, and squinted at the picture again. The flash of skin between the officers unnerved her. She scanned the environment. Not much was visible; the edge of the dirt road took up the lower-left corner. A farmhouse was visible in the distance to the right. Behind the gaggle of officers was a small tree—Keira couldn't see the leaves well, but she guessed it might be an oak or something similar. The rest of the picture was either grass or distant woods.

It wasn't much to go on, but she had the street name—Farrier—and knew the crime had happened on the outskirts of town. Keira exited the papers, shut the machine down, and went back to the reception desk.

"Thanks," she said to Hanna, and earned a sleepy smile in response. "I'll pick up that card tomorrow."

"Lovely, looking forward to it."

Keira left the library, glanced each way down the street, then returned to the crossroads marked by the fountain. The street sign wasn't easy to find. A tree had grown up around it, half swallowing the names in thick leaves.

A spark of surprise ran down her spine as she glanced toward where the faded yellow sign pointed. She already knew Farrier Street: it led toward Dane Crispin's house.

# CHAPTER 4

THE TOWN CENTER WAS so small that it only took Keira a couple of minutes to walk through it. Farrier Street was lined with cozy residential homes that soon gave way to farmland and empty acreage. Keira, realizing she'd gone too far, stopped and backtracked.

The landscape had changed a lot in the time between the hollow-faced man's death and that afternoon. What had once been cleared land had since been left to nature, and the ground was peppered with bushes and small trees. Keira walked up and down the path twice before stopping in front of a dead stump six feet from the road.

*Maybe…?*

She stepped back and scanned the environment. The stump was close to the street. Newer houses had been constructed behind it, but when she peered between those she caught a glimpse of an older farmhouse. It had been repainted and expanded since the photograph, but the structure was still familiar.

She looked back at the stump. *This is it. This is the small tree from the photograph. This is where he died.*

While trying to save Emma Carthage, Keira had discovered she had the ability to glimpse a person's last moments by touching something tied to the place where they died. For Frank Crispin, Emma's fiancé, that had been the chair he'd stood on to hang himself. For Emma herself, it was the memorial tree planted at her murder site.

Keira flexed her fingers, braced herself, and closed her eyes as she reached toward the stump. Her hand touched cool wood and found traces of dying moss. She waited, but her mind remained dark.

She squinted one eye open. Nothing had changed. She shifted her hand over the tree's remains, touching different parts of the stump, and eventually dropped to her knees to pat at patches of exposed earth. When that didn't help, Keira rocked back on her heels.

"Well." She dusted her hands on her jeans. "That was anticlimactic."

*This has to be the right place—there's nowhere else that could match. Is it because the tree's dead? Is there a time limit on this sort of thing?*

"Nice mornin'," called a croaky voice.

Keira jumped. A man, led by a leashed Doberman, walked along the lane. He nodded politely.

Keira managed a weak smile as the stranger passed. She couldn't imagine what sort of impression she made, kneeling by the side of the road and staring at a dead stump with furious intensity. Heat rushed over her face as she quickly stood and turned back toward town.

*So, not my best day. I've spent hours on John Doe but haven't learned anything I didn't already know—or at least suspect: He was murdered. He wasn't from town. His killer wasn't caught.*

Keira chewed over the situation as she neared the shops. If the faceless man lingered because he wanted justice, there might not be much Keira could do. His death had occurred so long ago, his killer would now be occupying a grave of his own.

But she hated the idea of simply ignoring the hollow-faced man. He'd been standing there, waiting, for more than a hundred years. There had to be some way to bring him relief, surely.

Keira passed the florist, strategically positioned before the turnoff to the cemetery. She stopped, then backtracked and bit her lip as she stepped into the store.

The bell above the door jingled, and Keira was assaulted with an intense concoction of scents and pollens. Rows of bouquets and buckets of individual flowers surrounded a rack of cheerful greeting cards. Keira turned to the counter. Normally the shop was run by its owner, the shrewd, pince-nez-wearing Polly Kennard, who so far seemed more interested in finding a girlfriend for her gloomy, death-metal-loving son than in selling flowers. That morning, instead of being greeted by Polly's cheerful welcome, Keira found herself face-to-face with the son in question: Harry.

His jet-black hair, pallid skin, dark eyeliner, and black nail polish contrasted beautifully with his pastel floral apron. The disgusted twist to his lips told Keira he wasn't there of his own free will.

"Hello." His voice was a resentful monotone. "Welcome to Two Bees, the florist with the happiest flowers; please kill me."

Keira couldn't stop grinning as she felt in her pocket for some of the money Adage had given her the previous day. "Hey, Harry. Good to see you again. What can I get for ten dollars?"

His eyes rolled toward the ceiling. "Anything. Loot the store, please. Then maybe she won't leave me in charge anymore."

"Cool. Thanks." Keira slapped the bill onto the counter and turned toward the buckets of budget bouquets. The arrangements were small—just a handful of flowers wrapped in bright paper—but Keira thought they looked nice. They were five dollars each, so she picked out two.

Then the entire bucket was lifted and thrust into her hands. Keira gasped and fumbled to hold it without sloshing the water.

"I'm serious," Harry said, his face a mask of disgust. "Get these awful flowers out of this awful store."

"I—I can't afford—"

"Don't care. Goodbye." He planted a hand on Keira's back and shoved her onto the sidewalk. The door slammed behind her. Keira, disoriented and stunned, looked from the bucket of flowers to the window at her back. Harry glared at her through the glass, then flipped the small, flowery placard to read *Closed*.

"Oh. Okay." She carefully set the bucket on the sidewalk, then took the bouquets out. There were eight in total. Keira balanced them in her good arm for the walk back to her graveyard.

Between the research and hunting for John Doe's murder site, she'd eaten through most of the day. Long shadows grew over the street and the temperature was starting to drop as fresh mist rolled in. She walked quickly to keep warm and tried not to shudder as water trickled off the flowers' stems and onto her arm.

The lights were on in Adage's parsonage, but she passed it and went directly to her cottage first. She dropped the bouquets onto the low stone fence surrounding the property, then chose a bunch of lilacs and stepped into the fog.

Mist plumed around her with every breath. The hairs rose on the backs of her arms, a series of uneasy prickles that warned her spirits were present. She searched for, found, and pulled on the muscle behind her eyes. The transparent shapes shifted into focus.

They were camouflaged in the mist and barely visible in the low light. A handful watched her. Most ignored her, staring into the distance or pacing between the rows of headstones.

Keira made her way toward the unnamed grave. The spirit wasn't visible. Keira waited for a moment, then bent and placed the flowers at the base of the headstone.

"I want you to know that I'm trying." She knotted her fingers together and stared at the stone, feeling equal parts awkward and nervous. "I looked up the newspapers about your death and went to see the place you passed away."

A sensation like ice ran over her shoulder. Keira flinched. The faceless spirit had appeared just behind her. The tattered edges of his coat brushed over Keira's back, forcing chills through her clothes.

Keira fought the impulse to pull away. The empty man didn't face her but stared into the distance somewhere to Keira's side. His back was to the sun and heavy shadows flooded the hollow gap where his face belonged. Keira tried not to stare at the way the flesh inside seemed to pulse.

The cold radiating off the specter was turning the dew on Keira's clothes into frost. She bunched her hands into her pockets to preserve their warmth. "You were killed by a stranger, weren't you? I don't think he was ever found. He would have passed away decades ago. I'm sorry."

The faceless man gave no reaction.

Keira tried again. "If you can find some way to communicate with me—raising your hand or nodding or anything—I might be able to help more. But, well, you're not giving me much to work with right now."

In the quiet following her words, Keira thought she caught a distant noise. Something whistling or gurgling or gasping, but so faded that it seemed to be coming from across an endless divide.

Keira realized what she was hearing and felt sick. The hollow-faced man had no nose and no mouth, but he was still trying to breathe through the throat that ended abruptly in the hollow interior of his head.

She turned aside to get a second of relief from the specter's presence, but when she looked back, he was gone again.

"Hello?" Keira tried to slow her breathing. Minutes passed, and the frost surrounding Keira began to thaw as the energy in the air dissipated. The spirit didn't return.

*He's weak,* her subconscious whispered. *He can only manifest for a few moments at a time.*

Keira rubbed her arms to return some feeling to them as she followed the path back to the cottage. She'd lost all memory of her past life and what it might have entailed, but since arriving at Blighty, she'd learned to trust her subconscious. It knew a lot more about survival and spirits than she thought it had any right to.

Her head swam with unpleasant thoughts. The John Doe either didn't want to communicate…or couldn't. But something was tethering him to the earth. Something prevented him from seeking relief in the next life, and it had been that way for so long that his existence must have become one unending stretch of painful longing.

But that left her with the same problem: if the specter couldn't communicate and if she couldn't find his name, Keira had no way to learn more about the dead man.

She stopped at the stone fence where she'd left her collection of flowers and picked up a new bunch. She had seven left. That meant she could show some kindness to seven long-ignored resting places.

Keira placed a bunch below Marion Cobb's headstone, then the grizzled older man's, then Tony Lobell's. At each grave, she paused and bowed her head in respect, as though she were visiting a missed family member. Most of the ghosts hid or watched from afar, except for Tony Lobell. He appeared next to the grave as Keira laid the flowers, hands pressed to his orb-like cheeks in wonder. As Keira backed away, he bent over at the waist, making a show of smelling the flowers and exposing himself shamelessly.

"You know *exactly* what you're doing," Keira grumbled.

He peeked over his shoulder at her, hands clasped together as a cheeky smile brightened his face.

The final bunch went to the elderly Victorian woman. She'd made it clear she didn't care for Keira's attention, but there was something about the opulent, dignified grave marker being so horribly neglected that cut into Keira's heart. The woman might be frosty, but no one deserved to be forgotten.

She bowed her head respectfully, then stepped back. The spirit refused to appear. Keira didn't let it bother her as she made her way back to the cottage.

As she stepped through the open gate, Daisy bounded into view. The cat arched her back and headbutted Keira's leg, so she bent to scratch behind her ears. "I bet you want dinner, huh?"

Keira stopped at the doorway. A row of glass jars stood on the mat, each holding a small branch or sprout. A note had been pinned under one.

*Cuttings to brighten your garden! Leave them in the jars for a few days to start the roots. I could tell you what they are, but I think I'll let it be a surprise.*

*—Mason*

*P.S. Zoe and I want to have coffee with you. Tomorrow? At ten? Call if that's not convenient.*

Keira smiled and tucked the note into her pocket. She unlocked the door and moved the six jars inside, placing them below the window, where they would get natural light. Then she served up dinner for Daisy, who was making urgent, repetitive squeaking noises, not unlike an alarm. The cat buried her face in her bowl, tail flicking happily.

Keira still felt chilled after being in the graveyard but reluctantly left the fireplace alone. The cottage had stayed warm enough from the morning's fire that she could leave it unlit until she returned from Adage's.

"I'll be back in a couple of hours," she called to Daisy. She took a donated scarf out of the closet, wrapped it around her neck, and gave the cat's head a brief scratch. Daisy, still buried in her food bowl, ignored her. "Don't wait up."

As she stepped back into the yard, Keira reflexively glanced toward the graves and pulled on her second sight. Transparent shapes moved into focus.

The elderly Victorian woman stood in front of her gravestone, one hand pressed to her lips as she stared at the flowers Keira had left.

# CHAPTER 5

"I CAN ASK AROUND if you like." Adage, seated at his small dining table, passed Keira the gravy before picking up his own cutlery. "I don't think it will be too suspicious. You're supposed to be groundskeeper now; I can simply say you're curious about an unmarked grave."

"Thanks, that would help a lot." Keira poured the gravy over her slices of roast. Adage's cottage, crammed full of mismatched secondhand furniture, had a way of making her relax. Soft rumba music came from the record player in the living room, and the whole house smelled like spices. "I was hoping I wouldn't have to ask Zoe, but I'm getting desperate. If I can't find any leads soon, I'll see what she knows."

Adage was silent for a moment while he chewed, then said, "If you don't mind me asking, why this ghost? You've a graveyard of options. Maybe it's my inherent laziness showing, but I would go for the low-hanging fruit first."

"Ha." Keira swallowed a mouthful of food that was still slightly too hot. She'd missed lunch and hadn't realized how hungry she was until the pork had touched her tongue. "It's the way he looks. A lot of the others seem resigned or even peaceful—and most of them are avoiding me for some reason I can't understand. But this one's suffering. And he's been trapped in this state for more than a hundred years. It may be difficult to help him, but something tells me he needs it the most."

Adage sighed heavily. "I respect that, and I can empathize. My only fear is that you're setting an unachievable goal."

That was exactly the anxiety that had been dogging Keira too. Instead of admitting it, she said, "I'll worry about that when I've exhausted every option."

Adage tapped the tip of his knife on his teeth. "You've made an impression in town, by the way. I went on my calls this afternoon with the intention of spreading the news about my new niece—and found out half the town already knew."

"Wow, yikes. News travels fast here. How'd they find out?"

"Through the library, of course. Hanna is a wonderful lady, but keeping her quiet is like trying to silence a siren. Miss Millbury came in to drop off a book, heard all about you, and spread it through her own network." He popped a piece of potato into his mouth and shrugged. "I don't mind. It's saved me an awful lot of time."

"And they believed it?"

"Oh, yes. Many have even started to form opinions of you. Mostly positive, but Mrs. House thinks you might be an odd one because her husband saw you talking to a tree stump while he was walking their dog."

"Oh no." Keira covered her face to stifle her laughter. "This town is the worst. Or maybe the best. I can't tell anymore."

"I'm very familiar with that sensation."

The kitchen phone rang. Adage excused himself and rose to answer it. Under the gentle hum of his voice, Keira, lost in thought, nudged peas across her plate. Maybe Adage was right. She'd been hired to help the graveyard's spirits; maybe she needed to be more pragmatic. It made sense to start with the easiest jobs and work her way up. She didn't know how long she had in Blighty; she needed to do as much as she could in the time she had.

Then she pictured her faceless man, close to unresponsive, lingering a hundred years beyond his death.

*No.* He was still worth trying to help, even if failure was the most likely outcome.

Adage's voice had dropped to a low, intent murmur. Keira leaned back in her chair to catch a glimpse of him in the hallway. The pastor was hunched over the phone, his head shaking slowly. Before Keira could catch any of the conversation, Adage ended the call and returned the receiver to its hook.

"I'm so sorry, child." Adage ran a hand through his thinning, white hair as he returned. His joviality had evaporated. "One of my parishioners has been in an accident. It's serious. They asked if I could visit them in hospital. Would you be very upset if I cut this evening short?"

"No—of course you need to go." Keira rose, but Adage waved her back to her chair.

"Please stay and finish your dinner. It would be a shame for it to go to waste." Coat hangers rattled as he pulled a jacket out of the closet. "I likely won't be back for a few hours. You're welcome to stay as long as you like; there's ice cream in the freezer. Just turn the lights out when you leave."

"I will," Keira promised. "Is there anything I can do to help?"

"Thank you, but it's in the Lord's hands now." Adage took his keys off the sideboard and crossed to the door. "Good night, and stay safe."

The door shut with a muted click. A moment later, the sound of an engine floated through the open kitchen window.

Keira looked back at her plate. The roast was delicious, but it seemed painfully lonely to eat it by herself. She picked at what remained on her plate, then set about packing up the leftovers.

Blighty's trademark mist thickened outside the window as Keira washed, dried, and put away the dishes. It was late evening by the time she wiped the countertop clean and began moving through the parsonage and turning out lights.

The air was cold enough to send a shiver through her as she stepped out of the house. The moon's light wasn't strong, but it was enough to see a dozen paces through the fog. She was growing familiar with the path back to the cottage and put her head down as she moved through the wet gravestones and cowled statues.

A thin, high-pitched cry cut through the air. Keira froze and stared into the night. The sound had come from the forest. She held her breath as she listened. For a moment, the world was silent. Not even the insects dared make a sound.

Then the call repeated. Shudders tracked down Keira's spine and her mouth dried. The sound wasn't natural. It was so high-pitched that it seemed to bypass her ears and claw at her brain. The prickles running over her skin like electricity told her it had a supernatural origin.

*A smart person would go to her cottage and lock the door.* Keira swallowed and took a step toward the sound. *A smart person would stay sheltered until morning.*

Spirits almost never made noise, though. Something in her thundering heart told her she couldn't ignore it. What if it was a call for help? It felt urgent, almost desperate.

The sound came again, cutting through her more effectively than an icy wind.

"Damn it," she whispered, and folded her arms around her. She jogged toward the cry, weaving between the stone monuments as she tried to avoid stepping on graves. Trees creaked as aged branches flexed. Tendrils of mist clung to her limbs.

The prickles grew stronger as she neared the end of the cemetery. She slowed, her lungs burning from the cold. The forest's edge rose like a wall ahead of her, the dark branches cutting across the sky like knives. She braced herself and pulled on the muscle to open her second sight.

Nothing appeared. Keira took a step closer to the trees, straining as she hunted for motion between the shadowed trunks.

Nothing. She turned to glance behind her. The graveyard was perfectly still save for the billowing fog. The familiar flickers of hazy light were absent. She frowned and pulled on the muscle harshly enough to send a stab of pain through her skull.

*My ghosts are missing. Are they asleep? Do ghosts even need to sleep? Or are they hiding?*

The noise came again. It was clearer now—a howling scream, its tone beyond human hearing. She felt more than heard the agony in the spirit's cries.

"Hello!" Keira had reached the forest's edge. She placed a hand on a tree trunk and felt dew wet her palm. "I'm here!"

She'd been in these woods twice before. The first time had been the night she'd stumbled into Blighty, fleeing the strangers with guns. The second time, she'd been exploring the wilderness behind her new home. Instead of ending at the edge of the cemetery, the graves spilled into the woods. The sight struck her as unnatural.

The stones were far older here than in the main cemetery. Their dark surfaces were worn down like rotting teeth, sometimes crumbling into piles and other times sunken deep into the earth. Some jutted out at unnatural angles as the tree roots exhumed them.

She kept her movements cautious and her breathing quiet as she stepped between the trees. The air was thicker there. Wet, full of the scent of pines and decay, it clung to her.

Something seemed to move in the distance. Keira squinted to keep it in sight, but it was like watching a shadow drift over deep black. As soon as she thought she'd fixed on the shape, it was gone again, veiled by the dense trunks and graves.

"Hello?"

Whatever it was seemed to be holding its breath. Keira's skull ached from maintaining the second sight. She reached a hand forward, fingers extended into the darkness as she tried to feel the energy. The air thrummed.

Keira exhaled. The moisture turned to frost on her lips. The static in her fingers was enough to make her heart pound.

*Whatever's here is strong*, she realized. *It's immensely, terrifyingly strong…but it's trying to hide itself.*

She came to a halt. Fear flowed through her veins and filled her mouth with coppery dread. Her instincts begged her to retreat, but she hesitated.

*It was crying. It needs help, and I'm the only one who can hear it. I can't just leave it, can I?*

She tried to swallow, but a lump caught in her throat. Ice crystals threaded up the moss hanging from the nearest tree.

*It's only a ghost. It can get angry and it can panic, but it can't hurt me.*

She seized that belief and wrapped it around her heart in an attempt at courage. Her fingers shook as she stretched them farther into the darkness. Dead pines crunched beneath her feet as she stepped forward.

"My name is Keira." Her voice was tight. She swallowed to clear her throat. "I'm here to help."

A hint of motion drew her attention forward. Her heart

knocked against her ribs in a painful tempo. She pulled on the second sight as hard as she could, swallowing the pain as she strained to see.

Thick moss hung from a branch like a curtain. Keira swept it aside, shuddering at how unnaturally cold it felt, and stepped past. A circle of four massive trees created a hollow between them. Inside was a grave covering. The structure had been ground down by the shifting forest floor and tree roots until what had once been a solid, six-foot-long slab of stone was now cracked in half.

Keira knew, as soon as she saw the grave, that she'd found the source of the disturbance. Energy prickled off it until it felt like being near an electrical current. And yet, despite keeping her sight open as wide as she could, the spirit still wasn't visible.

She moved into the hollow, crouching as the sloped forest floor threatened to slide beneath her. Her searching hand was now outstretched in supplication, like she was greeting a skittish cat. Keira kept her voice as gentle as her tight throat allowed. "I heard you calling earlier. You don't need to be afraid. I want to help you if I can."

The spirit bloomed into view. Keira took a sharp breath. The blood in her veins turned to ice as the unnatural figure rose toward her.

She tried to scramble back, to climb out of the hollow, but her shoes slipped on the frosted leaves. She hit the ground hard. Keira recoiled, braced on her elbows, as she stared in horror at the apparition.

# CHAPTER 6

THE SPECTER BARELY RESEMBLED a human. Unlike the white-tinted, transparent ghosts from the graveyard, the creature before Keira was a pure sooty black. Its form shifted like ribbons of smoke, billowing and coiling in on itself. Its eyes were dark pits. Its jaw stretched wide, exposing an empty maw that seemed to plunge into eternity.

Keira couldn't breathe. Malevolent energy poured off the apparition in waves. The sickening, cloistering evil was the same energy that had terrified her the last time she'd stepped into the woods. It hit her with enough force that her heart began skipping beats, filling her ears with a high-pitched whistle.

The spirit rose from its grave, the black smoke spilling between the cracks in the stone. Its eyes fixed on Keira as its jaw shifted into something resembling a lipless, grimacing smile.

*It can't hurt me. It's a ghost. It can't hurt me.*

The specter tumbled forward. Inhumanly long arms stretched out to claw at the earth, dragging its body closer in increments. Keira opened her mouth to cry out, but no sounds escaped her. She couldn't so much as breathe. She was frozen, incapable of even blinking as the specter dragged its hideous form nearer.

*It can't hurt me. It can't hurt me!*

The spirit's cracked grin was widening. A near-hypnotizing intensity hung around the deep pits where its eyes belonged. It was pleased…and Keira instinctively knew that was a bad omen.

It was nearly on her. Keira forced her limbs to move, to kick her farther away from the apparition. She rolled onto her knees and reached for a tree branch to pull herself out of the hollow as her mantra ran on a loop through her head. *It can't hurt me. It can't hurt—*

The specter lunged forward in a sudden burst of speed. Its long, bony fingers fastened around her wrist. Keira screamed. The touch was excruciating: both burning her and freezing her skin in one awful second.

A flash of light pulsed out of her, and Keira gasped at what felt like a punch to her chest. The specter lurched back. Hurt or merely startled, Keira didn't know, and she didn't want to wait to find out. Her wrist stung as though it had been freshly burned, but the fear made it easier to push the sensation to the back of her mind. She grasped the branch, gained her feet, and lurched into the forest.

Behind her, the specter wailed. The high-pitched, unnatural scream held all of the longing and desperation from before, but she now knew what it wanted. It wasn't crying for help. It was calling for a victim.

Keira plunged into the forest. She moved recklessly, nearly blind as the last traces of daylight faded. Branches scored across her exposed skin, so she raised her arms to protect her face. Her foot hit something solid and sent her to the ground. She heard a crack and, for a second, thought she'd fractured a leg, but when she looked behind herself, she saw she'd broken the headstone she'd tripped over.

The fog was far thicker than before and growing denser with every moment. Keira could barely see the trunks around her. She clawed her way to her feet and staggered forward. Her muscles had never failed her before, but now they shook as though she'd been running for hours. She'd lost her sense of direction. The trees surrounded her on all sides, their angular branches sinking deeper into a web of uncertain shapes as night spread over Blighty. She would be as good as blind soon.

A shrill cry came from somewhere ahead of her, and Keira flinched. A shape moved between the trees, filling Keira with near-mindless panic. *It followed me. It's not going to let me leave—*

She couldn't feel any trace of the malevolent energy, though. Two circles of color appeared in the dark. Keira blinked, and liquid-amber eyes blinked back.

Daisy emerged from between the trees, tail held high in a greeting, and threaded her lithe body between Keira's legs.

"Daisy!" Keira reached for her cat, but she had already left her again, bounding back into the gloom the way she had come.

Keira scrambled after her. The creature jumped over fallen branches and darted between trees effortlessly. Even moving as quickly as she could, Keira wasn't able to keep up with her, but Daisy seemed to sense that and always paused a second before she disappeared from sight.

Keira couldn't control her shaking. Her lungs hurt and her head throbbed. But Daisy had led her home before, so she kept her head down and trusted the little cat to guide her again.

Daisy's paws made gentle pattering noises on the leaves on the ground. The unnatural fog drenched everything. Trees passed in a blur as Keira lost herself in the steady rhythm of thudding footfalls and rasping breaths. It wasn't until her foot snagged on a root that she was shaken back to awareness enough to feel concern.

*We should have been home by now. Well, before now, actually... How long have we been running? Twenty minutes? Thirty? Is she lost?*

Keira staggered to a halt. Her mind felt as though it had been drowned in the fog that saturated the forest. She couldn't think. Couldn't even guess which direction she would need to turn to get home. The trees all looked the same, and as night thickened, it became harder and harder to see.

Ahead, Daisy frisked in a circle, her mouth opening in a silent meow. She was begging Keira to follow. With no other options, Keira complied.

She was exhausted, though. Her legs trembled and even breathing had grown difficult. She'd never lacked endurance before, but that night she felt ready to collapse.

Then the trees thinned. The relief was overwhelming. Keira trailed a few steps behind her cat as she staggered out of the forest and into soup-like fog.

Daisy looked like a mirage skating through the white. Keira had to fix her eyes on the shape to not lose it. Grass underfoot changed to some kind of asphalt. Keira didn't have long to question that before Daisy took a sharp left, followed a short driveway, and leaped up three steps.

Keira blinked. The fog parted. She could see a door and a stone wall, and even a square of light coming from a window. Daisy had led her to *someone's* home, just not her own.

Daisy scrabbled at the door, her nose buried in the corner as her claws scored the wood. Footsteps echoed down a hallway. Then the door opened, and a tall man looked first at Daisy, then at Keira.

Mason's eyebrows rose with shock. "Keira?"

Her throat closed. She reached forward, just wanting to be close to him, and Mason met her halfway, his arms surrounding her as he led her into his home.

"Are you okay?" One hand ran over her wet hair, stroking it out of her face, then pressed against her throat to find her pulse. His fingers felt hot against her chilled skin. Mason swore under his breath, then his arm went around her shoulders as he guided her deeper into the house.

Keira caught glimpses of a piano, bookcases, and numerous potted plants. Then Mason pressed her into a large couch. Heat rolled off a gas fireplace in the wall beside her, and Mason turned it up before disappearing through a door.

Keira rubbed at her eyes as she tried to fight off the weariness. Mason returned with blankets and towels and wrapped them around her. "Can I call someone?" His voice was soft. "Adage or…?"

"Adage is out," she mumbled. "I'm fine now. Just tired. Sorry for worrying you."

He muttered something she couldn't hear, then left again. Keira's headache was fading, and the room gradually came into focus.

The space was more eclectic than she'd imagined Mason's home would be. Bookcases were crammed with dusty, faded titles. Most of the furniture was made from dark, polished wood, though not all of it matched. A massive glass case in the back of the room seemed to hold an animal skeleton.

A thought occurred to her, and she looked over her shoulder toward where Mason had disappeared. "Hey, uh, did you see Daisy? She came here with me."

Clinking noises echoed from an unseen room. "Look in front of the heater."

The black cat lounged there, her lithe body twisted into a pretzel-like contortion. One eye was squished closed, but the other peeked open.

"Thank you," Keira whispered.

The cat squirmed happily. Her tongue poked out, and she didn't bother pulling it back in.

Mason returned carrying a steaming mug of what looked like milk. He pressed it into Keira's hands. "Drink that. It will help."

"Thanks." Her fingers shook around the cup, no matter how much she willed them to be still. Mason retrieved a towel and sat next to her as he began rubbing it over her hair. For the first time, Keira realized she was dripping wet. She put the mug onto the coffee table beside her and tried to stand. "I'm getting water on your chair—"

"Doesn't matter." He pushed her back into the seat and continued to dry her hair. Goose bumps rose over Keira's skin, despite the gas heater. She still wasn't used to physical touch, but Mason moved carefully as he dabbed around her eyes and brushed stray strands away from her face. "What happened?" he asked. "Did someone hurt you?"

"No." The familiar gnawing guilt accompanied the lie. "I just…got lost in the forest. The fog was really thick. I guess I must have found a back way to your house."

Mason sighed and lowered the towel. He suddenly looked very tired. "Don't lie to me. Please don't."

She couldn't meet his eyes. "I'm not— I—"

He took hold of her hand and lifted it. Vicious red marks scored her wrist where the spirit had grabbed her. Keira's heart skipped a beat.

"These are *finger marks*." Mason's voice was low and raw, a barely restrained whisper. He held her hand gently—almost tenderly—but she felt the tension in his fingers. He was furious. "Someone did this to you. Who was it?"

She couldn't speak.

Mason finally lowered her hand, but he didn't let go. His

fingers wrapped around hers as he bent closer. His words were soft, pleading. "You can tell me, Keira. I won't judge you or doubt you. I just want the truth, I want to help."

Words flooded her mouth. She clamped her jaw shut to keep them inside.

She wanted to tell him. It was a tangible, desperate need, and suppressing it felt like choking off her air. But more than wanting to tell him, she wanted to keep him as a friend. And no matter what he promised, her story would only sound like an elaborate lie.

She tried to imagine how it would go, what words she would use, how she could possibly phrase it so she didn't sound like she was lying. Each time she pictured him recoiling, his gentle face slowly growing cold. Mason was kind. One of the most compassionate people she knew. But he was also enmeshed in the world of science. He wouldn't—couldn't—believe her.

His dark eyes searched hers, imploring her, and Keira had to look away. "I'm sorry."

Mason sighed, and his head dropped. She could feel the disappointment and frustration rolling off of him.

She tried to worm her hand out of his. "I should go."

"No. Please stay." He released her but didn't move away. He ran his fingers through his hair and closed his eyes. "It's okay. You don't want to talk, and I won't force you to. But please stay. If you're here, at least I'll know you're safe."

They were sitting too close. Keira was acutely aware of everything—she could feel his body heat, hear every inhale, count the individual lashes framing his eyes. Then he stood, and Keira felt like something precious had been torn away from her.

"You're still chilled. I'll get more blankets." An emotion she couldn't identify dulled his voice as he left the room. "Don't forget your drink."

Daisy shifted in her place by the heater. Keira knew she was probably projecting her own emotions, but she thought the cat wore an incredibly judgmental expression.

The mug sat ignored on the table beside her. Keira picked it up. She made herself drink some of it, even though she could barely taste it. The red marks on her wrist stood out like brands. Keira pulled her sleeve down to hide them. They still ached.

"Here, I got some pillows too." Mason's voice was cheerful again. If he was forcing it, he was good at hiding that fact. He placed the bundles beside her, then, instead of resuming his place at her side, he sat in the chair opposite.

"Are you sure I should stay? I don't want to be a nuisance."

He laughed, and it almost sounded natural. "Don't be ridiculous. It's nice to have some company. On that note—how did you find me? I don't think I ever told you my address."

"Daisy led me here." Keira glanced at the small, sleeping cat. The creature had been to this house once before. On the day she'd thought she was leaving town, she'd given Mason the cat to look after. "I guess she remembered the way."

"Remarkable."

Keira picked up one of the blankets and fidgeted with the

tasseled end to give her hands something to do. She hunted for a neutral topic and landed on "You've got a really nice house."

"Thanks. It's my parents'; they're letting me stay here while they're in Bolivia. My mother is a zoologist and travels a lot for work. Dad always goes with her. He calls himself a botanist, but really I think he just likes walking through forests."

"Wow. I had no idea." Keira gazed at the furnishings with a new appreciation. "I guess I always imagined your parents would be pharmacists or surgeons or something."

He grinned. "Yeah, I think they were a bit disappointed that I decided to become a boring old doctor."

"So, um, I guess that explains the skeleton in the corner." She nodded to the glass case behind them.

"That's a good story, actually." He rose and crossed to the case. "My mum found it in Iceland. The basic structure belongs to a bird, but the vertebrae and clavicle are like nothing documented before. Mum is convinced it's a previously undiscovered species in the Cracidae family. She took it to her scientific society, but they say it's just a duck with a birth defect. Mum refused to accept their findings, so they kicked her out."

"Bummer." Keira tilted her head as she examined the skeleton. "That's a pretty broad risk-reward spectrum, though. Either it's a major discovery that will shake the scientific community...or it's a duck. And not even a good duck."

He broke into deep laughter. Instead of returning to the opposite seat, he took the place beside her, his shoulders still shaking. "I guess so. She'll never ever admit that she's wrong, though, so we'll probably have those bones on display forever."

They were close—their shoulders nearly touching—but the earlier awkwardness had been broken.

She sipped her drink while Mason told her stories about his parents—about his mother becoming hysterically angry when someone sewed a dead crow's head and salmon's body together and tried to sell it to her as a mercrow, about how his father had always been the house's peacekeeper, about how they would disappear into foreign countries for years at a time and come back laden with souvenirs like goat testicle necklaces and painted tortoise shells.

For a moment, the idea passed through Keira's mind that she might have misjudged Mason. What if he'd been receptive to her story? What if he had believed her? Maybe the distance between them would have disappeared completely.

But the moment was gone. She put it from her mind as thoroughly as she could and focused on enjoying Mason's smooth voice.

# CHAPTER 7

KEIRA WOKE EARLY. HER neck was sore, and she tried to rotate it before realizing she was leaning against a warm body.

She and Mason had fallen asleep on the lounge, propped against each other. The gas heater was still on, keeping them warm despite the frigid morning, and the first traces of early-dawn sunlight flitted through the curtains.

Keira eased herself away from Mason as gently as she could. He stirred but didn't wake. She covered him with the blankets, then tiptoed out of the room.

The door she chose led her into the kitchen. It was scrupulously clean and sparse, but she found a notepad and pen stuck to the fridge with magnets. She popped the pen's cap off and wrote.

*Thanks for letting me stay. Decided to have an early morning.*

Keira paused, wondering if the message sounded too distant, and finished it with,

*Looking forward to coffee with you and Zoe.*

Keira tore the page off, crept back into the living room, and placed the note on the coffee table beside her empty cup. Then she retrieved Daisy, who continued to sleep in front of the heater. The cat stretched, then flopped bonelessly in Keira's arms. Keira draped the cat over her shoulder and retreated to the hallway.

The outside air was brisk, and Keira huffed a breath as she shut Mason's door behind herself. Even Daisy shivered.

"Don't suppose you want to show me the way home?" Keira asked. The cat began kneading her claws into Keira's back. "'Kay. Didn't think so."

She turned to examine the street. The forest pressed against the end of the cul-de-sac to her right—*that must be the path we came through last night*—and the drive seemed to lead toward the town in the opposite direction. Keira doubted she could find her way through the forest, so she figured she'd have to brave the townsfolks' stares.

It took less than ten minutes to reach the fountain marking the shops' center. It was still too early for many people to be on the road, but Keira caught flashes of movement as curtain corners were lifted. She knew she must look out of place, carrying her cat through town so early in the morning.

Keira kept her pace brisk. Despite the chilled air, she was

warm by the time she made it back to the graveyard. Adage's car was still missing and the parsonage's lights were out, so Keira bypassed it and continued to her own home. She hoped the night hadn't been too harrowing for him.

Daisy had been a rag doll for the entire walk back but abruptly squirmed out of Keira's grip as they entered the graveyard. The cat tumbled to the ground, righted herself, and frisked into the grass to chase insects. The sudden solitude left Keira feeling vulnerable. She paused by the low stone fence ringing her cottage's garden and pulled on her second sight. Vague shapes shifted between the gravestones. She couldn't see any sign of the twisted spirit.

She let herself into the small cottage. The open-plan room felt dim and neglected. She started the fire to get some warmth in the building. Dried sweat still caked her, and she could feel tiny leaves in her hair, so she prioritized showering over food. The warm water felt incredibly good on her sore muscles.

The fire had started to warm the cottage by the time she returned to the main room. She tipped a can of beans into a saucepan and was fiddling with the stovetop when something small and black headbutted her ankle. Daisy peered up at her, golden eyes sparkling in the fire's light, and gave a silent meow.

"Ready for your breakfast, huh?" Keira left the beans to serve up a plate of cat food. As Daisy buried her head into the bowl, Keira looked toward the cottage's door. It was closed. *How did she get in? Did she sneak in after me? I would have thought I'd see her...*

Keira narrowed her eyes at the cat, who remained wholly occupied by her food. *She got me away from that twisted spirit.*

*She led me to Mason's house. Even if she remembered the way, that's still beyond the abilities of a normal cat, right?*

The beans were hissing, so Keira took them off the stove, grabbed a spoon from the drawer, and curled up in a chair by the fire to eat.

*On that topic, what was the deal with that twisted spirit? I've never seen anything like him before. And he could touch me. Normal ghosts can only ever make me feel cold.*

"You know your life has gone off the rails when you start differentiating between normal ghosts and weird ghosts," she said to Daisy. The cat finished her meal, took two steps toward the fire, and faceplanted into the rug. Keira sighed. "Even my *cat* is weird."

*I have the spirit's name, though.* The marks on the stone slab, so badly faded, had been barely visible, but the image had cemented itself in Keira's mind. *Gerald Barge, 1839–1892.*

She looked at the mantelpiece clock. It wasn't quite nine; she'd promised to meet Mason and Zoe at ten. That gave her just enough time to visit the library.

"I'm heading out; do you want to stay here?" she asked Daisy. The cat rolled over to expose her belly to the flames' heat. Her tongue protruded, and she seemed content to leave it that way. "I'll take that as a yes."

Keira pulled her jacket on, then hesitated. The marks around her wrist were still bright and angry. She rummaged through the closet of donated clothes until she found a light summer scarf, then tied it around the wrist. It looked like an ugly, gaudy fashion accessory, which suited her just fine.

"Be back soon, Daze," she called to her cat, then slipped out into the mist.

As had become her habit, she kept her head down and made herself small as she walked through Blighty's streets. Her natural inclination was to make herself invisible, but it wasn't working that morning. Store owners poked their heads out of their shops to call, "Good morning, Keira," and strangers waved to her in the street. The news that she was staying with Adage had spread quickly. Keira waved to anyone who greeted her but breathed a sigh of relief when she entered the nearly empty library.

"Good morning." Hanna's deep, slow voice echoed through the otherwise-silent room. The librarian fished a small square of cardboard from under her desk and held it out. "You came to pick up your library card, I suppose."

"Yes! Thank you." Keira had almost forgotten about the card but took it. The square had been filled out by hand in a neat, carefully spaced print. In the square that was supposed to show the bearer's photo, Hanna had drawn a stick-figure smiley face. Keira grinned and tucked it into her back pocket. "I'm just going to read through some more newspapers."

"Of course. Have fun."

Keira could feel Hanna's eyes on her as she returned to the digital archives, but she didn't have enough time to disguise her purpose by flipping through random papers like she had the day before. She went straight to 1892, the year Gerald Barge had died. It didn't take long to find him.

She was expecting some horrific catastrophe. Maybe Gerald

had been tortured to death, or fallen into a vat of radioactive waste—anything to justify what he'd become. But the paper's news was, at best, dull. The front-page story was about how a cow had won a local competition. Keira had to flip to the third page before finding any mention of Gerald.

Gerald Barge passed away peacefully in his home on the evening of January 9. A memorial service will be held on the 15th. All are welcome.

"That's it?" Keira reread the article twice, but there was nothing to glean. He'd died peacefully. There were no mentions of his occupation, family, or life. Keira tried both the newspaper before and multiple newspapers after, but none held any mention of Gerald. She slumped back in her chair, rubbing at where her neck had grown stiff.

*Maybe he had a bitter personality? And yet…plenty of people are bitter. What made Gerald twisted when every other ghost I've seen is fine?*

She'd lost her sense of time while absorbed in the papers and bit her lip when she saw the clock on the nearby wall. She was already late for her meeting with Zoe and Mason. Keira hurried to power down the machine. Hanna waved to her on the way out, and Keira waved back, wishing she didn't feel so lost.

# CHAPTER 8

KEIRA JOGGED ACROSS THE small space separating the library from the café. She'd run late and could only hope the others hadn't been waiting for too long.

Has Beans, the corner coffee shop, was unusually busy. The line extended to the door. Marlene, the sallow barista, saw Keira enter and raised a hand over the crowd to point at the corner. Keira followed the gesture and saw Mason and Zoe already seated in the nook by the window, engaged in some kind of heated debate.

"Hey," Keira said as she squeezed through the crowd to reach the table. "I'm so sorry I'm late."

They both smiled, but there was something strange about their expressions. Zoe's held more than the usual amount of intense eagerness. She seemed to think she'd concealed it but most certainly hadn't. Mason looked anxious. Keira was used to seeing him concerned, but this was the first time she could remember seeing him look so uncomfortable. Keira had a sinking sense that they'd been talking about her before she'd arrived.

Mason stood and pulled a third seat out for Keira. "I ordered you a drink and sandwiches, but I can get something else if you like." He spoke so quietly that Keira could barely hear him over the café's other occupants.

"Any kind of food sounds good right now, thank you. Uh, I can pay you back—"

She fished the money out of her pocket. Mason wrapped his hand around hers and pushed it back. "My treat."

His fingers dwarfed hers. Keira cleared her throat and carefully extracted her hand. "Sure. But I'm paying next time, deal?"

He finally smiled, though it still looked strained. Zoe, meanwhile, had propped her chin up on her hands, a tight-lipped smile dwarfed by owlish eyes as she fixed her gaze on Keira with all of the intensity of a predator.

Keira took a bracing breath, then released it in a rush. "Okay. Out with it. What is this?"

"We wanted to talk to you," Mason began.

Zoe slammed her open palm on the table. "This is an intervention, damn it."

"Zoe." Mason's tone held a note of warning, but she ignored him.

"You're keeping secrets. Also, you still don't have a toaster, and honestly it's bordering on disgraceful at this point."

"*Zoe. Please.*"

"I'm working on the toaster thing," Keira said. "And this really shouldn't be a news flash, but my whole life is kind of a secret. Even from me."

Zoe folded her arms, eyes narrowed with suspicion. Mason cleared his throat. He seemed to be picking his words carefully.

"I'm very conscious that your business is your own, and I'm not entitled to know what parts of your life you choose to keep private or even why, but at the same time, I'm worried. Something's happening that I don't understand. And the more pieces of the puzzle I put together, the less it makes sense. And…"

Keira braced herself. "And…?"

"And I think you can speak to dead people." The words rushed out of Mason so quickly that even he seemed caught off guard by them.

Keira's heart felt like it might have stopped. *How could he know? Did Adage tell him?*

She kept her eyes fixed on the wooden tabletop, but she could feel both of her friends staring at her. Her tongue was too dry. "Why…uh…"

"Tell me I'm wrong." Mason's voice was soft but insistent.

She considered laughing it off. She could call Mason ridiculous, say he'd been spending too much time in Zoe's company, and deny any accusations he tried to levy at her. But just the thought of it made her sick. She was tired of lying. And betraying Mason would hurt more than anything else.

"Um." She knew what she needed to say, but the words wouldn't form. "I, uh, technically…they don't really talk much…"

Zoe sucked in a sharp breath, shooting out of her seat, her voice rising into a shrill cry. "What! You actually—"

"Drinks." Marlene appeared behind them, her arms full of plates and cups. Keira, her nerves taut, flinched. "And sandwiches."

The three of them stayed frozen in their arrangement— Mason resting his chin on his knuckles, his dark eyes unusually serious; Keira resolutely staring at nothing; and Zoe half-standing, fingers splayed on the table and mouth open in a silent exclamation—while Marlene took her time arranging the plates on the table.

"Enjoy, folks," Marlene said as she set the last cup down. "And, Zoe, don't scream in my café."

"Okay," Zoe managed.

The barista had barely turned around when Zoe flattened herself back onto the seat and grasped Keira's shoulders. A near animalistic hunger lit up her face. "Ghosts. You can communicate with ghosts. He was right. Oh, hell, this is amazing. Wait, no—this is a joke, isn't it? You're pranking me. You've got to be. Please say you're not."

"Slow down." Mason batted at Zoe's arms until she let go of Keira. "This is why I didn't want to tell you. I knew you'd go wild. Keira, I'm sorry for broaching it like this. And I didn't mean to force you into this discussion. But if you feel able to talk about it, I'd like to listen."

Zoe shuffled her chair as close to Keira's as she could physically manage. "Yes. Please. Tell me everything."

Keira pressed her hands over her eyes. Hysterical, terrified laughter bubbled up inside of her, but she managed to suppress most of it. "How did you know?" she managed.

Mason shrugged. His eyes still held the quiet concern. "Many things that I couldn't explain accumulated into a revelation, I guess. But I only really started thinking about it when I saw the marks on your wrist last night."

The discoloration was hidden under a scarf, but Keira still moved her hand under the table before Zoe could stare at it.

"Those marks are shaped like fingers," Mason continued. "But they're not bruises; they're burns. You wouldn't tell me where they came from. After you fell asleep, I stayed awake for hours trying to find an explanation. I went over every option I could think of, but nothing made sense."

"Hang on, you stayed at his place last night?" Zoe's eyes narrowed, then she waved it away. "Never mind, I'll interrogate you about that later. Back to the ghosts, please."

Mason cleared his throat as he traced patterns over the table-top. "Then I started thinking about everything else strange that's happened since you arrived. The town is burning up with rumors about an infant's bones being found in the old mill on the same night you went missing for hours. It was too much of a coincidence; that *had* to be you. And then finding you collapsed in front of a gravestone…" He lifted his eyebrows. "All of a sudden, I was considering the possibility that ghosts might be real. I kept trying to laugh it off, thinking I was just overtired, but it was the only thing that made any kind of sense. And here we are. You haven't denied it."

"No," Keira admitted.

Mason gave a weak chuckle. "If I'm being completely honest, ghosts was a lucky guess. I'm kind of glad it's that and not, say, vampires."

Zoe sucked in a quick breath. Hope lit her face. "Can you talk to vampires too?"

"No." Keira choked on embarrassed laughter. "I mean, maybe. I've never met a vampire to know."

"But you *can* talk to ghosts, right?"

"I can see them. I can't hear them very well."

"That's so cool." Zoe leaned back in her chair. "Are they every-where? Are we, like, swimming in a sea of ghosts? There's got to be billions of them—"

"No, nothing like that. Not everyone stays after death. It mostly seems to be spirits with unfinished business."

Zoe's eyes grew even wider. "Wait, if you can see ghosts, what if *I'm* a ghost? What if I've been dead this whole time and this is your way of easing me into it?"

"Uh, no, I can promise you're very much alive."

She didn't seem to hear Keira but was staring at her hands. Very slowly, she lifted her head, a look of wonder plastered over her face. "What if we're *all* dead? What if Blighty is *purgatory*? Oh. This makes so much sense."

Keira didn't even know where to start with that theory. She glanced at Mason. He was staring at his coffee, the spoon moving in slow circles as he stirred it. Keira swallowed. "I'm sorry I didn't tell you."

"Mm." He smiled but it looked strange. "I know why you didn't. It's not the easiest thing to believe, is it?"

"But…you do?"

The strange expression left him, and he straightened his shoulders. "Of course. Sorry. It's just…a lot to absorb. And it has a lot of ramifications I'm still trying to come to terms with. But I *do* believe you."

She felt as though a weight had been lifted. She'd wanted to share her secret with Mason and Zoe for days, but the fear of being mistrusted—or, worse, rejected—had kept her silent. But they were both taking it better than she'd ever expected. Mason seemed rattled but resolute, and Zoe looked like Christmas had come early. She clasped her hands under her chin, eyes shining.

"Are there any ghosts here, right now?" she asked.

"Uh…" Keira hadn't thought to use her second sight in the town yet. Part of her was afraid of what she might find. But Zoe was staring at her with such expectant hope that she couldn't disappoint her. She pulled on the muscle. They were alone. She breathed a sigh of relief. "No, no one is here right now. From what I can figure out, they tend to gather either at the place they died or where they're buried. There are a lot at Blighty Cemetery and the old Crispin Mill."

Mason frowned, muttering furiously. "That's right. You're living in the cemetery. That must be the worst place on earth for you—"

"It's fine, actually." Keira wrapped her hands around her mug. "It's kind of cozy when you get used to it."

"No, don't worry, we'll get you away from there. You can stay with me. My house has a spare bedroom. Or if you prefer, I'm sure Zoe can find space for you at her place."

"That's okay." She shrugged. "I like the cemetery. But thank you for the offer."

Mason stared at her. "But…the graves… I'm sure Adage would agree you should be moved if he knew."

"He already knows," Keira said. "That's why I'm staying there. He hired me to help the spirits move on."

"*Adage* knew?" Zoe pressed a hand to her heart, pretending to be wounded. "*Adage* knew before your best friend? Never has the world known such a betrayal."

Keira gave her a sheepish smile. "Sorry. I really thought you wouldn't believe me. Or if you did, you'd think I was a…a freak or something."

Mason rubbed at the back of his neck, confusion and concern flitting through his expression. "I don't understand. They're hurting you."

"They're not dangerous." Keira reached out to pick up her drink, then realized she'd used the hand with the burns. She withdrew it quickly. "Most of them aren't, anyway. The only bad one I've met is in the forest. He's different—he's been twisted somehow. Maybe from anger. Maybe from pain. I don't know. But the others are friendly. Ish."

Zoe's owl eyes shone with enthusiasm. "What do they look like? Are they all gross and decayed?"

"No—not decayed. They appear in the way that they died, so

a few of them are bloody. And one of them is completely nude." She laughed. "He keeps bending over when I pass him. I'm pretty sure he's an exhibitionist."

Mason's smile was fleeting. "I want to believe you when you say they're harmless, but you nearly froze to death by Emma Carthage's grave—"

"That was my fault," Keira said, doggedly sticking to her story. "I tripped on my knife and then felt too lazy to walk thirty paces back to my cottage. If you want to keep me safe, you'll need to find some way to save me from myself."

He grimaced, looking conflicted. Keira nudged him with her elbow.

"Hey. Trust me. Please. If I felt like I was in danger, I'd move. But the graveyard is a surprisingly nice place to live. And there's, like, no commute to get to my job, so that's a definite bonus."

Mason's expression softened. "What if you were hurt? What if you disappeared one night and we couldn't find you? I wouldn't be able to live with myself."

A memory ran on repeat through her mind: Gavin Kelsey attempting to ambush her as she walked home from the mill. That had been his plan—to make her disappear. He'd said no one would notice or care if she went missing. She pushed the thought aside.

"I can look after myself. I'm strong, and I'm fast, and I don't fully know how this ghost-affinity thing works, but I'm pretty sure I was using it before I lost my memories. I only got hurt because I didn't know what that twisted ghost in the forest was capable of. But now I do, so I can stay well away from him."

Zoe cleared her throat. "I don't want you to think I'm not concerned for your welfare or whatever, but can we get back to talking about the ghosts? Seriously, this might be the most interesting secret I've heard since I discovered there are reptilians living in the sewage systems."

That made Keira laugh. Mason exhaled slowly and ran his hands through his hair, then said, "All right. I trust you. Just…be safe, okay?" He leaned back in his chair, thumbs rubbing at the inner corners of his eyes. "I went to med school because I wanted to save lives. I'm so extremely underqualified for anything to do with the dead."

Keira snorted. "That makes two of us."

# CHAPTER 9

"WHAT'S THE OLDEST GHOST you've ever seen?" Zoe spoke through a mouthful of food, her owlish eyes wide and eager.

"Early 1700s, I think."

"Cool. That's around when this area was settled. What do they look like? Do they float?"

"They don't fly or anything, but they can move through things. They look like mist. Some are clear, but others are just fuzzy pale shapes. It's like some are stronger than others." Keira picked at her sandwich. Her stomach was too unsettled to let her eat much, but Mason looked concerned whenever she put the food down, so she kept at it. "I think they use the moisture in the air to create their forms. They're clearest on rainy days or days with heavy fog."

"It must suck to die in the desert, then. If they can't talk, how do you communicate? Pantomime?"

"In a way. I ask them questions, and they nod or shake their heads."

"Can't they just, y'know, lead you to the problem and point at it or something?"

That was an idea Keira had wondered about before. "I don't think they can go far from their tether—the place that connects them to earth. That's why the twisted spirit shouldn't be a problem if I don't go back into the forest. He can't follow me." *I hope.*

Mason spoke. "You said it's different from the other ghosts. That it's been twisted. Is it the only one, or are there more like it?"

"Not that I've seen. I feel like it's a rare form. It's"—the word fell from her tongue like she'd said it a thousand times before—"a shade."

"A what?"

"A shade. Don't ask me what that is, because I have no idea. I just know that's its name." She shrugged. "Sorry, sometimes my brain gives me puzzle pieces of information, but nothing to connect it to."

"I'll do some research." Zoe paused to swallow a mouthful of her lunch. "I'm not really plugged into the ghost segment of the paranormal researchers, but I've got contacts. Maybe someone knows what you're talking about."

"That would be amazing. Ah—and that reminds me. There's a ghost I'm trying to help. He was murdered in late 1891, but I don't know what's keeping him here."

"What's his name?"

"That's just it—the gravestone is unmarked. I looked him up in the newspaper. No one could identify him. He was killed near the outskirts of town."

Zoe frowned at the ceiling. "I think I remember the one you're talking about. But I doubt I'd have anything that wasn't reported in the newspapers. I'll ask around, though."

"Thanks." Zoe's tendency to be flippant meant it was easy to forget just how thoroughly she knew the town's history—especially the sensational or sinister parts. "It'll be a massive help if I can ask you for leads. I've been using the library's newspaper archives, but they're not as helpful as I would have hoped. They couldn't tell me much about Gerald Barge either."

Zoe blinked. "Gerald Barge?"

"That's the twisted one. The shade."

Cackling laughter shook Zoe as she slapped the table. "Hell, of course you wouldn't find anything about him in the papers. No one figured out he was a serial killer until years later."

A few of the closer diners turned toward the commotion. Keira hunched her shoulders to avoid the attention and kept her voice low. "Is this for real? He killed people?"

Mason rubbed at the back of his neck. "I think Zo might be right. The name's familiar."

"Of course I'm right! Gerald Barge is an integral part of this town's gory history." Zoe made no effort to soften her voice. "It's a story and a half. Want to hear it?"

"*Obviously* yes." Keira shuffled forward in her seat, impatient for Zoe to begin.

"Back in the eighteen hundreds Blighty was still a fairly young town. There were a handful of respected individuals that essentially ran the place under the Crispins' oversight. One of them was Gerald Barge. He'd never married or had children, but he was considered a good Christian man. He raised the money to repair the town hall, lent his workhorse to his neighbors when theirs fell sick, you name it. Everyone loved him. When he died at the age of fifty-two, it was considered a tragedy and virtually the whole town came to his funeral."

Zoe leaned forward, hands laced beneath her chin. "Years passed. A new family bought his home and decided to plant a fruit tree in the backyard. When they were digging up the ground, they found small bones. At first they thought it was just a chicken or a cat or something, but they kept digging, and then they found the skull—a *human* skull."

Keira, engrossed, put her sandwich down. "Go on."

"Everyone was in shock. At first people tried to claim dear sweet Gerald was innocent—maybe these new occupants were the killers, or maybe the body had been there before Gerald's time—but gradually people started to have doubts. The bones' age matched the time Gerald had been occupying his estate. And his neighbors remembered how, once every month or so, Gerald would go into the woods for a few days to 'hunt.' He rarely brought back game, and when he did, it wasn't as much as you'd expect. Maybe a rabbit or something. Never enough to justify the length of the trips or how dirty his clothes got."

Zoe paused to take a sip of her coffee, obviously appreciating her audience's investment. "Well, then it came out that the next town over—separated from us by the forest—had seen members of its population go missing on a regular basis for more than a decade. Mostly women, often widows or poor workers. There was no sign of foul play and no bodies; they just up and vanished. The police never put in a serious effort to investigate. But unsurprisingly, the disappearances had ceased around the same time as Gerald's death.

"Then they found his killing cabin. It was a little shack in the middle of the forest, halfway between this town and theirs. Inside were ropes, sacks, shovels, and this awful collection of knives. Patches of ground looked like they'd been dug up around the shack. And, of course, they found a whole bunch of bodies buried there. I think the final count was over thirty, including the two he buried in his back garden before he realized he would draw too much attention if he kept taking victims from inside Blighty."

Mason grimaced. "And all that time, his town admired him."

"Mm-hmm. He did and said exactly the right things to make people love him so he could maintain his sick habit undisturbed." Zoe swallowed the last of her sandwich and dusted her hands. "When all of this broke, people were understandably horrified. A bunch of teenagers created a mob of sorts and dug up his grave. They broke the tombstone and brought his skull into town to show it off. The police tried to intervene, so one of the teenagers kicked the skull into a cornfield. People searched for it but couldn't locate it. The theory is one of those kids got to it first and kept it as a memento."

"And they never found it?" Keira asked.

"Nah. After a few days, they moved the rest of his remains to a new grave inside the forest, where it was less likely to upset people visiting the cemetery. They buried him with a concrete slab on top to stop the teenagers from trying to get at him again. And he's remained there ever since."

Keira chewed on her thumb. "That explains a lot."

"And you're certain he can't follow you?" Mason asked.

"Yep." *Probably.* Keira seized on a change of subject. "Since you guys are in the mood to listen to wild stuff, would you believe me if I said I thought my cat was magic?"

Zoe narrowed her eyes. "I could be amenable. What's your evidence?"

"Twice now she's led me home when I've gotten lost." Keira ticked the points off on her fingers. "She enters and leaves the house even when I'm *certain* the door is closed. And, uh, sometimes I imagine she understands what I'm saying."

"Nope." Zoe gave a dismissive wave. "Sorry, not convincing enough. Have you actually *seen* your cat? That thing's barely functional. I've met smarter potatoes."

Keira pulled a face. "Hey, come on. She's a good cat. She's just a bit…"

"Special?" Zoe quirked an eyebrow.

Keira laughed and threw a napkin at her.

Marlene appeared at the table and began gathering plates. She gave them a pointed, lingering stare. Keira glanced behind them; the café was packed full. As Marlene returned to the kitchen, she whispered, "We've been taking up a table for a while. I feel like we should go."

"Nah." Zoe examined her fingernails. "She doesn't have any bouncers, and she's not strong enough to kick us out herself. I once stayed here for fourteen straight hours."

Keira stared. "How? Wouldn't you need the bathroom?"

"I'm resourceful."

"Great. No further details, please." She turned to Mason.

He gave her a tight-lipped smile and picked up his jacket. "I'm ready. Let's go."

They wove their way through the crowded café, Keira doing her best not to bump any of the chairs. It felt strange to have revealed such a dangerous truth in a public place, but somehow, she also felt secure. The small, cramped shop had an atmosphere that lent itself to secrets.

Zoe snagged Keira's sleeve as they left the café. "So Adage is hiring you to be his ghost expeller, right?"

"Sort of. I'm not really expelling them. I'm just trying to help them move on." Keira stretched as sunshine flowed over her, and the three of them turned toward the fountain in the center of the intersection.

"Have you had much success?" Mason asked.

"Um." She chuckled. "One. Emma Carthage."

Zoe's grin was irrepressible. "So you going to let me sit in on some of your séances or what?"

"I...I don't do séances. It will probably just look like me talking to thin air. But I guess you could watch if you want?"

"Sweet." Zoe hooked her arm through Keira's as they crossed the road. "I can be your sidekick and waft burning sage around the area or whatever."

"I don't do that either." Keira looked from Zoe to Mason. "Should I? Is that a thing spirit mediums do?"

Mason grinned. "Whatever you're doing now must work well enough. And, Zo, don't be rude. I'm sure she doesn't want people gawking at her while she works."

"Killjoy," Zoe muttered.

They came to a stop at the fountain. Keira looked at the sun; it had started its slide toward the mountains. "I should get home. My way-smarter-than-a-potato cat will want food."

"Actually, I had a thought." Mason was clearly trying to look casual as he scratched the back of his neck. "What if Zoe and I stayed at your place tonight? We could help with your research, and you could teach us a bit more about the ghosts."

Keira narrowed her eyes at him. "What were you saying earlier about not gawking at me while I work?"

He raised his hands, palms outward. "No gawking, promise! We don't even have to talk about the ghosts if you don't want to. I can bring pizza."

"Ooh." Zoe's face lit up. "Yes, let's make it a pizza party sleepover. We can tell ghost stories. It would be *so appropriate*."

Keira pointed a finger at Mason. "I know what you're doing. You don't think it's safe for me to be at the cottage alone. This is a blatant excuse to make sure I don't get eaten by ghosts."

"Guilty as charged. Is it working?"

"Fine. Sure." She flinched as Zoe whooped next to her ear. "Don't think this is a permanent thing, though. But it would be nice to have some company. See you around dinner?"

Mason looked relieved. "Dinner it is."

"All right, go team ghost extermination." Zoe lifted Keira's hand and forcefully high-fived it. "I gotta get back to the shop. Don't you dare talk to any ghosts until I get there. I don't want to miss the good stuff."

"I can't promise that—"

"Don't make me revoke your BFF status," Zoe yelled as she began her jog toward the convenience store.

Keira rubbed the back of her neck. "She's going to be so disappointed when she gets there and has to watch me talk to myself for an hour."

Mason smiled sheepishly. "Sorry for forcing the subject. I hope I didn't make you feel pressured."

"Nah. I meant what I said; it'll be nice to have some company."

"Good. Let me walk you home?"

"Thanks, but I feel like I need to be alone for a bit. I've got some stuff to process."

He hesitated and glanced toward the path leading to the cemetery.

"It's fine." Keira laughed. "I've been seeing ghosts since I first arrived in Blighty. They're harmless. Besides, I have Adage. And my cat, who is smart and probably magic, despite what Zoe says."

He smiled but still didn't look at ease.

"I'll call you if anything exciting happens," Keira offered.

"That'll have to do. Because I can't let you spend your life worrying about something you can't change."

"All right. I'll keep my phone with me. See you later tonight."

"I'm looking forward to it."

Mason waved as he left. Keira took a deep breath and turned toward the road leading to the cemetery. Her mind buzzed. Part of her wanted to curl into a little ball to recover. Another part wanted to laugh. It felt intensely satisfying to have the lies lifted from her, like peeling off a nasty scab. *No more secrets. Not from my friends, at least.*

She couldn't keep the smile off her face as she passed the bakery. Then a hint of motion caught her attention, and prickling unease brought her to a halt. She turned. Two figures stood on the opposite side of the road, watching her.

The younger one was immediately recognizable. Gavin Kelsey's glossy, blond hair had been styled to obscure part of his face, but the hint of a bruise was visible underneath. His pinched features were frozen into an expression of poorly concealed loathing.

The man at his side was new to Keira, but it wasn't hard to guess who he was. He had the same platinum-blond hair as his son, though it was turning white at the temples. His suit looked expensive and his glasses lent him an air of dignity, but Keira felt a chill of revulsion roll through her. Gavin wore his feelings on his sleeve, but Dr. Kelsey's eyes were ice-cold and emotionless.

They faced each other across the street. Keira felt like she was staring down a wild animal, as though turning away would be risky. She held her place and lifted her chin. Gavin's lips curled into a sneer and his eyes dropped to the pavement, but Dr. Kelsey met Keira's glare with a small, chilling smile.

Then a bell jingled and a voice called Keira's name. Polly Kennard stood in the florist's open doorway, waving to her.

"Oh, I'm glad I caught you, dear." Polly bustled forward to meet her, a large bouquet cradled in her arms. "Harry said you came by looking for flowers yesterday."

"Uh—yes." Keira glanced across the street. Dr. Kelsey and his son had disappeared. Uneasy prickles spread over her back. "I—I can pay for them."

"Oh, no, please don't worry about that. They were a gift." Polly pressed the bouquet into Keira's arms, then nudged her oversized glasses farther up her nose. "Harry wanted you to have these too."

*I'm sure he didn't.*

"He's such a romantic like that."

*He's very much not.*

"He's out right now; otherwise, he'd give them to you himself. But he wanted you to know we put this arrangement together with you in mind."

Keira couldn't help but glance toward the store's second floor. The light was on, which meant Harry wasn't out; he just didn't want to come downstairs. She couldn't bring herself to disappoint Polly, though, so she fixed a smile on her face. "That's really, really kind. He's a good friend."

She placed emphasis on the last word, but Polly didn't seem to notice. "I hope you'll think of him when you look at those flowers. I know he's thinking of you." She winked and nudged Keira. "Pop by anytime, my dear. We're always happy to have a cup of tea and a chat with you."

"Thanks." She watched as Polly trotted back inside her store, then exhaled and began the long walk to the cemetery. The flowers might not have come from Harry, but they were no less gratefully received. The bundle was huge and would provide some much-needed color for the graves.

# CHAPTER 10

KEIRA BROKE THE BOUQUET up into small portions. She wove among the graves, picking up the previous day's dying flowers and laying out fresh offerings.

She stopped when she reached her unnamed spirit's grave. The stone, simple and unadorned, donated by the town to someone they didn't know, seemed a lost, forlorn thing. *Did anyone attend his funeral? Or was it just the pastor, the undertaker, and the body shrouded inside the coffin?*

Keira placed the last of the flowers at the base of the stone, then traced her fingers over the date—1891. Her heart caught. Gerald Barge hadn't been identified until years later, but he'd been taking lives through the decade prior. Not much was known about the John Doe except that he'd been stabbed and strangled, and he hadn't been local. Gerald liked to pick his victims from out of town. It fit—almost too neatly.

"Hello? Are you here?"

Keira half expected her request to be ignored and shivered when a tendril of mist brushed her arm. The faceless spirit stood on his grave, within touching distance, as he stared blindly at the forest. Keira folded her arms around herself.

"Hey." It felt unnatural to try to make eye contact when the specter had no eyes. The dark pit where his face belonged seemed to crawl with shadows—dark, squirming flesh where flesh should not exist. Keira cleared her throat and fixed her gaze on his collarbone instead. "I think I know who killed you. Gerald Barge."

She waited for some kind of reaction: the head turning toward her or the twitch of a hand. Anything, really. But the hollow-faced man only swayed in fractions, gazing into nothing, as though Keira didn't even exist.

He could hear her, she was certain: he responded when she called for him, and his ears were intact, half-hidden under shaggy hair at the sides of his head. Keira forged on.

"He killed a lot of people. I don't know if this is what you need to hear, but he died. A long time ago. It's not the justice you deserve, I know, but Gerald is dead and can't hurt anyone else."

She thought she heard some kind of noise in his throat. Something wet, like a clotted moan. Keira fixed her gaze on the ground between them and leaned closer. "What?"

The moan faded into nothing. When she looked up, Keira found herself alone again. She frowned, working her jaw.

She'd hoped Gerald's death and an acknowledgment of what had happened to the faceless man would be enough, but apparently he needed something more. She just wasn't sure what yet—or whether she could even give it to him.

She'd scarcely gotten back inside the groundskeeper's home and connected her phone to the charger when an engine rumbled up the driveway. Keira crossed to the window. Adage's car pulled to a halt beside his house. He got out, his movements slow and weary, and ran a hand through his white hair. Instead of going inside, he turned toward Keira's cottage.

She pulled her coat back on and hurried to meet him halfway. His face was gaunt and gray, and his blue eyes had lost their sparkle. She knew what the answer would be but still had to ask. "Is it bad?"

"He passed away two hours ago." Adage drew a hand over his face. "Brody McCormack. I've known his family since before he was born. It's—it's a shock."

Keira threaded an arm around his and tried to move him toward his home. "Let's go inside. I'll make you tea."

"No." Adage took her hand and squeezed it tightly. "I have a request, child. It's not easy to ask, but I fear it's important. Will you come to the hospital with me? His body is in storage in Cheltenham Medical's morgue. I want to be certain his spirit has moved on."

"Oh." Dread threaded its way through Keira's insides like icy worms. Her subconscious screamed at her: hospitals were dangerous. But Adage's bushy eyebrows lay low over his eyes, which looked damp, the lids swollen. She swallowed. "Of course. Did you want to go right now or rest a bit first? You can't have slept much."

"Now, if you don't mind. I'd rather have my conscience at peace, and I don't know how long his body will remain there." Adage gave her a weary smile as they turned toward his car. "Thank you."

"Would you like me to drive? Wait—actually—" Keira caught herself. "I don't know if I *know* how to drive. Maybe it's better if I don't."

He chuckled softly. "Wise choice."

Keira pressed close to the car window as they left Blighty. All of her existing memories were from inside the town, and she had a faint hope that some of the roads outside might jog her mind. Patches of forests merged with undulating hills, then the road gradually climbed into the mountains. It was beautiful, but none of it was familiar.

Adage was a careful driver, but it was clear he was exhausted. He squinted over the steering wheel and kept below the speed limit. The roads were nearly empty; from what Keira had learned about the sleepy, little town, very few people found their way there unless they were looking for it.

The twisting road carried them over the wooded, gently sloping mountain range. As they came down the other side, Keira caught sight of buildings in the distance. "Is that Cheltenham?"

"That's right." Adage pressed the back of his hand over his mouth to stifle a yawn. "It's not a huge town, but it's a good size larger than Blighty. We use their hospital and their train station when we need them."

As the ground evened out, they began moving through

residential areas. The buildings were newer than anything in Blighty and were built closely together. Adage took a turn to the right, and they passed between two pillars bearing a sign reading *Cheltenham Medical.*

A wave of nausea rose in Keira's core. On the outside, the hospital appeared modern and respectable. Large, dark-tinted windows created blocks of glare running up its eight stories. Multiple separate buildings were connected by floating walkways and gravel paths. It seemed busy; the emergency doors rarely closed for more than a handful of seconds. She hated it.

*Hospitals are too risky*, the voice in her head whispered. *You shouldn't be here.*

Adage coasted into the large parking lot, pulled into the first spot he found, and turned the engine off. "Ready?"

She forced a smile and prayed her voice wouldn't shake. "Absolutely."

The building was enormous. Countless black windows seemed to stare at her like empty eyes. As they approached the automatic doors, Keira reflexively put her head down and slowed a fraction so she could walk behind Adage. She'd mostly overcome her reflex to hide from strangers in Blighty, but away from the familiar town, the impulse to make herself invisible was overwhelming. The pastor wasn't tall, though, and didn't fully hide her. She wished she'd brought a hoodie.

The doors slid open, and the scent of starched linens, hand sanitizer, and bleach burnt her nose. Her heart kicked into a higher gear and her palms grew sweaty.

"Ah." Adage came to a halt in the waiting room, surrounded by rows of hard plastic chairs. He turned to Keira and lowered his voice. "I should have asked. Do we go to the body or the room Brody passed in?"

"I don't know, actually. From what I can tell, ghosts can linger at either location."

"We'll go to both, then, if you don't mind. The morgue is a little closer."

The doors separating the lobby from the rest of the hospital were shut. Adage waved to one of the nurses, and the light next to the door turned green.

"They know me here," he explained as they stepped through. "Several of my parishioners have spent weeks or months in these wards, and I try to visit often."

He certainly seemed familiar with the hospital. The stark-white hallways felt like a maze to Keira, but Adage navigated them deftly, nodding to nurses and doctors he passed.

Keira's sense of revulsion increased the farther they moved into the building. Her shoes seemed too loud on the white tiles. The walls were squeezing and hostile. Worse than the graveyard and worse than the mill, the hospital was stained with decades of suffering. The emotional imprint was a tangible force that hit her like a train and made her want to crumple to the floor. It was all Keira could do to close herself to the sensations and hope her emotional barriers held up to the onslaught. Like a child closing its eyes when faced by a monster, the defense was paltry, but it was all she had.

*There's something here*, her subconscious whispered. *Worse than the emotions. Worse than the way these walls have been stained by the hospital's history. There's something dangerous in this building, and you need to get out before it finds you.*

Keira balled her hands into fists to keep them from shaking. Adage led her to the elevator, which they took down three levels to the basement. *The building's stomach.* Keira shook her head to dismiss the thought, but it still hovered around her like a fly she couldn't catch.

Unlike the more sterile hallways above, the halls in the lowest level were crowded. Spare beds and equipment had been stacked against the wall in lieu of proper storage, old signs tacked onto them, marking them for repair. Sickly lighting cast shadows around their legs, and it was easy for Keira to imagine that the dark shapes were watching her. Adage stopped in front of a set of unmarked double doors and knocked. A wiry, gray-haired man answered.

"Apologies for the disturbance," the pastor said. "Brody's family asked if I could say a final prayer for their child."

The man looked surprised but didn't resist. "Of course, come in." He held the door open and stepped back, then frowned as Keira trailed after the pastor. "May I ask...?"

"She's with me," Adage said.

The thin man only hesitated for a heartbeat, then he shrugged and led them forward.

The room was bitingly cold and smelled strongly of disin-fectant. A metal table took up much of the space. Indents ran around its edges. *To collect the fluids*, her mind whispered, and suddenly Keira couldn't breathe. She faced away from the autopsy table as she tried to block it from her mind. She could still feel its presence, though. Cold steel. Hard edges. Scalpels digging into soft flesh. She'd braced herself against the emotions imbued into the building, but for a second her defenses faltered and her legs threatened to collapse. She took a breath. Antiseptic burned into her lungs, and she focused on that instead.

Neither Adage nor the mortician had noticed her reaction. That was something she was good at, at least: hiding how she felt and not drawing attention.

The wall opposite the table had been fitted with rows of wide metal drawers. The mortician stopped near one at the far corner and drew it open.

Brody McCormack lay on the steel shelf. Severe mottling had spread over the man's face and torso, punctuated by sharp lacerations. His skin was unpleasantly white, his fractured jaw slack, and his open eyes turned upward, as though in supplication. Keira instinctually knew he'd been in a collision with another car.

Adage folded his hands in front of himself and bent his head. He began to murmur a prayer in a steady, soothing voice, then shot Keira a glance out of the corner of his eye.

Keira took a short, quick breath. She was supposed to open the muscle behind her eyes.

But that risked letting it all in—the emotions, the presences, exposing herself to other spirits that might endure in this cold, sterile room. The wall was full of drawers. How many other bodies might lie inside them? How many lost souls?

For a second she was tempted to grab Adage's arm and pull him out of the doors and back into the relative safety of the parking lot. But she couldn't. Adage cared for Brody, and he needed Keira in order to know that the man had safely passed over. Because while Keira could leave this white-tiled room at any moment, Brody might not have the same luxury.

She braced herself, planting her feet as firmly as she could, and pulled on the muscle. It ached as it opened. The emotions imbued in the room threatened to drown her. Slicing scalpels. Burning chemicals forced into veins. A mechanical blade to cut through bone.

Then it passed, and Keira could see again. The room held no unnatural presences.

Not fully trusting herself, Keira glanced over her shoulder. The mortician stood there, his head bowed respectfully as he continued to watch them with a wary eye.

Keira turned back to face Brody's body. The muscle burned as she pulled her second vision wide open, but the sterilized room was resolutely bare. She relaxed the second sight. Adage caught her eye, and she shook her head a fraction to answer his unspoken question.

The pastor finished his prayer, raised his head, and inhaled deeply. "Onward, then. Thank you, Allan. Brody's family and I appreciate your help." The last words were directed to the mortician. Allan gave a stiff, polite nod to both Adage and Keira, then slid the drawer back into its cabinet and gestured them to the door.

Keira only began to breathe more easily once they were in the elevator. Her heart still thundered, but her head was beginning to clear again.

"The ward isn't far," Adage said. "The nurses will have already cleaned the room and changed the bedsheets. A new patient will be moved in within a few hours most likely."

*That's right. It's not over yet.* Keira wet her dry lips, hoping Adage wouldn't notice her stress. "What about Brody's family?"

"I stayed with his parents for as long as they wanted me. They are in deep grief, as you can imagine. A family friend took them home and will be staying with them for a few days."

The elevator doors rattled open to an unfamiliar passageway. They resumed their formation: Adage leading the way, Keira keeping two steps behind him, her head tucked down.

Halls passed in a blur. The watercolor paintings started to blend together. A woman cried inside one of the rooms. Multiple TVs created a droning background noise. They passed a nurse's station and barely received a glance.

Adage pushed a door open. It was a private room, clean, with the bed already made in preparation for its next patient. Adage smiled gently as he held the door for Keira, then stepped out of her way and bowed his head as he waited for her to start her work.

Keira hadn't fully regained her composure. The atmosphere in the private room was less heavy than the morgue, at least, but it was still infused with the same low level of twisting, painful emotions that saturated the building. The muscle twinged when she felt for it. As she opened her second sight, the room blurred, then returned to focus.

A tall man stood beneath the window, his arms defensively wrapped around his shredded torso. Wan light shimmered across his features as he turned his mottled face toward her, and Keira's heart plummeted. "Hello, Brody."

# CHAPTER 11

ADAGE GAVE HER A sharp glance. "He's here?"

"Yes," Keira breathed, staring into a replica of the face from the morgue.

Brody rocked from foot to foot. He was transparent, the edges of his form hazy against the walls behind him, but his core was as bright as some of the stronger spirits in Keira's graveyard. Blood dribbled from the lacerations across his face, soaking into his shirt. Keira took a step closer to the specter. "Adage, would it be okay if I talk to him alone?"

"Of course." He gave her shoulder a reassuring squeeze. "I'll keep guard in the hallway. Call me if you need anything."

Keira waited until the door clicked shut. Her eyes burned, and she realized she'd forgotten to blink. The deep unease that had plagued her since she'd arrived at the hospital intensified, solidifying in her stomach like a tainted meal that was making her sick. She swayed, then pushed through the sensations, focusing on the man ahead of her. "Brody, we haven't met before, but my name's Keira. I'm a friend of Adage. He asked me to help you."

Brody looked from Keira to the window and back, then opened his mouth. No sound came out. Instead, the man's broken jaw quivered. He tightened his hold around his chest. Keira thought he looked lost, like a child abandoned in a crowd. The temperature was dropping in time with his growing distress. Her breath plumed when she exhaled.

"Brody, do you have any unfinished business keeping you on earth?"

He stared at her as though he couldn't understand what she'd said. She took a step nearer and softened her voice.

"Is there something you need to do, something you need to complete, before you feel ready to move on?"

He shook his head. The motion momentarily turned his features into a smudged blur, like a poorly developed photo.

Anxiety pulsed with Keira's heartbeat She didn't know how long Adage would be able to keep people out of the room, but the hospital was busy, so she doubted she'd have long. Ten minutes, maybe twenty. Nowhere near enough time to help a ghost who didn't even know what he needed help with.

"Brody, you know you're dead, don't you?"

The specter looked down at his bloodied hands. He clenched them and nodded.

"You need to move on to the next life. You..." *How does this even work?* "Can you see a light? Or a door to walk through, or anything like that?"

She already knew the answer: he was lost. He turned in a circle, searching the room, but when he arrived back at Keira, his face held growing panic.

"It's all right. Don't be afraid." She struggled to keep her own fear out of her voice. She took another step toward the ghost, her hand outstretched to calm him. "We'll figure this out."

As she moved nearer, she began to sense the energy rolling off him. She tasted the misery of shattered dreams and a lost future. His fear at what might be waiting for him in the next life. The encroaching terror that he might not be able to reach it.

There was something else, though, something just beneath the surface. Something familiar but, at the same time, unique. *His essence*, her mind whispered. Keira reached toward it.

Adage, waiting outside the room, spoke. His voice was muffled by the door, but the words were quick, and Keira detected an undercurrent of nervous energy. He was trying to stall someone. They were already out of time.

"You're ready to move on, aren't you?" Keira dropped her voice to a rapid whisper. "You *want* to move on."

The nod was shaky but certain.

"Okay. Hold still. I'm going to try something." She reached for the essence she'd felt. She could picture it—a bundle of tiny, glowing threads, knotted together in a tangle. It existed in the center of Brody's chest, just to the side of where his heart had once been. The source of his light, keeping him corporeal, holding him together.

A distant concept rose from her subconscious: the Greek Fates. The three women who wove, measured, and cut the thread of a human's life. She hadn't imagined it would appear so literally, but there it was ahead of her—a thread that, either by design or by chance, had become snagged.

She closed her eyes and took the end of the string between her fingers. It was warm, almost unpleasantly hot, and made her skin prickle. She pulled. The knot unraveled.

Keira took a quick breath and stepped back. Brody's eyes fluttered. He looked down at himself, then back up, and a hesitant smile grew over the broken jaw. And then, like a cloud of mist caught in a breeze, he evaporated, shreds of himself disintegrating until there was nothing left.

The door opened, and Adage's words became audible. "Please, if you'd just wait a moment—"

"I've got a job to do," an older nurse snapped. She stopped and stared at Keira, who still stood in the middle of the room, one hand outstretched and fingers pinched where she'd pulled the thread. "What are you doing here?"

"Just saying goodbye." Keira ducked her head and hurried to Adage's side. "Let's go."

Keira's heart thundered with mingled panic and relief as Adage led her back the way they'd come. They walked in silence until they stepped around the corner and found themselves in a small waiting room. Adage turned to her, one hand pressed over his heart. "I'm sorry. I couldn't hold her back any longer."

"It's okay." Keira kept her voice quiet, aware that staff and patients were still moving along the hallway only a few paces away, but was incapable of holding back her smile. "He's moved over."

Adage's bushy eyebrows rose. "Truly?"

She looked at her fingers, then clenched them. They itched when she thought about touching the ball of thread. "Yes. Brody didn't have any unfinished business, but he couldn't move on for some reason. But I...I don't exactly know *what* I did, but it worked. I think I found a way to clear stuck spirits."

"Thank goodness." The stress seemed to drain from Adage's face. His shoulders slumped as he took his glasses off for polishing. "He was a good, kind boy. I know he will be welcomed into the Lord's embrace. At least now I don't have to worry about him. Are you ready to go home, child?"

"Yes, please." Every fiber of Keira's being begged for her to leave the hospital. She wouldn't feel safe until she was back in the car and the imposing building had disappeared from the rearview mirror.

Adage led the way. Following in his wake, Keira finally had a moment to examine the unease that tormented her. *Why do I fear hospitals?*

She remembered the little photograph she'd found in her jacket pocket on the night she arrived in Blighty. In it, three people had worn a type of uniform she hadn't been able to identify. Keira had initially thought it must have been some kind of government or military outfit, but now she wondered if it could be medical. It looked nothing like the scrubs the nurses wore, but she could imagine the high-collared, low-hemmed jackets being worn in a prestigious, private institute.

That still didn't explain the inscription on the back side: DON'T TRUST THE MEN WITH FLAKY SKIN.

A shiver crawled up her spine. Keira shook her head to clear the unpleasant thoughts, then abruptly realized her reaction was physical, not psychological. The temperature had dropped.

"Adage?"

He obligingly stopped, his eyebrows raised in a question. White walls lined with equally white doors stretched in all directions. An elderly woman and her daughter were walking along the space, arms looped together as they chatted. A nurse pushed past as she examined patient notes. Keira pulled on her aching second sight, but nothing appeared.

Even so, the skin on Keira's arms rose into goose bumps. "Does it feel cold to you?"

"Perhaps a little. But hospitals are often kept chilly. I like to bring a cardigan to stay warm." He plucked at the turquoise sweater he wore. "You can borrow it if you're cold."

"Thanks, but…" Keira's attention drifted to the door to their left. A tiny wisp of mist curled out from the gap beneath it. She frowned and slowly lifted her eyes. A narrow rectangular window was set into the door. As far as she could see, the room inside was empty; a single bed was neatly made, waiting for a fresh occupant.

Keira took a step closer, holding her breath as she pressed against the door. An angular face appeared on the other side of the glass, its drooping eyes barely inches from Keira's.

She gasped and jolted back, pressing a hand to her jumping heart. It was a woman in her late seventies or early eighties, her skin wrinkled and crepe-like, her face still holding on to a sense of hardness. Thin lips were pressed together, and the unblinking eyes stared blindly forward.

The specter was shockingly bright. Keira had grown to associate the strength of the apparition with the intensity of its emotions. Even though the woman didn't try to speak, Keira could feel the desperation bleeding out of her. Her lips twitched as the thin eyebrows pulled lower over empty, black eyes.

"Keira?" Adage approached her side. "Is something the matter?"

"I… There's a spirit…" Keira was riveted. The strange woman wasn't moving, and her gaze didn't waver. She seemed to be waiting.

*For what? Me?* Keira hesitated. She was so close to escaping the hospital. Both her body and her subconscious wanted to keep moving and not stop until she was through the automatic doors.

Faint wisps of hair flowed about the woman's creased face, like seagrass caught in the tide. Her eyes had no pupils and no irises, but Keira felt them fixed on her, unyielding. She spoke without turning her head. "Would you mind if I take a moment with her?"

"Of course. Have all of the time you need."

Keira pressed her hand on the door. The woman stepped back, allowing Keira to enter.

The room felt at least ten degrees colder than the hall. As the door swung shut, its motion disturbed a layer of faint mist that lingered across the icy tiles.

"Hello." With the door shut, the noises of the hospital faded until they were barely audible, and Keira was able to fix her whole attention on the woman. She was a little taller than Keira, but lean. Her drooping eyes looked inexpressibly sad. *Not just sad*, Keira realized. *She's frightened.*

Brody had been afraid—both of what had happened to him, and of what was waiting for him on the other side. But something about this woman was different. She wasn't panicked, and she wasn't frantic. Her terror didn't come from confusion.

Keira tilted her head, searching the woman's expression. "Are you unable to move on?"

The woman gave a single, curt nod.

"I can try to help." Keira reached out and opened her senses to the woman's emotions. A shudder ran through her as she tasted pure, desperate dread. Underneath it was a sense of urgency, like a ticking clock that was running out. Anger at an injustice. Grief.

Keira found the woman's essence. She closed her eyes and pictured the ball of glowing, entwined threads. She reached for a loose end, but before she could touch it, the essence faded. Keira opened her eyes. The woman had her hands pressed over her heart. She shook her head, frowning.

"Sorry." The emotions were intensifying, and Keira struggled to breathe through them. "I understand. You have something you need to do before you'll be ready to pass on. Am I right?"

A nod. The woman crossed to the window and stopped there, waiting for Keira to follow.

She gave a final glance toward the door. A corner of Adage's shoulder was visible through the little glass pane as he faced the hall.

*You've stayed too long already. There's something dangerous here. Leave before it finds you.*

Keira gritted her teeth and followed the ghost to where it stood by the window, its bony hand pointing to the ground outside.

# CHAPTER 12

THE ROOM OVERLOOKED A parking bay where two ambulances and a black van sat idling. A broad oak tree grew close to the window and cast shade over the room, but Keira's view was still clear enough to see a delivery vehicle pulling out from the bay. Farther away, past a small ridge of shrubs, was the parking lot where Adage had left his car. Beyond that were main streets dividing the hospital from the town, with wooded mountains rising in the distance.

"What do you want me to see?" Keira's gaze turned from the parking lot to the ambulances, to the road and back. Nothing appeared out of place.

The woman pointed more vigorously to something in the nearest parking bay, but Keira couldn't tell what.

"I don't understand."

The woman tapped the latch at the base of the window,

sending flakes of frost creeping over the metal. Keira opened it, then pushed the window up. The opening was barely large enough for an adult to fit through. The woman pressed past her, making Keira gasp from the sudden cold, and crawled through the gap.

Keira knew the motions were a pantomime. The woman could pass through the wall if she wanted. But she clung to the outside of the building, her white hospital gown floating in a phantom wind, her heavy-lidded eyes unblinking, and Keira knew what she wanted.

"No. Not a chance." She ducked through the window to hiss at the spirit. "I can't just—"

The woman threw a hand behind herself, pointing toward the ground, and Keira swallowed a frustrated sound. She glanced at the door, then back to the parking lot. "Can't I just take the elevator?"

The gesture was repeated, more forcefully this time. Ice grew where the specter touched the brickwork. The chill rolled over Keira, unpleasantly harsh.

She thought she understood why the woman was being so insistent. Just like the shade, she couldn't stray far from her anchor, the place where she'd died. And the fury of her emotions was burning through her energy. Even in the seconds since Keira had first seen her, she'd grown paler. She needed to show Keira something, and she didn't have much time.

"Okay. Okay." She rubbed numb fingers over the back of her neck. "Just…give me a second."

She crossed to the door and cracked it open. Adage stood outside, hands folded ahead of himself. He turned as Keira appeared, a hopeful smile brightening his face. "All sorted?"

"Not quite." Keira cleared her throat. "There's a bit more to do. I don't know how long it will take. Can I meet you at the car?"

He raised his eyebrows. "Don't worry, I have no objections to waiting, especially since you're not familiar with the hospital yet."

Keira didn't exactly know how to explain that a ghost was asking her to climb out a window. She glanced behind herself. The woman's creased face peered at her over the sill. "No need. I'll find my way down and meet you as soon as I can."

"If that's what you want, child." Adage took his glasses off and rubbed them on the edge of his coat. His blue eyes continued to watch her from under bushy brows. "You look nervous. You have since we first arrived here. Is everything all right?"

"I hope so." She managed a chuckle. "See you soon."

Keira closed the door firmly and waited until Adage's footsteps had faded down the hall before returning to the window. The woman clung there, her eyes keen. Keira gave her a thin smile. "All right, I'm in your hands. Show me what you want me to see."

The ghost moved from the sill to a water pipe that ran down the hospital's side. Keira scanned the parking lot, hoping none of the visiting families were looking in her direction, then hoisted herself up and swung her legs through the window.

The opening was small, and Keira had to wiggle to fit her hips through. She braced her arms on the room's white walls as she lowered herself out, then her feet found purchase on the ledge that framed the window below.

The oak tree had crowded close to the hospital's brickwork as it grew, shielding Keira from the parking lot's view. One of its limbs spread just a few feet below the window and looked solid enough to hold her weight.

Keira glanced toward the ghost, half hoping that it might have just wanted to show her the brick wall's peeling paint or a nice bird's nest, but it only scuttled farther down the wall, appearing unpleasantly reminiscent of an insect.

*Well. Too late to go back now.*

Keira grit her teeth, braced herself, then leaped. She hit the branch harder than she'd intended, and a small flurry of leaves cascaded past her as she straddled it, her fingers digging into the rough bark. She squinted an eye open to check that no one had seen her. Only a few visitors wandered through the parking lot, and none were looking toward her.

She twisted herself around to reach the trunk. The tree was growing old and knobbly and was easy to scale. She managed to keep her drop to the grass smooth and silent.

A row of bushes sheltered Keira from view of the parking bay. She didn't even need to activate her second sight to keep track of her guide. The older woman stayed at her side, chilled air radiating from her and drying the sweat on Keira's back. She waited until Keira straightened, then she led the way forward.

The spirit had been shockingly bright in the hospital room, but now, each step seemed to bleed light from her. She stopped at the bushes. Keira had to push her second sight as hard as she could to keep the specter in view, and the familiar tension headache flared in the back of her skull. The woman pointed past the shrubs, and Keira pushed their branches aside.

They were facing the black van she'd seen from the window. It was still idling, apparently waiting for some kind of delivery. A driver sat in the front seat, his cell phone's screen lighting his face as he scrolled through a newsfeed, a black cap pulled down over his shaggy gray hair.

The uneasy feeling that had dogged Keira since her arrival at Cheltenham Hospital redoubled. Her breath hitched, and adrenaline poured into her limbs in preparation for a fight or a flight.

But she still didn't know why.

The man wasn't familiar—at least, nothing about his face seemed to jog a memory. The van was nondescript and windowless. But simply being near it made Keira want to scream.

Her legs felt like they were made of stone. They dragged as she stepped out from the cover of the bushes and circled the van. Its back doors were closed and held shut by a silver bolt. A white emblem had been painted across the doors: a hexagon made of thin, curling leaves.

*That's it.* The emblem was familiar. It tore at the emptiness in her mind, digging into the space where old memories had once lived, but not connecting with anything except raw emotion.

She hated the emblem. She dreaded what it meant.

*Why?* Keira tried to hold herself together, faintly aware that she was hyperventilating. The only thing she could hear was her own incessant pulse. She looked toward the shrubs near the hospital wall; her guide remained there, now barely more than a glimmer. Grief pulled on her thin lips. She turned away and vanished.

Keira took an unsteady step closer to the van. The sigil on the back doors loomed above her, harsh white on a black backdrop, excruciating and terrible in ways she didn't comprehend. The lost memories were there, just beyond Keira's reach.

She needed to know. To know why the ghost was so desperate for her to see this. Why she feared it so furiously. What was hidden behind windowless doors.

Keira's hand shook as she reached for the silver bolt.

A door slammed, making her flinch. She took two staggering steps back. The driver stood beside the van, eyes wide as he stared at her. The same horrible logo was embroidered in the center of his black cap. He still held his cell phone in one limp hand, and now that he was closer, Keira could see the skin around his fingers was ragged and shedding off in clumps.

*Beware the men with flaky skin.*

Keira turned and bolted.

"Hey! *Hey!*" Heavy boots beat the pavement as the man raced after her. He swore, then Keira heard him speak in a clipped voice. "It's Sarah Tomlin. She's still alive. Outside Cheltenham."

Keira chanced a glance over her shoulder. The driver was speaking into his phone. His strides were long, but he was out of shape and already winded. Keira had the speed advantage.

She leaped over the shrubs dividing the parking bay from the main parking lot. She could see the far corner where Adage had parked. He stood by his car, facing the wrong way, unaware of the commotion. Keira didn't dare run to him. If the man from the van wanted her dead—and she was sure he did—she didn't want to think what might happen to Adage if she was caught with him.

Keira veered toward the hospital's fence and the road dividing it from the residential area. She deliberately ran between cars, choosing narrow gaps that she could squeeze through but would slow the van driver. She heard him swear again. Then she hit the chain-link fence, scaled it in a flurry of energy, and dropped to the sidewalk on the other side. She was at the opposite curb before he even stopped at the fence.

Her lungs ached and adrenaline made the headache throb, but she couldn't afford to slow down. She wove down a side street that would shield her from the man's line of sight. A pair of children playing in a yard and a man weeding his garden stared at her as she ran past, but otherwise the area was quiet.

*Fewer witnesses will make it easier to disappear.* Her subconscious seemed to know what she needed to do, so she trusted it and let it lead her toward the mountains.

# CHAPTER 13

KEIRA FOLLOWED THE STREET to its end. A row of houses acted as a barricade between her and the forest, so she vaulted a fence to get into a back garden. It was occupied. Two men laughed over a sizzling grill as they cooked sausages. Their backs were to Keira, and they hadn't heard her near-silent landing, so she lowered herself into a crouch and slunk along the property's edge. She used an overturned garden pot as leverage to get over the fence and dropped into the woods.

The trees were thinner and sparser than the forests around Blighty, but patchy cover was better than no cover. Keira sped up as she wove through the trunks. The ground inclined upward, and while the first few minutes of running had felt effortless, it didn't take long for dizziness to crash over her and force her to slow to a jog.

*This must be the blood loss Mason keeps worrying about.* She wanted to sit for few minutes, but her subconscious warned her there wasn't time. The people hunting her were fast, and they were ruthless. They would fan out through the streets and quickly progress to searching the forest. There was no time to rest, not even for a minute.

She took her jacket off and tied it around her waist as she picked up her pace. Bird chatter echoed around her. That struck Keira as a good sign, though she couldn't guess why. She followed the incline, trying to move in as straight a line as possible, and saw a gap in the trees ahead. A boulder had fallen down the mountainside and crushed foliage to create a natural lookout. Keira dropped into a crouch and crept onto the stone.

She could see Cheltenham Hospital from her vantage point. The parking bay, which had only held one black van and several ambulances when she'd been there, was now filled with eight black vans. They'd parked at odd angles, having pulled up in a hurry. Men in dark uniforms milled through the parking lot. Most carried walkie-talkies.

Keira searched for Adage. She recognized his sky-blue car near the back of the parking lot. The pastor stood next to it, both hands running through his white hair as he watched the men. She wondered if he suspected the commotion was for her. His body language certainly seemed worried. At least the men weren't paying him any attention, which meant they probably didn't know she was connected to him. Yet.

*Get out of here*, she silently pleaded. *Don't wait for me. Please.*

One of the men passed near Adage. The pastor raised a hand

to hail him as he called something inaudible, but whatever he said was ignored. Adage rubbed the back of his neck, the motion looking increasingly agitated.

*Please don't ask about me. Don't draw attention to yourself.*

She felt sick to her stomach. The gentle pastor wouldn't give up on her quickly. But she didn't have her cell phone, so there was nothing she could do for him without physically stepping back into the parking lot. And that would be certain death. They'd made that clear enough when they'd shot at her outside Blighty, on the night she'd lost her memories.

She could only hope Adage would put the clues together and leave without making a scene. Keira lingered as long as she dared before creeping back into the tree cover. Seconds were precious.

She kept her pace as quick as she could without exhausting herself. The slope uphill was grueling and the dried leaves layering the ground continually threatened to slip from under her. She used her arms as much as her legs, grabbing branches and trunks to physically drag herself up the trail, but always being careful not to snap anything. Broken branches could be used to track her path.

A whistle in the distance startled her. Keira crouched and listened. Deep, booming barks echoed from farther down the mountain. She closed her eyes, her mind flashing back to the night she'd arrived outside of Blighty. They'd been using dogs to track her then too, but that night she'd had the rain as an advantage. It had washed away her scent, something she didn't have in her favor today. Still—they weren't close. Yet. She kept moving.

She didn't have a concrete idea of where she was going, only that she needed to put as much distance between herself and the hunters as possible. A helicopter passed overhead. Its droning blades were audible well before it reached the mountain, and Keira hid under thick tree cover. Moments later, a second helicopter joined the first, and together they looped around the mountain range. The sound became heavy and bone-shuddering when they passed too close and set Keira's teeth on edge.

Time blurred. Keira kept moving, pushing through lingering dizziness and tiredness to maintain her lead. The helicopters refused to stop. They were like bees humming just out of reach, infernally frustrating.

The sun dropped in increments, and twilight smudged the landscape. Her adrenaline had long since faded, leaving her queasy and shaking. Keira leaned against a tree as she considered her options.

She could continue moving through the night, but it would be painfully slow. Worse, it would leave her too tired to do much once the sun finally rose. The alternative was finding somewhere to camp, trying to get some sleep, and hoping she wasn't found.

*Climb a tree*, the subconscious part of her mind whispered. *You'll be safer off the ground.*

Keira paced through the woods until she found a huge oak. Its canopy was thick enough to give her cover and the branches looked stable, so Keira climbed it, clambering over the lowest footholds and eventually stopping on a forked branch halfway up. It was wide enough to sit on comfortably, and Keira used her jacket to tie herself to the limb so she wouldn't roll off during the night.

The sun finally set behind the mountain, and Keira's eyes adjusted to the moonlit darkness. She needed sleep, but she still felt too on edge to close her eyes. Birdcalls were replaced by bat chatter and a distant owl, and as evening gradually progressed, Keira caught sight of wild animals among the trees. A fox crept under her. It paused, its snout turned toward the wind, then skittered away as it detected some distant threat.

The bat chatter ceased. Even the night insects fell silent. A sense of dread crept over Keira. She pressed her back to the tree's trunk, breath suspended as she listened.

The footsteps came first: heavy boots breaking through clumps of leaves and dry twigs indiscriminately. One pair to her left, another pair farther to her right. As they drew closer, she heard the dog's panting. The men didn't carry flashlights, but something told Keira they didn't need them.

A hint of motion to her right. Keira didn't even dare turn her head, but her eyes tracked the figure as it moved into view. He wore a skull mask and had a massive canine at his side. Its gray fur rippled across bunching muscles, and its tongue lolled over teeth as long as her finger. It looked more wolf than dog.

They passed by at least twenty feet from her tree. Keira knew that was her saving grace; the dog would have smelled her if it had been much closer.

She kept perfectly still. The men and their dog passed, and gradually their footsteps faded. Time ticked by. The men didn't return, but the image of their dog, saliva frothing over its jagged, white teeth, kept Keira awake well past midnight.

Her mind was a mess. It kept cycling through the same impossible questions again and again: *Is Adage safe? Why did the ghost need me to see the van? How do they know me, and what do they want with me?*

And, worst of all: *Where do I go now?*

Blighty had become her home. The idea of never seeing it again—of giving up Mason or Zoe or Adage—felt like a knife slicing into her heart. But her subconscious also warned her that being close to them would put them in danger. The van's driver had been surprised that she was alive. Now that she'd been spotted, the hunt would be renewed.

At least she had one thing to be grateful for. She'd been seen in Cheltenham, miles from Blighty. They would concentrate their search there…at least for the near future.

Zoe and Mason had made plans to meet her at the cottage that night. She wondered how long they'd waited. Would they have called her cell phone only to hear it ringing from where she'd plugged it in to charge? Mason had promised to bring pizza. Keira's eyes burned, and she pressed her palms into them.

A slow, smoldering fury burned inside her chest. In the span of an hour, the strangers had stolen her friends, her home, even her freedom to stand in the open without fearing for her life.

She'd had cause to dislike people since arriving at Blighty— Dane, firing after her and her friends as they ran from his property; Gavin Kelsey, callous, cruel, and a murderer—but she had never hated anyone or anything as deeply as she hated the unknown men at that moment.

The helicopters continued their search until the early hours of the morning, their spotlights cutting through the canopy. Keira slept patchily, muscles growing steadily sorer from having to hold still. The tree's cover was dense and she'd been lucky to wear clothes in earthy colors that day. The searchlights never lingered over her position.

Renewed thirst dogged Keira when she woke the following morning. The horrible chugging helicopters were gone at least. She untied herself from the tree and lowered herself to the ground, swallowing moans as sore muscles objected to their use.

She doubted the search had stopped, but it seemed to have moved on from her location at least. The birds were lively again, and that was a good sign.

Keira let her instincts guide her over the mountain. She had a vague idea of where Blighty lay in relation to Cheltenham, so she kept track of the sun's position and corrected her course according to it.

It was midafternoon before she found water. Keira collapsed beside the spring to gulp down mouthfuls of the cool liquid. She allowed herself an hour to rest beside it before continuing the hike.

Her mind felt strangely blank. She wondered if this was how she'd been before she'd lost her memories: constantly on the move, ignoring the aches in her feet and the emptiness in her stomach, nothing to look forward to, simply focused on surviving another day. It certainly felt familiar.

She passed over the mountain's ridge about an hour before sunset. Like the night before, she made a bed for herself in a tree. This time, she was tired enough to fall asleep instantly.

A drizzling rain woke her shortly before sunrise. Keira reluctantly dropped out of the tree, wrapped the jacket tightly around herself, and set out again.

She was ravenous. She knew she could go at least another few days without eating, but it would be unpleasant. At least the ground was leading downward.

Then, abruptly, the endless wall of trees ceased. Keira stood on the edge of a narrow asphalt road. She pulled on her memories of the drive out of Blighty, then turned left.

She couldn't risk being spotted, so she stayed inside the forest, walking parallel to the road—close enough to keep it in sight but protected by a layer of trees and vines.

Occasionally cars passed. Each time she heard an engine, Keira lowered herself to the ground. The likelihood that any of the vehicles belonged to the men hunting her was slim, but even slim chances could be dangerous.

Rain continued to drip over her. It wasn't heavy, but it was cold, and Keira hunched her shoulders. More light began filtering through the trees as the forest thinned. She followed the faint glow, weaving between trunks and scratching branches. She pushed through a final curtain of leaves and found herself standing on the edge of the woods and staring down at Blighty.

The clouds dampened the sun, and even though it was only midafternoon, many of the houses had their lights on. They twinkled through the rain like beacons. Two days had passed since she'd left. She hadn't realized how much she'd missed Blighty until her throat closed over.

She skirted around the edge of the town, moving toward the cemetery and parsonage. More than anything, she wanted to be inside her home, warm and safe, with her friends and her cat. But caution tried to pull her back. It would be dangerous to reenter Blighty, it said. It could get her friends killed. That was a high price for a little comfort.

*Maybe I can come and go without them knowing. Stop by the groundskeeper's cottage, pick up some clothes and food, and leave a note so they know I'm all right. I can be back inside the forest in less than ten minutes.*

*And then what?* Keira's heart ached. She assumed she would be back to the life old Keira had known: running, hiding, barely scraping by. Sleeping in trees. Stealing food. Only this time, she wouldn't know what she'd done to deserve being hunted. The burning fury in her chest grew hotter.

The church's steeple came into sight and Keira slowed, keeping herself hidden inside the forest. The parsonage's windows were cold and empty. But a small rectangle of light glistened across wet gravestones. The light in Keira's cottage was on.

# CHAPTER 14

KEIRA FLATTENED HERSELF AGAINST a pine tree. She had a clear view of the dripping, fog-clouded graveyard and her cottage, but anyone looking toward her would have trouble seeing her in the gloom.

The cottage door opened. A figure appeared on the step, golden light flowing over his back and tousled hair. His face was invisible in the darkness, but the posture was unforgettable, and Keira pulled in a sharp breath. Mason.

She broke out from the trees before she could second-guess herself. Her legs shook as she quickened into loping strides, but they carried her steadily as she wove between dark stones and dead trees.

The mist coiled around her limbs and the tinge of burning frost on her tongue warned her that she would be surrounded by the dead if she opened her second sight, but she didn't try to look for them. The cottage was close. Mason either heard her or sensed her, when she was still twenty feet out, and turned. He squinted into the gloom for a second before recognizing her, then a sharp cry broke from him as he left the porch's cover and ran to meet her halfway.

"Hey," Keira managed. Mason caught her by her shoulders and pulled her close. She pressed her face into his shirt and mumbled, "Sorry I missed the pizza party."

"Forget that. I can't believe you're back." His voice was full of shocked laughter. He swept her toward the cottage. They made it as far as the doorway before Zoe met them, throwing herself at Keira and squeezing her tightly enough to wind her.

"I *knew* you hadn't spontaneously combusted," Zoe gasped into her ear, then pulled back slightly, her nose wrinkling. "Wow, you're wet. Maybe you spontaneously liquefied instead."

"In, in." Mason ushered them out of the rain and into the cottage. The fire in the far wall was lively, and by the amount of soot gathered around the grate, it had been running for a while. Daisy lay on the rug before it, stomach exposed to the heat. At Keira's entrance, one eye lazily opened, then slid closed again.

"Are you hurt?" Mason plucked at Keira's hands, eyebrows heavy as he took stock of all the scrapes she'd accumulated in the forest.

Keira tucked her hands behind herself to escape his quick eyes. "I'm fine, just a bit tired and hungry."

"Of course you are. Zo, can you find her some dry clothes? I'll fix the food."

Zoe saluted, then threw open the closet doors and began riffling through the donated offerings. "What on earth happened to you, anyway? We were waiting for you when Adage turned up, almost out of his mind. He said he'd lost you in the hospital."

"Is he okay?" Keira knew she was ignoring the question, but her own felt too pressing. "Is he here?"

"He's in Cheltenham now, searching for you." Zoe pushed a bundle of clothes into Keira's hands. "Don't worry, I'll call him. Get changed first. We have *so* much to catch you up about and, from the sounds of it, vice versa."

Keira allowed herself to be shepherded toward the narrow bathroom-slash-laundry. She stood on the tiles for a moment, shivering, until she heard the muffled sounds of Zoe calling and speaking to Adage. The fire's heat hadn't managed to reach the chilliest room, so she changed quickly, forfeiting the shower in favor of getting some food and sleep. As she pulled a sweater over her head, she caught a glimpse of herself in the mirror. Her cheeks had hollowed out again. Dark circles encompassed her eyes. Her hair, tied back, was tangled and heavy with water. She looked feral.

*It's more than looks. I* feel *feral.* Being away from Blighty— away from her friends—had changed something inside of her. She was back to the Keira that had woken up in the forest with no memories: running on instinct, wary of everything and everyone, a wild animal that shied away from help until it was desperate.

Then she looked down and finally noticed the clothes Zoe had picked out for her. Green sweatpants, many sizes too large so that she had to cinch the waistband and let the legs billow around her, and a Christmas sweater making an appearance several months too early. Rudolf led a charge of reindeer over a glittery Christmas tree. Santa followed in his sleigh, one hand raised in greeting. His eyes, like the tree's baubles, were made of sewed felt, only one had come off and left just a strand of black yarn behind, giving him a deranged squint.

Keira started laughing at the absurd Santa and couldn't stop. It was so Zoe, so Blighty, so much of everything she'd come to love. The old Keira, the Keira that had woken in the forest, no longer existed. She'd grown. The dislodged part of her snapped back into place, and just like that, she felt like she was home again. Even if home meant a suspicious Santa Clause peering up at her from her sweater.

She doubled over the sink, relief and joy mingling into her mirth until she couldn't breathe through ragged chuckles.

The door rattled as someone knocked, then Zoe's voice floated through the wood. "Hey, so, Mason wants to check on whether you're having a mental breakdown or what, but I guess he's scared of seeing you in your underwear, so he sent me instead."

"I'm good." Keira wiped moisture off her cheeks, then opened the door, arms spread to showcase Zoe's fashion choices. "And I'm flattered that you think this is what suits me."

Zoe gave her an appraising once-over. "What, did you want me to dress you in black? Maybe add some leather to really lean into the tragic-backstory aesthetic? Nah. Green's your color, girl. Embrace it."

Mason, near the fireplace, cleared his throat. He held a large bowl of stew toward her. The scent of herbs flooded Keira's senses, and she almost ran to take the food.

"Wow, I needed this."

"You look it." He ran his hand across the back of his neck as Keira sank into the chair. "It's been two days since we last saw you. Did you get enough to eat? Adage thought you had some money with you but didn't know how much."

"Mm." The question barely registered as she shoved spoonfuls of food into her mouth. "No shops in the mountains. None that I found, anyway."

"The...mountains?"

"I saw some berries but didn't try them. Figured the risk-reward ratio wasn't in my favor."

Mason exchanged a look with Zoe. "You don't mean...you walked back?"

"Sure. Not much else to do."

He shook his head, looking stunned. "I thought you must have hitchhiked or something. Those mountains are big. You must have been moving constantly for the last two days."

"Couldn't risk hitchhiking. People were looking for me."

Zoe collapsed into the couch beside Keira. "I walked for two hours once. Mum wanted us to go on a hike. I legitimately thought I was going to die."

Keira laughed, stew flooded her nose, and Mason ferried her tissues while she coughed her airways free again.

Daisy stretched in front of the fire. Her toes spread toward the ceiling as she flexed her back. Keira used her foot to give the cat a chin scratch. "Thanks for looking after Daze too."

"Well, actually—" Mason grimaced. "She went missing the same night you vanished in Cheltenham. And she didn't turn up again until literally an hour before you did. That's why I kept going to the door to look for you; it seemed like too much of a coincidence."

"Huh." Keira frowned at her cat as she drained the last of the stew. Mason took the bowl from her and carried it to the kitchen.

Zoe pulled her feet up under herself. "I admit to being skeptical when you said the cat might be magic, but there *is* something weird about that critter. She had just enough time to gorge herself, then fall asleep before you showed up."

"You still haven't told us what happened either." Mason returned, the bowl refilled, and Keira murmured gratefully as she took it.

Her first instinct was to tell them a sanitized version of events—omitting the ghosts and holding her secrets close to her chest, like she'd grown used to. But they already knew about the ghosts. They knew about the people hunting her. It was a sharp surprise to realize she didn't have to lie any longer—at least not to the people in her cottage. Still, she braced herself before speaking. "Adage must have already told you why we went to the hospital."

"Brody. Yeah." Zoe nodded. "He was a few years older than us, but we knew him. Poor guy."

"Adage said you were able to clear his spirit," Mason added.

"Right. And I was eager to get out of there, but then another spirit caught my notice. She wanted—needed—to show me something. So I told Adage I'd meet him at the car and followed her down to the parking bay."

"Adage mentioned a lot of vans arrived at the hospital. He didn't know if they were connected to you. He didn't want to ask too many questions just in case."

*Good. Smart Adage.* "That was them."

Keira quickly recapped seeing the van, the emblem on its rear doors, being spotted by the driver, and her flight into the mountains. Mason listened in silence, running his hand across his mouth, his eyebrows low and jaw set as he watched her. Zoe repeatedly drew breaths, apparently desperate to interject with questions but reeling herself back under control each time.

"One final thing." Keira rose to find the photo she'd tucked behind the fireplace's clock. Other than the clothes on her back and a crumpled twenty-dollar bill, it was the only thing she'd brought with her from her past life. A message was penned on its back side in a hand that Keira recognized as her own. *Don't trust the men with flaky skin.* "The driver's hands were peeling."

She passed the photo to Mason and Zoe and gave them a moment to take in the figures and the message.

The image was grainy, its details less distinct than Keira would have wished, but it showed three people standing in front of a stone building, wearing long, white coats, each with some kind of name tag on their lapels. Her subconscious pinged every time she laid eyes on the central figure: a gray-haired, gaunt man, his eyes seeming to bore into her through the photo. She knew him, and she never wanted to cross paths with him again.

Mason scratched his chin. "Please don't think I doubt you, but I have to play devil's advocate."

Keira nodded, encouraging him to continue.

"Skin conditions are hugely common. Eczema, rashes, and psoriasis can affect anyone—and even adverse working conditions can dry someone's skin enough to flake."

"This is what we get for inviting a doctor," Zoe muttered. "Van guy wouldn't have called the CIA or whoever those goons were unless he was connected to it all."

"He recognized me too." Keira finished her second bowl of stew and put it aside. "He said, *Sarah Tomlin is still alive.*"

Mason raised his eyebrows. "Do you think that might be your real name?"

Keira let the idea sit with her for a second, then shook her head. "It doesn't feel familiar. When I woke up, I knew my name was Keira. It was one of the *only* things I knew."

"Sarah Tomlin was probably a fake name," Zoe said. "It's a good sign if they don't know your real identity."

"Keira suits you better." Mason passed the photo back to Zoe, who held it up to her face, squinting at the grainy details.

"I wish I had my corkboard," Zoe murmured, her voice so faint that Keira had trouble catching the words. "There'd be so much red string crisscrossing it that it would pass for embroidery."

Keira leaned forward, propping her chin up on her knuckles. "I have this deep-seated dread of hospitals. The whole time I was walking the halls, I had the sense there was something dangerous inside, and I needed to get out before it caught me. And…" She trailed off as her heart missed a beat.

"What is it?" Mason asked.

"The hospital was empty." Keira shook her head. She couldn't believe it had taken her so long to make what now seemed like an obvious connection. "I mean, it was full of people, but the ghosts—I only ever saw two. There should have been more than that. A lot more."

Zoe looked intrigued. "How many people die in Cheltenham every day? And how many would stay there, instead of anchoring to their eventual gravesites?"

"I can answer the first question," Mason said. "Cheltenham has an active ER unit. It would probably see between five and ten deaths each day."

The cottage was warm, but a shudder ran through Keira. She'd kept her second sight closed for as much of the visit as possible, but certain ghosts—like the elderly woman who had wanted her to know about the van—could still make themselves visible, if they had enough energy. Even keeping her vision closed, the halls should have been thrumming with the dead.

Daisy rose from her place by the fire and made a muffled chirruping noise as she stretched. Then she sprang into Keira's lap. Keira scooped her arms around her small cat, cradling her as she lay down to resume her nap.

Keira focused on the warm weight as she took a slow breath. "The hospital was empty. The organization that's hunting me was parked out front. I'm not reaching to think they're related to the low spirit activity, am I?"

"Ghost hunters?" Zoe guessed. "Maybe they go into hospitals and, I dunno, clear out the dead so that it doesn't get too crowded?"

"Then why chase down someone doing the same work?" Mason asked.

Zoe shrugged. "Maybe there's, like, grants for ghost-hunting work, and they don't want Keira to get them first. You'd be amazed how competitive businesses can be."

It was more than that, though. Keira recalled the pure revulsion she'd felt when facing the sigil. The taste of coppery dread coating her tongue. The terrified expression on the elderly spirit's face a second before she faded away.

Professional competition didn't warrant hunting dogs and rifles. There was something more going on.

Daisy had gone boneless and started to slide out of Keira's lap. She carefully repositioned the cat to sleep at her side, accidentally exposing her palm. Mason reached for it and turned her hand to catch the fire's light, then muttered something under his breath. "You have splinters. Hold still a moment and I'll get them out."

The red spots hadn't been bothering Keira, but she knew Mason too well to think he'd listen to objections, so she stroked her cat while Mason retrieved his kit from the corner of the room. "Have you two been staying here the whole time?"

"Mostly," Mason said. "While Adage was out looking for you, we wanted someone waiting here in case you came back."

"We've been taking it in shifts," Zoe said. "Gotta admit, seeing a graveyard out your window each morning is cool, but knowing there are ghosts out there is starting to give me the creeps."

Keira managed a sheepish smile. "I'm sorry. I didn't mean to make you worry like this."

Mason pulled his chair up beside her and took her right hand. "You're back now. And you're safe. That's what matters."

Keira flinched as Mason used tweezers to poke at one of the splinters. She hadn't even realized she'd collected so many; she'd been in a fugue of anxiety when she'd climbed the trees and hadn't paid attention to what the branches were doing to her hands. "It might not be safe here for long."

"Seriously?" Zoe crossed her arms, her eyebrows dropping murderously low. The effect was ruined by the way she sat on the chair; with both her legs and her arms crossed, she reminded Keira of a pretzel. "You're not going anywhere. We only just got you back."

Mason kept his attention focused on her hand. He was bent so low over it that Keira couldn't see his expression, but the tweezers' progress slowed.

Keira tried to swallow her guilt. "It's not that I don't want to stay. I do. This place is all I have for a home. But those men are going to be looking for me again, and eventually, they'll come here. I might need to leave—and it might be sudden. We have to be ready for that. I may not get a chance to say goodbye."

"So help me, Keira, if you try to run off into the night, I'll come looking for you." Zoe jabbed a finger toward her. "I'm lazy and easily disoriented, so I probably won't catch you, but I *will* be looking for you. And I'll definitely get sick since I don't know how to survive in the wilderness. I'll get dysentery, most likely. Is that what you want? Do you want your best friend to die of dysentery?"

Mason glanced up briefly. "I'm with Zoe. Minus the dysentery part. But I don't want to think about you trying to survive on your own."

Keira struggled to laugh. Her throat felt too tight. "I can look after myself."

"Of course you can. You managed fine before us. But right now, you're skin and bones, without money and without memories." He fished another splinter out, wiped it off on a towel at his side, and returned for more. Even though his voice was bright, there was a tightness around his eyes that told Keira he was disturbed. "If you leave, know that I'll be looking for you. And probably doing a horrible job of it too."

"We can be dysentery buddies," Zoe said, nodding sagely.

Mason frowned. "You just need to boil your water. You know that, right? It's not like dysentery is some mythical, unavoidable disease these days."

"Boy, if you think I'm going to be doing anything more advanced than slurping water out of puddles, you're vastly overestimating my wilderness survival abilities."

Keira dragged them back on topic. "I'm grateful. Incredibly so. But I won't have much of a choice. I was spotted in Cheltenham, which is only a few hours' drive from here. When they can't find me in the forest, they're going to start spreading out. And unlike when I first arrived in Blighty, I'm not exactly a secret anymore. They just need to ask someone who's spoken to Hanna in the last week and they'll know exactly where to find me." She tried to keep her smile bright, even though it felt like it was breaking her up inside. "It's dangerous, not just for me, but for both of you, and for Adage as well."

Mason and Zoe exchanged a glance. Then Mason cleared his throat. "Better show her."

# CHAPTER 15

ZOE ROSE AND PICKED up a stack of papers from the small writing desk below the window. She offered them to Keira, the corners of her mouth pulled up into a bitter smile. "I took these last night."

Mason still worked on her right hand, so Keira took the papers with her left. Her mouth dried as she leafed through them.

They were photographs taken through a window at night. The images were blurry but showed two men walking along an alley. They wore some kind of dark cloak. In the second picture, one of the figures had turned his head far enough for his face to be visible. Where there should have been skin was something angular and white. A skull mask, Keira thought. They had a massive canine on a leash. The angle was bad, and the dog was barely visible, but Keira was certain it was the same creature she'd seen from her vantage in the tree.

"Remember how I saw a skeleton outside my window on the night you arrived?" Zoe settled back into her chair, but her usual high spirits had dissipated. "That's them. They've already been through Blighty looking for you."

Keira tried to swallow, but there was a painful lump blocking her throat. An instinctual panic was rising in her as she stared at the figures. Mason must have felt her anxiety; he pressed her hand, then took the photos and put them facedown on the side table, where she couldn't stare at them any longer.

"Zoe took those pictures at about three in the morning," he said. "She was staying up late and watching over the town. I thought she was being paranoid, but turns out it paid off this time."

"Not going to lie; those two minutes were probably the highlight of my life."

"We've been keeping our ears to the ground," Mason continued. "No one has seen any strangers in town. It's like when you first arrived; they only looked for you at night and seem to have moved on when they couldn't find you. I don't think they want anyone to know they're here."

"So you're safe from the rumor mill," Zoe said. "I mean, as far as this shady organization is concerned. The rumor mill on its own is pretty brutal. One time when I was eleven, I made a hat out of banana peels. Even to this day people refer to me as Zoe, the Banana Girl."

"Zoe's point is...we don't think they're going to ask about you around town. At least, they haven't so far."

Keira chewed her lip. She dearly, desperately wished she could share her friends' confidence. The stakes were horribly steep, though. "We can't be sure it will stay that way. And if they find out you're helping me, they'll hurt you."

"Let them try." Zoe held up two fists. "I've never taken a karate class, but I've watched, like, three dozen martial arts movies, and I'm pretty sure that counts for something."

"Doubtful." Mason smiled as he stuck a bandage over a scab on Keira's hand. "But I support Zoe's sentiments. We talked about this while you were gone. We agreed that, if you didn't come back, we'd do what we could to find out what happened to you. Even if it meant confronting some kind of secret government department."

"I—"

"We're not going into this blindly, Keira." He closed his kit. "We're making a conscious choice to become involved, with or without you. And truth be told, I'd rather face whatever this is *with* you."

Zoe nodded. "We're not a force to be taken lightly."

Keira lifted her eyebrows. "If you say so, Banana Girl."

"Okay, you know what? That's fair. I gave you the weapon; I can't blame you for using it."

Keira flexed her hands. Mason had been thorough; tiny red marks showed where splinters had been excised. The larger ones had bandages over them. She laced her fingers together as she tried to think.

She'd promised herself she wouldn't put her friends in danger.

At the same time, Mason had a point. She'd survived on her own before. But back then, her memories had been intact. She was working with a lot less now.

"We're not going to be reckless," Mason said. "You'll lay low for a while until we're sure the danger is gone. In the meantime, Zoe might be able to find some information on this organization. You said you saw an emblem on their van, right?"

"Right!" Keira reached for the photographs on the side table. "Do you think you could research it if I gave you a sketch?"

"I can sure as heck give it a try." Zoe pulled a pen out of her pocket and passed it over.

Keira did her best to re-create the image: a hexagon made of narrow leaves. Even though the proportions weren't quite right, just drawing the image left her feeling grimy. She handed the finished sketch to Zoe, who examined it closely.

"Yeah, it's not familiar to me, but it's a place to start. It looks kind of modern, doesn't it?"

"I guess." Keira rubbed the back of her neck. "I didn't really think about that."

"My bet is on a private organization, not government. Maybe a subsidiary of an umbrella corporation." She saw Keira's and Mason's curious looks and shrugged. "Government cares about prestige. If they use logos, they go for classical stuff like serif letters and coat-of-arms-style arrangements. But something like this, all modern and sleek? It's a business that has to present a pretty face for its customers."

Keira frowned. "Is that better or worse?"

"Hard to say. Government departments have deep pockets and like to bury their mistakes. And they tend to be petty." Zoe pursed her lips. "Not to say businesses aren't petty, but keeping their bottom line in the black has a tendency to distract from obsessions that don't have a financial reward. Which suggests you're doing something that hurts their income in a major way. I hate to say it, Keira, but you should have more brushes with death. They're kinda useful."

She chuckled and scratched behind Daisy's ears. The cat stretched, sticking all four of her legs out and letting them quiver. Then she pulled back into a ball with a yawn.

Mason checked his watch. "Adage is on his way back. He'll be glad to see you. But I'm sure you're tired. And I distinctly remember promising you pizza last time we spoke. If I go to pick up some food, will you still be here when I get back?"

Keira glanced at the window. The curtains were closed. Beyond was her small domain: the graveyard, stretching into the forest. It would be drowning in mist and shadows, and anyone approaching the cottage would have plenty of cover. She hoped she was making the right decision. "Okay."

"Good." He smiled and tilted his head to the side in the way only Mason could. "Try to get some rest. I'll be back soon."

He pulled on his raincoat before exiting into the night. Keira listened to his footsteps crunch through the dead grass until he was out of hearing.

"He was a mess," Zoe said. She'd pulled her feet up again, but this time rested her chin on her knees as she stared at the fire.

"Mason?"

"Yup." A smile touched her lips. "Apparently Captain Capable doesn't know how to deal with something he has no control over. He even started listening to some of my more outlandish theories. That should give you an idea of how desperate he was."

Keira groaned. "Sorry again. If I hadn't forgotten my cell phone, I could have stopped you from worrying so much."

"Eh, it gave us something to think about." Zoe stretched, her spine popping. "I'm gonna get a coffee. Want me to make you some tea?"

"Thanks."

As Zoe moved into the kitchen, Keira gently nudged the cat's paws off her lap and rose. Now that she'd had a chance to sit and warm up, she was starting to feel all of the aches and bruises she'd accumulated.

A cardboard box had been positioned near the stove. Keira noted a depiction of a yellow toaster on a brightly colored star design. "Really?"

"Maybe Mason wasn't the only one feeling helpless, you know?" Zoe tapped the box as she set up cups. "At least now I can stop worrying about your toaster-less state."

"Wow." Keira couldn't hold back laughter as she retrieved her envelope of money from where she kept it in the cupboard. "Okay, sure. But I'm paying you back."

"It's a welcome-home present." She indicated Keira's festive sweater. "Or a Christmas present. Either works for me."

"Nope." Keira leaned back against the cupboards, eyebrows

raised. "It may not have been by my own volition, but this is the first piece of furniture I'll fully own, and I'm not going to let you cheat me out of that. How much?"

Zoe grimaced. "My store has a mean markup, and not even my employee discount puts much of a dent in it. Trust me, you'll want to take this as a gift."

"Zo." She tilted her head forward, looking as stern as she could manage. "How much?"

"Forty."

"Forty? What, does it play show tunes while it cooks?" Keira emptied the envelope and shoved the money into Zoe's pocket, feigning disgust. "This toaster better wash the dishes too."

"Maybe Hanukkah presents are more your style—"

"No, no, I paid for it, which means it's my toaster now. No refunds." She poked her tongue out at Zoe, who laughingly returned the gesture before switching back to filling their mugs.

Keira crossed to the window nearest to the door and lifted the curtain out of the way.

The drizzling rain continued. It was prime weather for the ghosts; they always appeared stronger when there was moisture about. She pulled on the muscle behind her eyes and blinked into the mist.

Her graveyard was empty. Keira frowned, skipping her gaze between the dark-gray stones as she hunted for a glimmer of movement. Even on days when the spirits were being quiet, there was usually at least a couple of them about, pacing between their grave markers or staring into the sky.

A sudden panic hit her. *Did I lose the ability? Can't I see them anymore?*

She searched with increasing desperation, pulling on the muscle until a headache started to throb through her skull, and finally caught a glimpse of motion.

The graves merged with the forest to her left, creating a maze of trees and stones. Something tall and dark stood at the edge of the woods. It swayed, long arms swinging at its side as it gazed across the cemetery.

Keira's heart turned cold. She impulsively pressed back against the wall, minimizing her form and trying to blend in with her surroundings. It took her a moment to realize she wasn't seeing one of the men who had chased her, though. She was seeing the malformed spirit from deep in the forest.

*Gerald Barge.*

He turned to stare at her, and she felt like his pit-black eyes were boring into her soul. A cold sweat washed over her as she closed the curtains.

# CHAPTER 16

ADAGE ARRIVED SHORTLY BEFORE midnight, bedraggled despite his raincoat, his eyelids heavy but his smile as warm as always. Keira, at least, had managed to nap; Adage looked like he hadn't slept properly in days.

"I'm glad you're safe and well, child." He clapped her on the shoulder. "Whoever said miracles ended with the New Testament was very mistaken."

"Sorry I couldn't get back to you—"

"That's all fine." He shook water off his coat. "Zoe gave me the gist of it. You can fill in the details tomorrow, if you feel up to it. But not too early. I don't often indulge in sleeping in, but don't expect me to be up before midday."

He took a slice of pizza from the box Mason offered him, then, just like that, he was gone again, stepping out into the rain and disappearing in the direction of his own home.

Zoe, who had been working furiously at her laptop in the corner by the fire, made a show of stretching and looking at her watch-free wrist. "Wow, it really is late. Are you going to ask us to spend the night or what?"

Mason poked her as he passed, carrying empty mugs to the sink. "Zoe, don't be rude."

"I thought it was a given. I'd love some company." It was the truth; Keira felt as though she'd only just regained her humanity after the days in the forest. She wasn't ready to be left alone with her thoughts yet. "One of you can take the bed. I'll set up spare blankets in front of the fire."

That started an argument, Mason trying to insist that the bed belonged to Keira, Zoe claiming that she didn't even really need sleep, technically, and that it was all a hoax perpetrated by Big Mattress. Keira argued back as she unstacked piles of spare quilts from the closet.

The battle ended when Zoe interjected, "I may not have brought you into this world, but I can still take you out of it." Keira held up her hands, accepting her defeat.

She'd been tucked into bed, half slipping into dreams, when a sleepy, cranky Zoe prodded her awake. "Move over. Your floor is too hard and your stupid cat keeps trying to lick my face. I'm going to share with you."

Keira made room for Zoe in the narrow bed. They both fit—just barely. Only, to her horror, she discovered Zoe was a cuddler. She survived a total of three minutes cinched in a bear hug, Zoe snoring quietly in her ear, before she tapped out, extracted herself from her friend's embrace, and slunk into the messy bed by the fire.

Zoe hadn't been joking about the cat. Keira had barely closed her eyes before a wet, warm tongue started dabbing at her forehead. "No-o-o," she'd grumbled, batting at Daisy, then pulled her blankets over her head. She'd thought Mason was asleep, but she distinctly heard his laughter as she tried to fight off her overly affectionate cat.

Now, with moonlight stretching over the ceiling and Daisy asleep at her side, Keira's mind raced in circles.

*Is it really okay to stay?* Zoe had made a good argument. The groundskeeper's cottage was well hidden, forgotten even by many people in the town. Plus, she'd last been spotted in Cheltenham. The unknown organization didn't have much reason to look too closely at Blighty.

Still, she felt like she was being selfish. *But, then, it would be just as selfish to leave, wouldn't it? People are relying on me here. And not just my friends.*

She'd made promises to the spirits. Even if most of them were refusing to talk to her, and even if some were beyond help, she'd still said that she would try.

Keira held her hands above her head and stared at them through the pale moonlight. Old Keira would know what to do. Old Keira must have been well practiced at excising difficult spirits. She'd know all of the methods, all of the best tactics, maybe even have some tricks up her sleeve...

*I can unravel them. Reach inside, find that tangle of thread, and pull it free. It untethers them and they have no choice except to move on. I could probably go through the whole graveyard in half an hour and clear the lot of them.*

*But is that what I'm supposed to do?*

Many of the ghosts were lingering because of unfinished business. As far as she could tell, some didn't even want to move on. Forcing them would be like evicting them from a home they'd lived in for fifty years.

*And if they're staying for unfinished business, don't they have a right to find their peace?* Keira rolled onto her side. Mason was sleeping within arm's reach, his expression peaceful and his breathing deep and steady. One hand was cast over his head, reaching toward the warmth of the fire.

A shrieking wail rippled through the night air. Keira jolted out of her bed, her heart racing, but neither Mason nor Zoe moved. Silence fell over the graveyard for eight painful seconds, then it came again: a brutal, shrieking wail. Frustration and blind anger thrummed through the noise, sending a shiver down Keira's spine.

The shade was calling for her.

Keira ran a hand over her face, but she couldn't stop her heart from thumping. The wail had been so sharp and felt so close, it was hard not to imagine it was right outside the door. She lay back down and pulled her blankets up around her chin. A second later, the scream repeated. This time, there was an undercurrent of something else inside it. Something that caused nausea to rise through Keira. It was raw desperation, or blinding terror, or some nameless emotion caught between the two.

Against her better judgment, she rose and silently crossed to the window. The curtains shimmered as she pushed them aside, allowing moonlight to flow over her.

The world outside was a confusing battle of starlight and shadows. The largest stone statues stood tall above the fog, which washed over the ground and swallowed the smaller headstones. Water trickled across the windowpane, and Keira's breaths spread condensation over the glass as she stared into the dark.

Hints of movement near the edge of the forest teased Keira's eyes. She opened her second sight, and the scene blinked into clarity.

The shade tangled with a spirit near the trees. Shreds of mist exploded across the ground as the ghost tried to fight off the black, smokelike creature.

Keira's heart plunged. It wasn't the shade screaming: it was the ghost. She ran for the cottage door, slammed it open, and skidded into the mud outside.

Her bare feet slapped through the rain-churned ground and sparse grass. The humidity was so high that every breath felt like drowning. As she ran, she glimpsed ghosts flickering in and out of sight around her. They were frantic, their faces contorted in terror as they dashed between the gravestones. Some of them waved her on, urging her toward the scene of the fight.

The shade was tearing into the ghost it had caught. Keira had never thought of the spirits as solid, changeable beings, but now she realized she'd been wrong. The ghost was being destroyed. Its jaw stretched open in a voiceless scream. Its arms had been reduced to stumps, the hands and forearms consumed, and the shade's head was buried in its stomach. Mist plumed out of the wounds as the ghost's eyes rolled back into its head.

"Get away from him!" Keira snatched a rock off the ground and hurled it at the shade. The stone passed through its coiling, smoky body, but it lifted its head. A substance that was half liquid, half smoke dripped from between its stretched lips and evaporated before it hit the ground. The bleak, empty pits of its eyes stared blindly. Then it released its bony fingers from the ghost and began crawling toward Keira.

*This is one spirit I'll have no qualms over unraveling, permission or no.*

She braced herself, planting her feet in the mud and lowering her body weight. The shade scuttled toward her, weaving around and over the gravestones. Its movements reminded Keira of a terrible, malformed spider. The mouth kept grinning. The empty eyes kept staring.

It hit her, and Keira felt as though every scrap of warmth had been sucked out of the world. She choked as she tried to breathe.

The fingers were sharp as they plunged into Keira, one clawed hand digging into her shoulder and the other into her lower ribs. She screamed. It was tearing her apart, goring massive holes in her chest, digging deeper to reach her vital organs. She fell back, jarred as she hit a slab.

Out of the corner of her eye, Keira saw the other ghost—the ghost that had been attacked—spasm. Its blank, pupil-less eyes fluttered, then its form dissolved, bleeding into the mist.

Keira tried to fight the monstrous creature bowed over her, but trying to touch it was like beating at air. The warmth was being drained out of her as its fingers curled deeper inside her. She tried to scream again, but her voice choked.

*Focus! Unravel him!*

Keira closed burning eyes. She fought to sense the ghost's essence through her pain and the cold that was consuming her. It was nearly impossible. She could see his coiling, smokelike form, but that was all. She reached a hand into him, blindly hunting for the tangled thread that had to be there.

She knew she'd found it when something sharp and prickling cut into her hand. The essence stuck to her fingers when she touched it; splinter-like pains needled into her.

Keira fought the urge to recoil. Instead, she clamped her fingers on to one of the threads, clenching her teeth as the spiny pain rippled up her forearm, and pulled.

The shade's head rolled, and a thin, hissing wail belted toward the sky. Then its head plunged down, the jaws biting into Keira's neck. She felt her skin split.

Keira convulsed. The essence wasn't unraveling. She pulled on the threads, but they slipped between her fingers, slicing up the skin as they passed.

*No. It has to work—it has to work—*

She tried to grab the threads again, but her fingers were numb and clumsy. It was as though the coil had been tangled into a knot that wouldn't budge. She could no longer breathe. She felt her heart slowing, skipping beats, leaving her light-headed.

But she was moving. Through the numbing effects of the cold, she realized something had grabbed under her arms and was dragging her. The shade wouldn't let go, though. Keira tried to scream as its fingers tore through her abdomen, but her throat was gone.

"What the *hell*?" a man yelled. She recognized Mason's voice, followed by Zoe's, which bordered on hysterical.

"What? What is it?"

"I felt something. Cold. Hold the flashlight still," Mason said.

The tearing, shredding fingers raked down Keira's legs. Then, suddenly, they were gone. Mason dragged her another few feet, then one of his arms looped under her legs, and the other went behind her shoulders. He lifted her. "Get the door," he said.

She forced her eyes open. Her vision swam. Dizzying glimpses of the sky, the ground, and the gravestones muddled around her. In among them, she saw the shade. It was no more than ten feet away, pacing across the rain-soaked ground. The empty eye pits fixed on her as it roved back and forth.

*That's as far as it can go from its tether*, she realized. *It's closer than before. Because it's stronger than before. But it's still limited.*

Not that the knowledge helped her much. Keira had a horrible suspicion she was on the path to being dead. Blinding pain radiated from where her ribs had once been, the chunk taken out of her throat, and the shredded stomach and legs. Keira had a high opinion of Mason's abilities, but she figured she was a lost cause, even for him.

*There were so many things that could have killed me, but I ended up being taken out by the only thing I discounted as not being a serious threat.*

She would have laughed if she'd been physically capable of it. Death wasn't so bad, she decided. She was in agony. She felt like ice had been used to stuff the holes in her chest, and chills radiated through every limb. But she wasn't afraid. That was a silver lining at least.

The cottage door banged open, and the sudden light made her squint. Mason carried her toward the fireplace with quick, smooth steps. Keira wished he would leave her outside. She was going to ruin a perfectly good rug.

Then she caught a glimpse of herself in the firelight.

There wasn't any blood. No protruding bones, no gaping holes. The torso which she'd thought was irrevocably rearranged seemed fine. Her clothes were muddy and wet but still intact. She lifted a hand to her throat. It was reassuringly unmangled.

Instead of cuts and gaping wounds, her skin was covered in red burns. Lines traced where the shade's fingers had raked her, and there were darker spots where it had bitten. The burns wouldn't kill her, though, and Keira managed a shaky smile.

Just that took more energy than her body could afford to expend. Mason lowered her, placing her onto the temporary beds they'd set up in front of the fire, and pushed a pillow under her head. His face was set in tight angles as he sent instructions to Zoe. "Boil the kettle. Get me some more blankets. And see if you can find a hot water bottle."

"Oh, yeah, no problem, I'll just pull one out of my butt." Zoe's voice had risen into a panicked squeak as she rattled through cupboards. "Because I'm pretty sure Keira doesn't have one."

"Ugh." Keira scrunched her eyes closed as Daisy came up to lick at her face. "While you're poking around in your butt, see if you can find a rulebook for how this ghost stuff works. Because I'm tired of blind guessing."

# CHAPTER 17

KEIRA DIDN'T REMEMBER MUCH of the rest of the night. Mason kept heaping wood on the fire and trying to get her to swallow warm, sweet drinks. She guessed she must have eventually fallen asleep, because when she finally opened her eyes again, light was streaming through the windows.

Mason rested on the floor near her. He'd propped his back against the couch and stretched his long legs out as he stared at the fire. Daisy sat neatly in his lap, curling the tip of her tail with joy and occasionally headbutting his hand when he didn't stroke her fast enough.

*He looks exhausted. He didn't stay up all night, did he?*

A quiet, scraping noise came from the kitchenette. Zoe, dressed in the same outfit she'd worn the day before, was cooking at the stove. Eggs, Keira thought, based on the smell.

Keira still felt half-frozen. A clammy sweat covered her. She was wrapped in an incredible number of blankets, and she could feel some kind of bandages on her feet where she must have nicked herself on rough stones the night before.

The stabbing pains that had burned through Keira's body were reduced to a dull ache, not too different from overexerted muscles. She knew moving would make them worse, but it was unavoidable. She set a calm, pain-free expression on her face and maintained it as she sat up. A quiet chant played in the back of her mind. *Ow, ow, ow, ow...*

Mason's face brightened when she moved. He placed Daisy on the floor and scooted closer. "How are you feeling?"

"Great, just great," she lied. "Sorry about last night—"

He pressed a hand to her forehead, then moved it to her neck, and frowned. "You're still chilled. It's been hours, but I can't get your temperature back up. What happened?"

Zoe approached, juggling three plates, which she placed on the floor between them with a clatter. "Yeah, you'd better tell us, because he wouldn't let me wake you and I'm literally dying from curiosity."

"Literally dying, huh?"

"Yeah. Like how curiosity killed the cat." Zoe sat on Keira's other side, her expression deadpan. "Except cats at least have nine lives to waste on curiosity. I have one. So spill the beans. Except maybe not literally."

Keira glanced down at her plate and saw she did, in fact, have a serving of warm beans next to the scrambled eggs.

Both Zoe and Mason were watching her. She didn't know

what to say. *I thought I was dead. I felt like I'd been torn open. The shade is a very, very long way from harmless, and I still don't know what the consequences of coming in contact with it might be.*

Mason wanted her to live somewhere other than the cemetery. But Keira couldn't leave, not now, not when the shade was devouring her ghosts. The twisted spirit was her responsibility; she'd woken him when she'd stumbled on his grave. She had to find a way to put him back in the ground.

"It was Gerald Barge, wasn't it?" Mason asked. He hadn't touched his food but was watching Keira closely.

"Yeah," she admitted.

"Okay." Mason took a slow breath and held it, his eyes closed. "I don't want to sound like a jerk right now. But I *distinctly* remember you promising to be careful."

Zoe nodded. "And I *distinctly* remember you saying this ghost-busting business would be boring. I, also, am trying not to sound like a jerk, but I've known politicians who cared more about honesty."

"I made a pretty major miscalculation." She let out a sigh as she poked at the breakfast. "I heard him scream—Gerald Barge, I mean—and went to check on him. He was attacking one of my ghosts. Killing it. I thought I could stop him. But apparently, I can't."

"It's a ghost," Zoe said. "They're already dead, so they don't exactly need rescuing from being killed, right?"

"I was wrong about that too." Keira thought of the spirit she'd seen, his limbs torn off, his face contorted in terror and pain. Her throat ached when she swallowed. "The shade can hurt them. They hide if they see him, but when he catches them, he eats them. My best guess is he's absorbing their energy, and it's making him stronger."

"Bummer," Zoe said, which Keira thought was the understatement of the century.

Mason used his fork to break up his eggs. "You should have brought us with you. Or at least woken us to let us know what was happening. I heard the door slam, and before I could figure out where you'd gone, you were screaming. When we got outside, you were lying among the graves. I thought you'd slipped and hit your head. But when I tried to touch you, I felt something... I don't know what, but it was cold. Like icy air. And then this happened." He raised his hand. The skin was a deep red, just like hers, and Keira flinched. "Was that the shade?"

"That would be it. Mason, I'm so sorry. I didn't know it could hurt you as well."

"I got off easy, it would seem." He nodded to Keira. Her skin, normally pale, now carried a map of red scores.

"They'll fade," she promised. "So, you felt Gerald Barge. Could you see him too?"

"No. Maybe the mist was slightly thicker than normal, but nothing unusual."

Keira chewed her lip. Before, she'd assumed she was the only person who could be touched by the spirits. *Maybe it's related to how strong they are. When they're exceptionally agitated, they appear brighter and clearer. Maybe if they become powerful enough, they can be seen or felt by anyone.*

"What's our next move?" Zoe asked. "I have work in an hour, but I can totally blow it off."

"Don't do that. I don't want to get you fired."

"Oh, it's chill. The other day a drunk customer decided to make himself a cake in the middle of the store. I guess he saw a recipe on the back of a box of cocoa, and we sell bowls and utensils and everything, so he figured he'd try it out right then and there. He got as far as whisking the milk and eggs into the dry ingredients before I caught him. It was like the aisle had been baptized in flour. I spent four hours of overtime cleaning it up, so now my boss owes me a favor."

Keira chuckled. "If I were you, I'd save that favor for another time. Otherwise, you'll spend it watching me take a very thrilling nap."

"Roger that."

Mason wet his lips. Keira held up a hand before he had a chance to speak.

"I'm staying in my cottage. Thanks, though."

"After last night?" His eyebrows lowered. "What if the shade comes back?"

"I know what he's capable of now." Keira examined her reddened arms. "I'll be watching him. Besides, I *can't* leave. He's killing the ghosts, and I have to find a way to stop him."

"I swear, this stress is shaving decades off my life." He sighed. "At least I don't have anywhere else to be today. Can I stay for a few hours?"

"Yeah, that'd be nice."

"Call me if anything exciting happens," Zoe said. She stretched, then rolled to her feet and gave Keira a goodbye hug.

As the door clicked closed behind her, a high, fractured wail pierced the air. Keira flinched, but the cry had come from much farther into the graveyard. Gerald, calling for whoever was leaving the cabin, begging them to come closer.

Mason sensed the change in her mood. He touched her shoulder in a gentle question, and she shook her head. "I just wish I knew what I'm supposed to do."

His smile was warm as always, but thin. "Get some more rest. You might be able to think better after. I'll feed Daisy."

Keira curled up by the fire while Mason closed the windows and turned out the lights. Her mind was uneasy. Each time she managed to fall asleep, anxious dreams clouded closer, chasing her back to wakefulness. The aches were still present. The clammy, chilled sensation lingered no matter how many blankets she wrapped herself in or how close she lay to the fire. But she could also tell she was getting better. Whatever damage the shade had done wasn't permanent.

*It ate your energy*, her subconscious whispered. Keira knew that made sense—if ghosts were made of energy, perhaps they could consume more to become stronger. She'd felt it before too—after the first attack, when the twisted spirit had burned her wrist, she'd been shaky and breathless for hours.

She didn't want to think about what would have happened to her if the twisted creature had feasted on her for much longer.

Eventually, Mason lay down in the second makeshift bed.

He fell under quickly. He had to be exhausted, Keira knew. She waited just long enough for his breathing to be steady and his eyelids to start twitching as he dreamed, then she crawled out of her own bed.

*I'm sorry for making you worry so much.* She adjusted his blanket, making sure he was warm, then rolled to her feet. Daisy rose from her place by the fireside and trotted after Keira as she crossed to the door. Mason had asked her not to leave without telling him, but he wouldn't like what she was about to do.

Keira pulled on her jacket and buttoned it tightly, then stepped outside. Daisy frisked into the long grass, her black tail raised like a flag as she chased insects. The sight made Keira smile, but the expression quickly faded as she turned toward the graveyard. She opened the muscle behind her eyes, and the spirits blinked into sight.

# CHAPTER 18

"HI," KEIRA WHISPERED. SHE stood before Marianne Cobb's grave. Marianne's form was faint, and she was a long walk from the cottage, but she was the closest spirit. Most of what Keira had come to think of as *the regulars* were hiding.

Marianne, only thirty-four at the time of her death, wore a simple dress. Wispy curls flowed around her face, held in place by a shawl. Even when her form was almost too transparent to see, Keira thought she looked unusually pale. Dark circles ringed the empty eyes. It wasn't hard to guess what had taken her: illness.

To her left, Keira could see the shade's twisted form lurking between two gravestones. Its territory had expanded, allowing it to edge into the cemetery. It paced restlessly, hunting for a new victim but unable to get any closer. Yet.

"You're afraid of him, aren't you?" Keira tilted her head toward the black spirit, and Marianne nodded. The woman's lips drew tightly together as she wrung her hands.

"He killed a ghost last night. Was that the only one?" A shake this time. Keira had been dreading that. "How many others?"

Marianne held up two hands, and Keira's heart plunged. "*Seven?*"

That was worse than she'd thought. Her memory regurgitated the image of the middle-aged ghost writhing in agony, his stump arms the only thing to show from his efforts to fight off the black monster as it devoured him. He'd been terrified and in agony. Keira felt sick.

"What do I need to do?" she asked. "How do I get rid of him?"

Marianne held her hands out, her shoulders slumped and her expression grief-filled. She didn't have any answers. Keira felt a stroke of panic squeeze her as she glanced back toward the pacing shade. He would keep eating, and each time he ate, he grew stronger, and he grew closer. Eventually the graveyard would not be safe for any of them—not the ghosts, and not Keira. *What happens after that? Could the shade reach the church? Adage's house? If Mason could feel him, will other people too?*

Keira guessed that human energy would nourish it far more than spectral remains. She didn't want to think about the potential consequences of letting it come into contact with other life.

"Stay as safe as you can," Keira said. "Does hiding work?"

Marian gave a brief nod, but there was hesitation in her expression. It worked, but it was an imperfect solution. Keira guessed that hiding might take effort. That was how the previous seven ghosts had been caught; they'd let their guard drop, just for a moment.

Keira shielded her eyes as she stared into the mist. The elderly Victorian woman stood by her gravestone, facing away from them. The others might cower, but her pride wouldn't let her. Tony Lobell, the naked spirit, still smiled and waved when Keira looked at him, but his usual enthusiasm was missing. A child darted between gravestones, its mouth open in laughter, before an older spirit nudged its back and it faded from view. When Keira looked back toward Marianne—the weak spirit had already faded.

*Earlier, when I tried to introduce myself to the dead, I had the sense that they were avoiding me. At least now I know why.*

She'd unleashed the shade. The ghosts, voiceless, couldn't even warn her about what she'd done—but she'd released it, and she'd fed it, and now it was coming for the rest of them.

It was no wonder that so few of them had been willing to speak to her.

That was changing now. As Keira moved through the cemetery, more spirits appeared, desperate for assistance no matter where it came from. They were all frightened. Some of them reached out to touch her, as though looking for comfort, and Keira couldn't bring herself to pull away even when the chill made her teeth chatter.

As though drawn to it by fate, she arrived at the nameless gravestone tucked near the forest's edge, close to her cottage. She touched the headstone, and a moment later, the man with the empty face bloomed into sight at Keira's side.

"Hey," Keira said. "I'm sorry. I promised to try to help you, but right now, that shade is going to have to be my most important project."

The hollow-faced man showed no reaction. To their right, half-hidden between the dark stones and coiling mist, stood Gerald. His lips were pulled back in what might have been a grimace or a grin.

"I guess you haven't seen anything like him before, right?" Keira wrapped her arms around her torso to protect herself against the figure's chill. "Or know of any way to get rid of him?"

Her companion was predictably voiceless.

"I can't unravel his essence like I did in the hospital." She chewed on her lip. "As far as I know, there's only one other way to untether stuck spirits…and that's resolving their unfinished business. But how am I going to do that? I'm having enough trouble figuring out *yours*. As far as I can tell, Gerald isn't even sentient anymore."

The shade's incessant pacing and blank stare reminded Keira of a tiger in a cage, ravenous and waiting for the chance to feast on the creatures just outside his bounds. He'd lost too much of his humanity to be reasoned with.

Keira rubbed the back of her neck. At least Gerald Barge had a known history. She should be able to find out some details from the newspapers. But since he'd died in 1892, there wouldn't be anyone alive who remembered him. No one to tell her about his hopes and dreams, or whether he had any unfinished projects.

*Unless…did he have children? Zoe didn't say. A grandchild or great-grandchild might know a bit about him.*

"It's a start," Keira muttered. "You might not be the greatest conversationalist, but at least you're a good listener." She directed the last words at the nameless ghost, but he was already gone.

She released the second sight and tilted her head back to stretch her neck. A pounding headache had grown from its overuse, and she rubbed her palm against her temple as she returned to the cottage.

The door's hinges creaked as she opened it, and Mason stirred by the fire. He raised his head, eyes blurred and hair messy, still in a fog of sleep. "Huh?"

"Shh, lie back down." Keira carefully shut the door behind herself and shucked off the jacket. "There's nothing to worry about. I definitely didn't go outside while you were asleep."

"Huh?" he repeated, still disoriented, then grimaced. "Don't do this to me, Keira."

"Shh, shh, back to sleep." She made her feet light as she moved to the kitchen to fill the kettle.

"Caffeine," he mumbled, partially a request and partially stating a fact of life, and clambered to his feet. Still squinting tired eyes, he began retrieving mugs and boxes of coffee from the cupboards.

Keira smiled as she watched him, but something ached deep inside too. "Hey," she said as Mason prepared a cup of tea for her and a cup of coffee for himself. "Are you getting enough rest?"

He cocked his head, the familiar, warm smile fighting through the tiredness. "I'd say so. I've had exactly zero responsibilities since coming home from the university."

"And yet, it almost feels like you never have time for yourself." She'd gathered that, before her arrival at Blighty, Mason had already been kept busy running errands for neighbors and his parents' friends. And now, Keira's appearance had stacked about twenty additional layers of complication into his life. He'd spent days away from his home waiting for her, and even now that she was back, he couldn't seem to allow himself to relax.

Mason must have guessed her train of thought, but he simply shrugged, passing Keira the finished tea. "I'll be a doctor eventually. If I can't handle a little bit of stress now, how will I survive in the real world? Speaking of—let me take a look at your injuries."

She let Mason lead her to the fire and sat while he undid the bandages, applied fresh antibacterial cream, and rewrapped the various cuts she'd accumulated. The work seemed to relax him. Keira thought that might be his personality. As long as he knew what to do, he was fine. It was only when he felt powerless that he began to drown.

Once he'd packed up his kit, Mason stretched. "How are you feeling? If you're still tired—"

"Don't worry, I think I'm napped out for the rest of the week." The persistent weariness and chill would take a while to fade, she knew, and more sleep likely wouldn't help. Especially not when she had more pressing concerns. "I was planning to go into town. I want to see what I can find out about Gerald Barge. You wouldn't know if he has any surviving children or grandchildren, would you?"

"Sorry, serial killer trivia is really more of Zoe's forte." Mason glanced at the clock on the fireplace mantelpiece. "She'll be getting a break for lunch soon. We could swing by the store and see what she knows."

"Perfect." The day wasn't cold, but her chill refused to abate, so she pulled on a thick jacket and hoped she wouldn't look too strange. She was grateful that none of the shade's attacks had reached her face. A scarf around her neck hid the only bruising that wasn't covered by her other clothing.

As they opened the cabin door, Daisy slunk inside, her body close to the floor to make herself look like a shadow. She had something in her mouth.

"Daze! No!" Keira dove after the cat. Catching Daisy was a chore in itself, and when she finally pried back the jaws, she released a held breath. "It's just a leaf."

"No way." Mason scratched behind Daisy's ears as the small feline snapped her jaws around the leaf Keira returned to her. "You know, I've been trying to give her the benefit of the doubt, but Zoe might be right."

Laughing, Keira jostled him as she passed him in the doorway. "Not a chance. My cat's smart. She's just…shy about showing it."

"If you say so." He matched her brisk pace as they turned toward the driveway leading to town.

# CHAPTER 19

THE DAY WAS UNUSUALLY warm, and with only a few minutes until midday, Blighty's main street was busy. As they passed the florist's, Harry backed through the door, his arms full of bouquets to display outside the shop. Keira guessed he'd had a rough morning. His shoulder-length, aggressively straightened hair was starting to frizz in the humidity, and his black lipstick had become smudged.

"Hi," she called as they passed, followed by Mason's cheerful "Doing okay, Harry?"

"My life contains nothing but a constant yearning for the eternal embrace of death." He dropped the bouquets into the water buckets and slouched back to the door. "Today especially."

"Okay, cool, good luck with that." Mason turned back to Keira as the florist's door slammed, its cheerful flower-themed *Open* sign swinging wildly. "I'm pretty sure he secretly likes working in the florist's. He gets to rain on people's parades if he thinks they're too happy."

As they passed other shoppers and families on the street, almost everyone called a quick, "Hello, Mason!" or "Hey there, kiddo!" Mason always responded in kind. It seemed to be a habit in the town, but Keira was caught off guard the first time someone called a hello to her.

"Uh, hi." She raised her hand in a half wave as the woman passed her. She was pretty sure she'd never met the lady before in her life. The second time it happened, she was a bit quicker with her reply but no less perplexed. She narrowed her eyes at Mason. "Am I the subject of gossip, or are people here just exceptionally friendly?"

"A bit from both baskets, actually." He grinned. "You're experiencing small-town mentality. People think well of Adage, and word will have gotten around that you're his niece, so they're going to like you, too, by default."

"Huh." Keira felt a pang of fondness for the town.

The happiness lasted until they reached the general store Zoe worked at. Even from a distance, they could hear raised voices. They exchanged a look, then jogged to the open doors.

There was a line at the checkout, every person looking irritated. Zoe seemed to be the only employee in the store that day. She stood behind the counter, her black hair held up by clips and her apron bearing a bright, if crooked, name tag. Her jaw was set in a way that suggested she was suffering from great mental anguish. "It. Is. *Expired.*"

The woman at the counter, middle-aged and with tightly permed hair, pursed her lips as she waved a piece of paper in Zoe's face. "It says valid until the end of November!"

"November of *five years ago*. Where are you finding all of these old coupons? Do you hoard them? Do you think they're going to appreciate in value like some kind of collectible?"

"I want to speak to your manager."

Zoe spluttered, hands waving futilely. "I *am* the manager! You *know* that!"

"This says I can get ten percent off milk! Why won't you take my coupon?" The woman shoved her scrap of paper closer to Zoe's face, as though Zoe would understand the argument better if she could smell the scrap of dusty newspaper.

"I *literally* told you." Zoe clutched the sides of her head. "Am I in hell? Is this what hell feels like?"

"Um…" Mason raised a hand, smiling weakly. "Should we come back?"

Zoe's face lit up as she saw them. She craned to see the clock suspended above the door and made a small crowing noise of triumph. She ripped her apron off and tossed it behind her, then scooted around the checkout. "Gosh, look at that, I'm on my lunch break. I'll be back in an hour."

An indignant man next in line thumped his shopping basket onto the counter. "I'm not going to stand here waiting for you to get back!"

"Okay. You know what? Everyone just take your groceries and leave the money in a pile on the counter. Honor system. I'm friends with the pastor, and he gets to decide if you go to heaven or not, so keep that in mind before you try to shortchange me."

"That's not how that works," the man grumbled, already opening his wallet.

"It is now. Adage goes by Santa Claus rules. He knows everything you do, good and bad, and he'll eat your toes if you're naughty. Be back in an hour."

Zoe stepped between Keira and Mason and draped her arms around their shoulders. "My dear friends, you came to save me in my hour of need. I am faint from hunger. Shall we pilgrimage to the café across the street?"

"Sure." Keira patted Zoe's hand. "Sounds like you've had a bad morning."

"Oh, nah, pretty mediocre. People are awful. Same as they were yesterday, same as they'll be tomorrow. I made my peace with that fact many years ago. Adage is going to be mad at me, though." Zoe's thin-lipped smile showed no hint of remorse. "He's already told me I'm not allowed to use him as a threat. But y'know what? I'm not scared of Santa Adage eating my toes, so whatever."

As they crossed the cobblestone street toward the café, Keira briefly filled her friends in on the shade situation. She skirted around some of the less-pleasant facets—like how many ghosts had already been consumed and how little time she suspected she had until the groundskeeper's cottage would no longer be her home—and finished on the most optimistic note she could manage. "So basically, I just need to figure out his unfinished business and find a way to finish it. Preferably soon. Really, really soon."

"Hmm." Zoe chewed on her thumbnail as they entered the café. The low hum of chatter and whirring coffee grinders surrounded them. Zoe took a breath and shrugged. "I have an idea. But it means research. You guys mind if we get our food to-go?"

"That's fine with me," Keira said, only to have her words drowned out by Zoe's yell.

"Oy! Marlene! Get us some to-go sandwiches or burgers or something, whatever's fast! I'm on a deadline!"

The people in line ahead of Zoe scowled at her, but Marlene, the sallow barista half-hidden behind the crowded serving counter, raised a thumbs-up.

"I'm pretty sure Gerald Barge didn't have any kids." Zoe leaned against one of the mismatched bookcases pressed against the wall as they waited on their food. "I researched him a couple of years back. He didn't have a wife, I know that much. At the time, all of his friends and neighbors said it was a crime that no woman would have him. He was *such* a nice guy, and all of that."

"Yikes," Mason said.

"Exactly. Serial killers seem to fall into two camps: the creepy, incompetent ones, and the charming, manipulative ones." Zoe pulled a face. "Gerald Barge was the latter. After his past was unearthed—literally—I bet a lot of women were thanking their lucky stars they hadn't caught his fancy."

"Do you have any idea what sort of unfinished business he might have?" Keira asked.

"No clue. Maybe he killed ninety-nine people and was super bummed he couldn't make it to a full hundred?"

"Well, I'm not killing anyone in his name, if that's what you're going to suggest."

"Sorry, but whatever it is, don't expect it to be easy. Blighty's always been a bit weird, but I can guarantee it was many times weirder back in the 1890s. Like, listen to this—the mortician at the time turned out to have more than a few screws loose. Apparently, he would prop his corpses up around his workroom, dress them in costumes, and pretend they were having conversations with one another. He'd inherited the business from his father, but dead bodies scared him, so that was his way of making them seem less grim. People knew what he was doing, but no one else wanted the job so they just left him to it for, like, thirty years. Props to Timothy 'The Barmy Embalmy' Weller."

"Wow," Keira managed.

"Exactly. These days, that would be a one-way ticket to canceled licenses and outrage and, y'know, actual jail. Morticians take their stuff seriously, except, apparently, in 1800s Blighty. But my point is, what if Gerald was one of those corpses? What if he never got over the indignity?"

"That leads to a good question," Mason said. "What will you do if Gerald Barge's unfinished business *can't* be finished?"

"I…" She swallowed and felt a small prickle of panic growing in her chest. "I don't know."

*This is your job*, her mind whispered. *You're the ghost hunter.*

*You're supposed to have the answers. You're supposed to make things better.*

"Hey." Zoe elbowed her in the side, distracting her from her thoughts. "Chill, you've got me to help now."

"Food." Marlene circled out from behind the serving counter and passed them a bundle of paper-wrapped meals. "I don't suppose you're paying for this, are you?"

"Put it on my tab I swear I'll pay it someday okay see you later love you." Zoe grabbed the food and scooted them to the exit. She released a whistling breath as they stepped outside. "Right. I've still got fifty minutes before customers start to riot. Let's hustle."

Keira took some of the parcels and increased her pace to match Zoe's. "Where are we going?"

"The one place where you can find immense knowledge and terrible lies in equal measure." Her grin was wolfish. "The *library*."

"Uh…" Keira glanced at the food. "Are we allowed to bring this in?"

"No one's found an effective way to stop me so far," Zoe said cheerfully.

Keira exchanged a glance with Mason. He shrugged helplessly.

Hanna looked up from her crossword just long enough to make eye contact with Zoe, then put her head back down. "No. I'm not ordering it."

"Wha-a-at?" Zoe sauntered up to the desk and leaned against it, peering down at Hanna's crossword. "Who said I wanted to order anything? Can't I just visit my good friend? Five down is 'rigor,' by the way."

Hanna narrowed her eyes at Zoe, then carefully jotted down the word. "You always want to order books. Always obscure. Always expensive. Half the time printed by some fanatic in his back garage. Always books that no one else would ever want to read. Well, you've been cut off. I have a limited budget, and it can't stretch to cover both you and the romance book club."

"Damn romance book club," Zoe grumbled. "Why can't they just read something sensible once in a while, like *The Lizardmen among Us*, instead of spending your money on *Poked by the Duke* volume eighteen?"

Hanna's eyes had narrowed into the thinnest slits imaginable. She slowly, carefully folded the book of crosswords closed, which seemed like a very ominous sign. Keira reflexively took a step back.

"Some people *enjoy* romance, and I won't have you shame them for it," the librarian hissed. "Now I will kindly ask you to remove yourself from my establishment—"

"Aww, you know I'm joking." Zoe pulled a sandwich out of her pack and slapped it on the desk. "The book club can't read *Poked by the Duke* volume eighteen because I already have it on my bedside table. And don't worry, no orders today. I'm here for a title you already have. That cool?"

Hanna hesitated a moment, glancing at Zoe's friends, then she pulled the sandwich closer as her expression relaxed. "Oh, all right then. Make yourselves at home. Nice to see you again, Keira. Mason."

Keira managed a weak smile as they skirted around the librarian's desk. Hanna watched them a moment, then reopened the crossword book as they wove deeper into the building.

# CHAPTER 20

"THE HISTORY SECTION'S OVER here." Zoe led them between shelves, squeezing past patrons browsing the well-worn books, as they made their way to the back corner. "We're looking for a book I requested years ago, back when Hanna still tolerated me. It was written by a local historian named Kenneth and, as Hanna very derisively noted, printed in his back shed. We have one of only eight copies ever created. He totally abuses the word *repercussions* and there's an entire chapter about a schoolteacher he had a crush on who has no relation whatsoever to Gerald Barge, but otherwise it's pretty good. He was obsessive and perfectionistic, which sucks when you're reading for entertainment, but is the absolute best combination of traits when you're doing research."

She stopped at a mismatched shelf full of somber-colored covers and scanned the books, running her finger along the spines as she muttered under her breath. Then she clicked her tongue and pulled out a spiral-bound book with a painstakingly handwritten title glued to the wire. She held it up to them, and Keira squinted to read the name.

"*Fox in the Henhouse: The Life, Death, and Mystery Surrounding Gerald Barge, the Posthumously Convicted Serial Killer: Horror in Blighty, Volume One (of One).*"

"Yep. This is one guy who does not believe in economy of words." Zoe grinned wickedly over the top of the book. "If you think the title is long, just wait until you reach the run-on sentence in chapter thirteen. It goes on for eight pages."

"Oh, good," Mason muttered weakly. "I'm already getting flashbacks to medical school."

The three friends selected a table near the back of the library and pulled their chairs close together. Zoe scattered the sandwiches across the table, so they could eat as they worked. As promised, the book was about as fun to read as a dictionary, but equally thorough. Kenneth Malone painstakingly recorded every detail he had uncovered, including a whole host of unnecessary information. Zoe, who had already read the book once, skipped the superfluous sections and zeroed them in on the important parts.

The book was exactly what Keira had been hoping for. She borrowed a pen and a piece of paper from a reference table near the windows and jotted down notes.

Gerald had grown up in Blighty. His home life was reported to have been largely peaceful until his mother left when he was twelve. The official story was that she'd passed away while visiting a distant sister, but Kenneth postulated that she'd had a fling and run away. There were reports of a woman bearing a striking resemblance to Gerald's mother living in a town several hours away.

After that, Gerald's father had done his best to raise his three children on his own. Gerald had taken over the family farm when his father passed away. He'd never married. He lived alone in a small but tidy house not far from the town center and had a garden, chickens, and a goat. He had reportedly saved a nice nest egg but chose to live frugally.

There were stories of Gerald staying up with neighbors until two in the morning to help them catch escaped chickens. Another account told of how Gerald spent hours and invested his own money into repairing a friend's farm equipment when it broke. He was described as a tall man, slim and unassuming, with a good head of hair and friendly eyes. He drank, but not to excess; he laughed a lot, told a lot of jokes, and was friends with almost everyone, no matter their social circle.

He sounded like a great man. Right up until they reached the chapter titled "The Crimes of Gerald, Part One."

Gerald had targeted women almost exclusively. His career as a killer could be sorted into three distinct periods, which Kenneth explained in great detail. The oldest bones didn't have any injuries to indicate a cause of death, which led Kenneth to believe the first victims may have been strangled or stabbed. Around the time he was forty, Gerald started bludgeoning his victims to death. Crushed skulls, crushed ribs, and broken legs marred those victims. Toward the end of his career, the bodies had been dismembered.

"Ooh no," Keira muttered, noting down name after name where Kenneth could confirm them. By the time the bodies were uncovered, most had decayed to the point that identification was difficult or, in many cases, impossible. DNA testing was still more than half a century away from revolutionizing crime investigations, and police manpower was limited. Less than a third of the victims had been positively identified.

"What a piece of work," Mason muttered. They'd just read through the account of Mary Talbott's death. Like many of Gerald's victims, she'd come from a poor farming family. Her body had been recovered in eighteen pieces, all stacked neatly into a square grave behind his hunting cabin.

Keira blew out her breath. The book had helped her get a clearer picture of Gerald. Perhaps a little too clear. But it hadn't done much to answer her only important question: What was his unfinished business?

According to the book, he'd lived modestly, had no big dreams or plans, and was happy to be a part of the community. He passed away in early 1892 after suffering a stroke.

Zoe flipped another page. A hand-drawn map filled the sheet. Keira leaned closer. Kenneth, perfectionist that he was, had mapped out the town. A tiny x marked Gerald's house. It was along the road leading to the Crispin family estate. Keira scanned the rest of the map and was surprised to see that not much had changed. The general store was still in the same place, as was the town hall, and even the café.

An idea occurred to her, and she said, "Turn the page."

Zoe did. It featured a second map, this one of the next town over, where Gerald had taken his victims.

"Next page," she whispered, and took a sharp breath. As she'd hoped, the final map showed the forest dividing the two towns. An *x* marked Gerald's killing cabin, the place he'd claimed he stayed in to hunt and where he'd butchered and buried the majority of his victims.

A long road snaked through the forest, connecting the towns. Gerald's cabin must have been at least two hours off the path. Keira chewed her lip as she pointed at the mark. "How long would it take to get there?"

"By foot? Probably a full day. With a helicopter? Three hours, tops. Teleportation device? Instantaneous."

"Well, I can't afford either of the latter, but I *do* want to visit that cottage."

Zoe squinted at her. "You think you'll find a clue there?"

"I hope. Sometimes, when I'm near places people died, I can…*feel* things. Sometimes even see things."

"Ah." Mason blinked at her. "*That's* why you wanted to see the tree on the Crispin property."

"Yeah. Emma Carthage left an imprint there. If Gerald killed his victims in his cottage, I might be able to see something from them too. Right now, it's my best chance to figure out what Gerald wants."

"A day to get there. A day to get back. Sounds like someone is in for a delightfully morbid camping trip." Zoe closed the book. "I've got a tent and a sleeping bag."

"So do I," Mason said. "How soon do you want to leave?"

Keira tried not to think about whether any ghosts had been consumed while she was away from the graveyard. They'd need to navigate around Gerald to even get into the forest. "As soon as possible."

"There's not enough time left today. Tomorrow, then," Zoe said. "It's my day off, so it works out perfectly. Let's meet up at your cottage. We can leave as soon as it's light."

# CHAPTER 21

KEIRA PARTED WAYS WITH Mason at the village's edge. She wouldn't have minded having his company that evening, and Mason had implied he was ready to return to the graveyard with her, but he'd neglected his own life for days. Keira had playfully pushed his shoulder and told him she'd had enough coddling for a lifetime and to make sure he got enough sleep to survive the hike.

She briefly stopped at Adage's parsonage to say good night, then turned homeward. It took until she reached her cottage for the loneliness to set in. She paused in the doorway, surveying her one-room home. Late-afternoon light, tinted by the encroaching sunset, lit up the piles of bedding they'd scattered by the fire.

Mason had left his medical kit on the table by the window, and she ran her fingertips across its lid. The wooden box could only be a few years old, but it was already becoming worn with frequent use.

*He cares too much.* Keira crossed to the blankets, shaking them out and folding them. *He hates to say no, and it's stretching him thin.*

*I can't add to that.*

Maybe it was a mistake to let Mason and Zoe search for Gerald's cabin with her. She had to admit, they would make the trip a lot more fun and a lot less lonely. But they had their own lives to tend to, and she'd been soaking up so much of their time lately.

Then she remembered how she'd felt while hiking over the mountains. Alone and driven by a desperation to do whatever it took to stay alive, she'd become something that was human in name only. Keira grimaced as she forced the quilts back into the closet. Mason and Zoe helped her feel grounded. As guilty as she felt for asking for more of their time, she thought she might need her friends for what she was about to face.

As dusk fell, Keira revived the dying fire and cooked an early dinner. She kept one eye on the window. She hadn't seen or heard from the shade since arriving home, and that worried her.

Very few spirits were visible. She hoped they'd taken her advice and were hiding. A handful were still present: the Victorian spirit, two of the children, and a couple of older ghosts. They all ignored Keira, so she thought it would be best not to pressure them. Everyone was trying to deal with the shade's presence in their own way.

As Keira ate her dinner, she scanned the maps and the list of victims she'd photocopied at the library. She would need to go through the list more thoroughly later, but she was pretty sure none of the names matched any of the graves she'd encountered in Blighty's cemetery. She supposed that made sense. Gerald had taken almost all of his victims from the next town; the ones who had been recovered would be interred in its graveyard.

A scrabbling noise at the door told her that Daisy was ready to be let in. As soon as Keira opened the door, the black cat shot past her, carrying a small stick in her mouth. Keira laughed. "What, are you building a nest?"

The cat's tail rose like a flag when Keira talked to her, but she didn't turn away from her target: the little nook behind the bed. Keira smiled and shook her head. She'd clean up the cat's collection when she got back from the forest.

Sleep pulled Keira under quickly that night. She drifted in and out of dreams until a prickling, uneasy sensation woke her.

She lay still as she blinked at the moonlit room, trying to understand what had roused her. The hairs on the back of her arms rose, and something uncomfortable buzzed at the back of her mind. She tilted her head back to look at the clock above the fire. One in the morning.

*Is it the shade?* She rolled out of bed, dragging a blanket with her and draping it around her shoulders to stay warm as she approached the window. The familiar mist flowed between dark headstones. Keira opened her second sight. A couple of the more stubborn spirits still stood near their graves. She couldn't see the shade, but she didn't think the ghosts would be out if he were too close. The muscle was still sore from the day before, and echoes of the throbbing headache poked at her eyes. She let it drop.

Keira turned to glance across her room. A flicker of motion came from the corner beside the closet. Daisy crouched there, almost invisible in the darkness except for her round, amber eyes.

"Hey, Daze," Keira whispered, bending down to reach the cat. Daisy's eyes turned to her, then flicked back to the window. Keira scratched around her ears and under her chin, but she didn't respond.

*That's not right.* Keira swallowed and looked toward the window again. She'd never seen Daisy spooked before. Her cell phone was within reach, propped on the kitchen counter as it charged. Mason had told her to call him if anything went wrong.

*No. I'm not the kind of person who jumps at shadows. Or who drags their friends out of bed over feelings of vague foreboding.*

"Is it the shade?" Keira asked, continuing to brush a finger over her cat's silky fur. Daisy's attention was unwavering, but Keira couldn't see anything outside the window, even when she pulled on her second sight until streaks of light flashed across her vision.

*I'll sit up a while. Put the lights on, boil the kettle. It's probably nothing, but it'd be smart to stay alert, just in case.*

Keira made it as far as the light but didn't turn it on. Something large moved across the window. Only its silhouette was visible, blocking out the moonlight and creating a streak of shadow across the floor.

*That's not the shade.*

Her heart turned to ice. The entity leaned closer to the window, scanning the insides of her cottage. Looking for her.

Keira didn't know if she'd been seen. She was in one of the darker parts of the house, but any protection the shadows could give her was fleeting at best. Motion would draw attention to her, so all she could do was make herself immobile and pray it would be enough.

Agonizing seconds passed. The figure stepped away from the window and disappeared from sight. Keira waited a heartbeat, then sank down and crept back, burying herself deeper in the hidden parts of the building.

Her cottage only had one way out and the windows were stiff. If the stranger blocked the door, she would be as good as trapped.

Keira's eyes turned toward the kitchen. There were knives in the drawers. Not that a knife would do much good against someone with a gun, but it was better than cowering.

Something hard hit the front door. The bang was loud enough to shake through the building and rattle the windowpanes. Keira flinched and turned the shock into motion as she darted toward the kitchen. She wrenched a drawer open, felt blindly for a knife, found something sharp, and snatched it out. She swung to face the door, but the outside world had fallen silent again.

Keira backed along the counter, feeling for her phone blindly while she kept her eyes on the door and window. Her fingers found the charging cable first. She yanked the cell phone free... then hesitated.

She could call Mason. But what would that achieve, except putting him in the line of fire? He'd promised he could reach her in five minutes. Keira's throat was too tight to make much of a noise, but she almost chuckled. Five minutes was no time at all in a fight. She would almost certainly be dead by the time he pulled up at the driveway. And even if he did arrive in time, what chance did he have against a presumably well-armed intruder?

She kept the phone in her spare hand. If things went sour, she could at the very least destroy the device before the strangers got to it. She didn't want the organization to have her friends' contact details.

*I never should have come back. I shouldn't have let them convince me to stay.* Except they hadn't. Keira, so desperate to have a home, had convinced herself. And she'd thought she'd been right. The cottage wasn't easy to find if a person didn't know where to look. She'd been careful not to leave any traces of her path across the mountain. They shouldn't have been able to track her to her home. And yet, apparently, they had.

Keira ran her tongue over dry lips. She crept back across the room, her feet silent on the dusty floor. Daisy continued to cower beside the closet. Through the sparse light, Keira could see the fur standing up along her back. Keira knelt in front of her, poised like a snake, ready to strike if someone tried to open the door.

Seconds passed, each one keying Keira's nerves tighter. Outside, a small animal ran through the underbrush. A bat chattered in the forest behind her house. Farther away, almost too far to hear, a car engine purred to life.

She held still until her muscles had cramped and her doubts were spinning like a tornado through her skull. Fear left a coppery taste in her mouth. She tried to swallow it as she rose and inched toward the door.

*They have to be gone. No human can be that quiet for that long. Right?*

Keira looked back at Daisy. The cat was still huddled into a little, wary ball, but she'd tucked her paws under herself to keep them warm. She was no longer panicked. Keira took that as a good sign, rallied her courage, and turned the handle.

She held the knife at the ready as the door drifted inward. There was no sign of anyone near her cottage—no sounds, no motion, no foreign scents. She stepped into the threshold, glancing in each direction, but all she could see was the mist and the familiar arrangement of shrubs and stones. She began to step back inside the house, but as she did, she noticed a piece of paper had been attached to the door.

A long, cruel-looking nail fixed it to the wood. *That explains the banging noise.* Keira tore the paper free, crept back inside, and pushed the door closed. She locked it before she dared turn her lights on and read the note.

It was simple and to the point. Small, neat script read:

*You're not welcome in this town. Leave, or there will be repercussions.*

"That's it?" Keira frowned at the message, then dropped it onto the table below the window. She took a slow, deep breath, massaging her shoulders as she waited for her galloping heart to settle.

She knew she probably shouldn't feel relieved. But she couldn't help it. She hadn't been caught by the strange men. The message had come from a disgruntled townsperson. Comparatively, that was a walk in the park.

A quick sense of sadness followed the relief. Keira looked at the paper, then turned away before it could hurt her anymore. Someone in town didn't like her. Someone in town wanted her gone.

She hadn't expected rejection to ache so badly, but it did. She didn't think she'd done anything to hurt anyone.

*No, that's not completely true. There are two people who might not like me much. I'd say this note came from Gavin Kelsey, but somehow this doesn't seem like something he'd do.* The blond-haired teen was a bully. The language was all wrong compared to the way he spoke. And Keira had been pretty explicit with him last time they'd met that she wouldn't tolerate further games.

*Maybe Dane Crispin? No, that doesn't make sense either.* She'd wronged Dane by entering his private property. He'd caught her and chased her through the forest. The note's formal tone was probably accurate for the way Dane spoke, and a nighttime pilgrimage was something she could see him doing. Only one thing ruined her theory—Dane had chased Keira and her friends blindly and hadn't managed to actually see any of them. He couldn't realistically know Keira was the person he'd been after. With how cut off from the rest of the community he was, he might not have even heard about her existence yet.

*But who else does that leave?* She ran the back of her hand across her forehead, which pricked with cooling sweat. She thought of everyone else she knew. Marlene, Hanna, Polly, Harry. Even the grouchy ones seemed too friendly to pull a stunt like this. *What does that mean? Have rumors been circulating? Did someone pass me in the street and take a disliking to me on sight?*

Keira couldn't tell which answer she was hoping for. She shuffled to her kettle and put it on. Daisy finally left her corner and cautiously returned to her place by the fire. Keira gave the cat a small smile as she watched her curl up. She was grateful that she hadn't been followed by the strange men from the hospital, but she still doubted she would get much more sleep that night.

# CHAPTER 22

KEIRA GASPED AS SOMEONE knocked at her door. She'd fallen asleep in front of the fire, but the memories from the previous night were still fresh enough to leave her nerves wound tight. The sun was up, but only just barely. Keira turned to face the door, keeping the chair between herself and the cottage's entrance, and held her breath as she listened.

"Oy, Keira, you in there?" The knocks repeated, and this time Keira let the tension slump out of her shoulders as she hurried to unlatch the door.

"Hey, hi, sorry, I dozed off." She laughed to hide her nerves. "Come on in."

Zoe and Mason had arrived together. They both wore thick jackets and scarves, and their cheeks were pink in the early morning frost. Keira shivered as the cold outside air swirled around her, and quickly ushered them in to where it was warm.

"I see you're all geared up and ready to go." Zoe winked as she strolled toward the fire.

"Don't worry, I just need a minute." Keira opened the closet doors and began rifling through it for clothes that might be appropriate for hiking. Her outfits were all donated. She owned a lot of T-shirts and scarves, but not much that could be called appropriate for a hike. Still, she was sure she could make something work.

"One minute?" Zoe grinned. "You and I must be kindred spirits. If you were my sister, you'd quote me an hour, then take three."

Keira snuck a peek at her out of the corner of her eye. "I didn't know you had a sister."

"Oh, I've got like a billion siblings. They're all awful. Luckily, you're going to be spared the agony of their presence because none of them live in Blighty."

"There's no rush." Mason placed his equipment on the floor. He had a proper hiking backpack. Based on how bulky it was, Keira guessed it had to be heavy, but the way he carried it made it look light. "I thought we could have breakfast together before we left. And feed Daisy too. Will she be okay for the next couple of days?"

"Don't worry. I called in on Adage on the way home last night. He'll be looking after her." Keira took two knit tops and a jacket out of the closet, then grabbed some fresh underwear from the drawer and made a beeline for the bathroom. She splashed some water on her face and changed in record time. The clothes weren't the most ergonomic or breathable, but they were comfy and would keep her warm, which were her two main priorities. Her trusty, well-worn boots would take care of her feet. She tied her hair up and, as promised, was back into the main room in less than sixty seconds.

Mason was already in the kitchen, cooking eggs. He called over his shoulder, "Grab some spare clothes to sleep in. It gets cold at night in the forest. I brought a backpack for you."

"Thanks." Keira collected a pair of corduroy pants and her new favorite sweater—the one with the one-eyed Santa Claus.

"I should have thought to bring you some spare clothes." Zoe stretched her feet toward the coals that still smoldered in the fireplace. "I was going to make some T-shirts that said *Murder Cabin Team-Building Exercise*, but I figured that was getting a bit morbid."

"Maybe a touch," Keira replied.

Mason scraped scrambled eggs into three bowls and passed them out. "I looked up the forest last night. It's fifty kilometers wide, and the cabin is about halfway through. That should take us—"

*Five hours*, Keira's mind whispered. *Four if we hurry.*

"Eight or nine hours," Mason finished. "We should get there with a few hours of sunlight left. We can set up camp near the cabin, give Keira some time to do whatever she needs to, and leave the following morning. Does that sound all right to everyone?"

"It sounds like hell," Zoe said. "Eight hours of walking. Ugh. I don't suppose I can bribe either of you to carry me on your back?"

"You don't have to come if you don't want to," Mason said.

Zoe held up her hands. "Whoa, those kinds of threats are totally uncalled for. I'm complaining, not volunteering for a joyless existence."

He chuckled. "That's fair."

Keira and Mason finished cleaning up while Zoe fed Daisy. Then Keira gave her cabin one last scan to make sure she hadn't forgotten anything and pulled her hiking pack on. It wasn't as weighty as she'd expected. She guessed Mason had taken the heaviest items, but it was too early in the morning to argue with him over it.

As they left the cottage, Keira drew a deep breath. The air was crisp, filled with ice particles, and the frosted ground crunched under their boots. Keira came to a halt at the low stone fence dividing her home from the graveyard and opened her second sight.

The shade stood barely fifteen feet away, pacing at the edge of his boundary. His head rolled as he shambled between the graves, alternating his gaze between Keira and her companions.

*Damn it. He's closer. He got another ghost.*

Scorching anger boiled through Keira's stomach, and she clenched her fists at her side. She didn't want to think which of her spirits were gone. She prayed it wasn't one of the children. Even in death, they appeared blithely unaware of danger.

Something else had changed about the shade too. His form, made up of what appeared to be coiling black smoke, seemed different. As he paced, his jaw opened in a voiceless hiss, and Keira glimpsed something pale inside his mouth.

"Everything okay?" Mason asked.

"I just need a minute." Keira circled the stone fence, moving carefully as she approached the stalking creature.

Off-white shapes moved through his form like loose tea leaves rolling in a freshly poured cup of water. They bobbed to the surface for a second before disappearing back inside. Keira only stopped when she was two paces from the shade—just barely out of reach of his grasping hands—and tried to track the shapes as they swam within him.

*Bones.* Her suspicion was confirmed when the tip of a femur broke free. It bobbed above the inky outline for a second before swirling back in.

*He's started carrying his bones. Just how much energy has he consumed?*

Zoe was speaking, but Keira was so absorbed in the sight that it took her a second to catch the words.

"What's happening? Are we talking to the ghosts? Is this how you communicate?"

Zoe circled her, face wide and curious, inadvertently putting her back to the shade. The creature lurched forward, bending its torso to reach as far as possible, and its clawlike fingers grazed the edge of Zoe's ear.

Keira grabbed Zoe's jacket by the lapels and dragged her away from the hands. Zoe staggered, and Keira put her arms around her friend's shoulders, holding her possessively so the shade couldn't reach her. "Careful. Gerald wants to say hello."

"Oh. Dang." Zoe had collapsed against Keira and her words

were muffled through her jacket. "Tell him I'll take a rain check."

"Hah." Keira stepped Zoe back to a safe distance before letting her go. "We'll have to circle around him to get out. Both of you wait here a minute. I won't be long."

Except for Gerald, the graveyard was very nearly deserted. Only one clear spirit remained. Keira took a breath and pushed her hands into her pockets as she approached the Victorian woman.

The elderly spirit's back was pin straight. Her hair had been piled into an elaborate arrangement on her head, but stray strands drifted in the otherworldly wind. Wrinkled hands rested on top of an elaborate cane. She barely deigned to glance at Keira before turning away. Keira cleared her throat, refusing to let the hostility get to her as she spoke to the back of the woman's head.

"Hey. I know this is my fault. I'm trying to fix it. I'll be a couple of days, at least. You seem like you're the most in control here, so…make sure the others stay hidden, okay? Don't let them resurface. For at least two days. I'll be back as soon as I can."

She hadn't expected an answer, and she didn't get one. The spirit tilted her head toward Keira—just a fraction—before stalking away. Keira managed a tight smile as she backtracked to where Mason and Zoe waited. The woman had understood her message at least. Keira prayed she would be strong enough to keep the others safe.

"Let's go." She hitched her backpack higher and turned toward the trees behind her cottage. Zoe and Mason took up places on her left side, away from the shade. Gerald's twisted form lurched after them, moving parallel as they walked into the woods.

The shade's sphere was large. Keira had to lead them a long way into the forest before they could start correcting their course. The tree's branches were damp with early morning dew, and every time Keira brushed one, it rained droplets onto her.

It took forty minutes to weave around Gerald. Keira felt a small spark of triumph as they reached the main road—a narrow, winding pathway that was mercifully free from obstacles—and were able to put their backs to the specter. He stood behind them, wild howls rising from stretched jaws as he wordlessly tried to call them back. It only took a minute for the bends in the path to put him out of sight, and soon after that, even his cries faded beneath the crackle of dried leaves underfoot and the sounds of chattering birds.

Keira could be fast. Weaving through the forest, she could twist around and under branches like a shadow. Her friends weren't quite as athletically inclined. Mason had good stamina but struggled when branches blocked their path. Zoe, not a fan of cardio to begin with, put up a good fight to keep pace, but it soon became clear that Keira needed to slow down.

The sun continued its steady ascent, but the trees were too thick to let much light through. Despite the chill, Keira soon took her jacket off and tied it around her waist. She could have moved faster—maybe shaved a few hours off the trip's estimated time—but the exhaustion from her unwanted contact with Gerald still lingered, and she was grateful for the steady pace they'd set. As they moved deeper into the forest, they began to hear larger animals moving through the brush. Deer, Keira suspected, along with plenty of rabbits.

"I gotta say, guys," Zoe said as they stopped for their first water break. She slumped down on a fallen tree trunk and unscrewed the lid from her water bottle, then poured so much into her mouth that it overflowed and dribbled down her jacket. She swallowed, wiped her hand across her chin, and sucked in a gasping breath. "I'm not complaining, but this is about as fun as being punched in the face repeatedly."

Keira laughed as she leaned back against a tree and sipped from her own bottle.

Zoe continued, "Do you want to know why people enjoy exercise? It's because it's literally so horrible that your body releases dopamine to help you cope with it. It's basically the equivalent of getting hooked on painkillers and stabbing yourself once a week to get a new prescription." She grimaced. "Our country has an epidemic. A *fitness* epidemic. We need campaigns to raise awareness. Hashtag just say no to exercise."

Mason faced the path ahead, but his smile was audible. "I think I'm obligated to disagree with that."

"Shut up, you're not even a doctor. You're a fake shill, and I can't figure out if that's better or worse than being a real shill."

Mason and Zoe traded snipes as they resumed the hike. Keira let the talk wash over her as she led the way. The forest was peaceful. The path was rarely used; since proper roads had been constructed to connect the towns, almost no one used the dirt track unless they wanted to experience nature. She kept her ears and eyes alert for signs of other humans, but enough spiderwebs and creeping vines covered the trail that she felt safe in the knowledge that no one had passed through in days, if not weeks.

They stopped frequently for drinks, food, and rest. Keira tried her hardest to relax and not let her impatience show—or her nerves. A niggling worry had grown that the shack might not hold what she needed. As she'd discovered from visiting the tree where the faceless ghost had been killed, not every death left an imprint.

*What if they fade over time? These murders happened more than a hundred years ago. There might not be anything left.*

"Keira?"

Mason's voice pulled her out of her reverie, and she snapped a smile onto her face. "Sorry, I zoned out."

It was nearly three in the afternoon. Their path had started to trend uphill, and they'd slowed to a speed Zoe could handle. Even so, Keira's friend panted as she leaned against a tree.

Mason tilted his head toward the forest to their right. "I was saying now might be a good point to leave the main path. According to the map, the cabin will be directly west of here."

"Good. Not far now."

Zoe groaned, one hand holding her side. "If either of you see any mushrooms, let me know, okay? There's probably a fifty-fifty chance of getting high or dying, and either of those options would save me from walking, so I figure I can't lose."

"I think I'm obligated to—"

"Mason, don't take this the wrong way, but if you continue that thought, I will personally grind your bones into dust." Zoe swiped sweat off her face as she pushed away from the tree. "Come on. This murder cabin won't find itself."

Mason grinned and shrugged as he passed a compass to Keira. She held it up, but, as they stepped off the dirt track and into the forest, she realized she instinctively knew which direction was west.

They had to slow further as the uneven ground made the trail harder to follow. The day was on the cooler side, and the heavy tree cover helped drop the temperature further. As the sun started to move toward the horizon, Keira put her jacket back on. The forest was alive with animals. They chattered and skittered away between the trees as the friends disturbed them, and several birds started an indignant screech.

Occasionally, Keira felt herself slipping back into the fugue that had engulfed her on the walk from Cheltenham back to Blighty. It never stuck, though. Anytime her mind started to detach itself, it was startled back into place by a muffled groan from Zoe as she stumbled over a concealed rock or a comment from Mason.

Her friends would likely never know how much they were doing for her, but Keira held on to the gratitude like a warm coal in her chest.

"It should be somewhere near here," Mason said, breaking through her thoughts again. The sun was growing low, and what sunlight made it through the trees came in at a hard angle. "But…I'm starting to think it may be harder to find than expected."

They were on a small patch of empty ground. The growth around them was dense, reducing visibility to less than twenty feet in any direction.

"I guess the pathways have become overgrown in the last hundred years," Zoe said, swiping damp hair off her forehead. "People found the cabin when they were investigating Gerald Barge's past, but no one bothered to write down the coordinates, huh?"

"Mm." Mason chewed his lip. "We'll keep walking for a while. Look for any signs of habitation: old paths, stones where they don't belong, buckets or discarded cutlery, anything like that."

He moved forward, but Keira remained frozen, her attention fixed on the dense cluster of trees to her right. The forest had been alive with sound as they moved through it. She could still hear shrill, indignant birds behind them and the whirr of insects ahead, but the area to her right was strangely quiet. She opened the doors to her second set of senses and felt prickles creep over her skin like trails of ants.

"Hey." Her voice was quiet, but it carried in the still air. "I think it's this way."

Zoe and Mason exchanged a glance, then fell in line behind Keira as she wove between the tightly packed trees. They didn't try to speak. Even their footfalls had become quieter. It struck Keira that they were trying not to interrupt her concentration, which was more entertaining than it had any right to be. Now that she'd become aware of the static in the air, it was impossible to ignore. Her friends could have produced bagpipes and broken into a resounding two-piece symphony and she would have still found her way.

The ground led downhill. Keira shoved branches out of her path, her movements growing more urgent as the static intensified and the sinking sensation in her stomach growing heavier. She'd felt these kinds of emotions before at the old Crispin Mill. There, the ground had been tainted by decades of suffering and death. It had nearly dropped her to her knees when she'd first felt it.

Now, even though she was prepared for the emotions, and even with her mental barriers in place, her limbs shook and her heart pounded out of control. She was afraid she was going to be sick, but it was too late to back away.

She swiped a curtain of vines away. An old clearing stood ahead, and in its center was what remained of Gerald Barge's killing shack.

# CHAPTER 23

ITS DOORWAY HAD BEEN made of stone. The narrow arch was the only part of the cabin that was still intact; the stones had developed cracks and some looked ready to collapse with a good shove, but despite a heavy layer of moss and lichen, they had survived their century of solitude in the forest.

The rest of the building had fared poorly. The ceiling had collapsed, bringing down most of the walls with it. The forest had recognized the fallen wood beams as part of itself and made progress churning them back into soil. Small trees sprouted from what had once been the living room, shielding another small stone shape—a fire pit, Keira thought—from view.

Her chest ached. Her ears rang. She took a shambling step toward the building, then stopped.

She could hear the dead. They didn't make any kind of earthly noise, but their memories screamed and screamed and screamed.

It was too much. Keira closed her eyes, breathing slowly, hands flexing at her sides.

*We can't leave. Not yet. This is what we came for.*

The sun was near setting, but it still stung her eyes when she opened them. Her vision blurred as she took another step toward the house.

Behind her, she was vaguely aware of Zoe's awe-filled voice. "This is really it, huh?"

Keira tried to nod, but she wasn't sure if her head even moved. She took another step closer, then another. Her world tilted. She paused, trying to get ahold of herself, before continuing on.

Layers of long-dead leaves crinkled under her boots. The space around the cabin must have once been a sparse clearing, but nature had worked in slow and steady steps to reclaim it. Trees from the forest had fallen, some creating rotted fences to step over. One felled goliath leaned on the remains of the cabin's rear corner. New trees sprouted wherever there was space, some carrying vines up toward the heavens, some nearly as tall as their ancient counterparts.

She took another step forward, then another, her eyes fixed on the gaping doorway. The space beyond that was dim, sheltered by the two remaining walls and the fallen tree. She thought there might be furniture still inside. A table. A hint of rusted metal. She'd imagined Gerald's cabin would have been razed to the ground after it was discovered, but it seemed as though everything had been left in its place.

She stepped onto a patch of dead leaves. They crumbled away

beneath her. Keira tried to jolt backward, but it was too late: she'd been focused on the cabin, not on where her feet carried her, and her balance was gone before she even felt it slip away.

A dry root scraped her cheek as she plunged downward. She heard a voice yell her name, but it faded as walls of dirt rose around her. Subconsciously, she knew she needed to twist around, to adjust how she fell to lessen the impact, but her limbs were like lead and her mind frozen—not in fear, but in shock.

Then she hit the ground. Layers of rotting leaves cushioned her fall, bowing at least a foot under her weight, and it hurt less than she'd imagined.

Not that she would have noticed the pain either way.

One small, insidious thought reached her: She'd fallen into a pit. A pit near Gerald's cabin. One that had been excavated a hundred years ago. Excavated because Gerald had hidden his worst secrets here. The moment she touched ground, the emotional imprint slammed into her, sucking the breath out of her, rending her mind in half as easily as a cleaver.

The pit had been filled with bodies.

As soon as the thought entered Keira's mind, she began to scream. She was no longer alone in the dark, but surrounded. Rotting bodies crushed against every side. A bleached eye, bulging out of its skull, pressed against her cheek. There were silks and linens and cottons everywhere, damp with sweat, damp with blood, damp with decay. And the limbs—limp and gray and spongy. There were so many. They covered her. She couldn't breathe. Couldn't see. Couldn't so much as move.

Then one of the bodies near her squirmed. Keira stretched her mouth wide, trying to cry out, but she had no breath left. A hand, desiccated, the skin peeling away from the bones, fastened around her ankle. She tried to kick free. There was no room to move. The press of bodies crushed her against the decay-soaked ground. The hand kept squirming, clawing over her knee, creeping between the other corpses to grasp her forearm, then following that up, toward her throat.

"Talk to me," whispered a bearded man pressed against her back.

A woman against her thigh shuddered. "Talk to me."

"Talk to me, talk to me," unseen mouths rasped, dried tongues twitching in unnatural rhythms.

The hand wrapped around the curve of her jaw, thumb resting near her lips, fingers coiling into her hair.

"Talk to me," Mason said.

Keira drew in a sharp, stuttering breath. The pit was empty. The bloated, crowded bodies had evaporated into the still air, leaving just her and Mason alone on the bed of dead leaves.

He held her steady as he tried to read her with a mix of desperation and rising panic. "Can you hear me? Where are you hurt? Did you hit your head? Talk to me."

Keira closed her eyes, the relief like a rush of warm water over chilled limbs.

"Hey, hey, stay with me!" Mason jostled her lightly. "Don't pass out."

"I'm fine," she managed. "You don't need to worry."

He reached his other hand around, feeling the back of her head for bumps or cuts, and Keira pushed it away with a grimace. She still didn't feel quite like herself. The bodies were gone, but they'd left their emotions behind: pressing, howling, overwhelming. Her mental barriers were crumbling as fast as she tried to get them back into place.

"Ahoy down there." Zoe's voice sounded distant. "Good news, I found a rope. Bad news, it rotted into nothing about fifty years ago."

"That's okay. We're going to get you out of here. Come on." Mason's arms went around Keira as he pulled her up.

Keira's feet took a second to remember how to work, but she staggered alongside Mason as they moved to the pit's edge. His head was very close to hers. "Reach up," he said.

The pit was too dark to let her see clearly. Keira stretched her hands across walls made of dried dirt and loose stones. Then she raised them higher, feeling for fingerholds, but instead Zoe's warm hands fixed around her wrists.

Mason moved his grip to around her waist. "Three, two, one," he called, then he lifted at the same time as Zoe hauled back. Keira's mind caught up to what they were doing a second too late and her boots scrabbled against the dried soil, breaking clumps free, as she clambered to freedom.

She ended up in a heap among the dead grass and fallen branches, a breathless Zoe at her side. The throbbing cloudiness in her head began to dissipate. Her heart, galloping helplessly behind her ribs, began to slow again.

Zoe crawled back toward the pit. She and Mason debated something in hushed tones. Keira sat up carefully, grimacing as the familiar headache flared into life. The whistling in her ears had abated, but it was now replaced by the steady ache of a pulled muscle.

"I'm telling you, you're too heavy," Zoe said, crouched at the edge of the trench.

"And you're sure there's not another rope?"

"Ask me that again and you can stay down there for good, Pit Boy."

Keira moved to join Zoe by the hole. She clenched her teeth as she looked over the edge, prepared for another barrage of the images and emotions, but they didn't come. It was now just an empty gorge in the earth, ten feet long and nearly as deep, with a dirt-smeared Mason standing at its base, hands braced on his hips as he squinted up at them.

"Here," Keira said, dropping onto her stomach and reaching both hands down. "We should be able to get you up together."

It took a moment, but they got Mason out, even if the end result was that they were all sweaty and exhausted. They sat with Gerald Barge's shack to their backs and the pit ahead, as they caught their breath and picked loose dirt and leaves off their clothes.

"You're okay?" Mason asked.

Keira's head was still feeling the press of the long-cold emotional imprints and the searing headache was growing worse. It took her a second to realize Mason had spoken to her, and another second to remember how to smile. "Yeah."

"I can't believe you just walked into a hole like that," Zoe said.

"Honestly? Me neither."

"It was hard to see," Mason offered. "Especially in the dim light. I think it must have been covered with wood or something similar back when the cabin was discovered, but it's all rotted away since then."

From her angle, Keira couldn't see the pit's base, just its flaking, stone-pocked side. She closed her eyes and felt the sensation again: lying among the bodies, fabrics and flesh pressed against her. The headache redoubled.

"Let's go." Mason stood and offered Keira his hand. "It's getting late. We'll set up camp somewhere away from here."

She let him help her to her feet. "But I still need to—"

"Not yet. We'll get some food and some rest and then think about returning in the morning."

It was a sensible plan. Keira was exhausted and the headache made it hard to see right. But she couldn't stop herself from looking back at the cabin even as Mason and Zoe guided her out of the clearing.

*So many memories. So much death. Where am I even supposed to start?*

# CHAPTER 24

THEY HAD TO WALK for nearly twenty minutes before the headache subsided enough that Keira could begin to think again. By then, the sun was teasing the horizon, and visibility was abysmal. There was something about the way the shadows stretched long and the slushy colors of twilight blended together that made it hard to judge distance or even pick out individual trees.

"Is here far enough?" Mason asked as they emerged into a patch of relatively smooth ground.

The static still buzzed at her back, but it was growing faint enough that Keira was pretty sure she could sleep through it. "Works for me," she said, slinging her backpack off.

Zoe began kicking debris out of their way as Mason unpacked their tent and set it up with Keira's help. Before long, they had to fish their flashlights out and wedge them between branches to light the area. The trees were too dense to allow for a campfire without risking burning the whole forest down, so they set up a small gas cooker to heat dinner.

Zoe slumped on the forest floor, her face going slack from relief as she took the weight off her feet. "I'm never going to walk ever again."

Keira was used to traveling long distances, but even her legs were sore. "It's the forest. The ground is never truly flat, so you're using more muscles to keep your balance than you would on a footpath."

"Ugh." Zoe tilted her head back, eyes closed as she faced the canopy. "Rainforests only have a thin layer of fertile topsoil. Much like I only have a thin layer of good humor covering my deep, deep loathing for this place."

Mason chuckled as he spooned heated beans and sausages into bowls for them. "My parents used to take me camping here when I was young. We never got as far as Gerald's cabin—not that they knew it was here—but it was a cheap way to have a family holiday."

"How are your folks, anyway?" Zoe accepted her bowl and poked a fork into the beans. "I haven't seen them in ages."

"They're in Bolivia right now. They send a postcard every few weeks."

Zoe tilted her head toward Keira. "He's a proper latchkey kid, you know. His parents were never at home."

Keira lifted an eyebrow. "He told me they travel a lot for work."

"Yeah. And they'd leave him for months at a time. I think the poor kid saw more of the Santa Claus at city hall than he saw of his parents."

"You're making it sound worse than it was." Mason sat with one leg bent, so he could rest his arm on his knee. "My parents spent at least a few months home every year, and when they were gone, I stayed with my grandparents. By the time my grandparents passed, I was old enough to look after the house on my own."

Zoe snorted. "You were fourteen. That's basically child abandonment."

"It's not like anything bad was going to happen. I always had plenty of money to get groceries, and the neighbors were watching out for me, even if I didn't realize it at the time."

Keira had been struck before by the way the town seemed to treat Mason like a communal son. That was starting to make more sense.

"Anyway, the alternative would have been to bring me on their trips," Mason continued. "Dad was all for it, but Mum overruled him. She thought it was better for me to have the stability of one school and one set of friends."

"That still doesn't save you from being a latchkey kid."

Mason shrugged, leaning back. "If we're on the topic of parents, how's your mother?"

"Mm." Zoe took a spoonful of beans, but it seemed to hurt her to swallow them. "She's fine."

"I know she was waiting for some test results. Have they come back yet?"

"Nope."

There was something in Zoe's expression that didn't sit right with Keira. Her face, normally so open and eager, had tightened, like she was trying to hide inside herself. Keira had spent too much of her time in Blighty lying to the people closest to her. This was the first time Zoe had lied back.

Mason's voice sounded nonchalant, but Keira thought he must have picked up on the emotional shift too. He still stirred his fork through his dinner but the movements had become slow and careful. "Sometimes they can take a while. I know I'm only a fake shill, but if you ever want advice or a referral or even just someone to talk to—"

"Not a chance, nerd." Zoe grinned, and she nearly looked like herself again. Except there was still something underneath, something she was trying furiously, desperately, to conceal. Fear. "What are your folks doing in Bolivia anyway? Didn't they already visit there years ago?"

It was a desperate grab for a change of topic. Keira and Mason glanced at each other and, by unspoken agreement, went along with it. "Sure," Mason said. "But my mother thinks she can write a paper on the waterfowl she saw in a natural spring…"

Within minutes they were back to their usual banter. Zoe joked and laughed, seemingly herself again. They argued about one of her latest theories, that cheese was becoming less cheesy and the government wanted to see how far they could take it before people noticed. Zoe quizzed Keira about some of the ghosts in the graveyard, while Mason reclined and listened with an easy smile. It felt the way a camping trip should: fun.

But Keira couldn't shake the quiet sense of dread that had taken root in her stomach. Something was wrong in Zoe's world.

As she lay awake in their tent that night, the thoughts wouldn't stop crowding her mind. Above, the tent's blue walls billowed lightly in the wind. Keira raised one hand over her head and let the fingertips trail over the synthetic material. She'd been lying there for hours but still couldn't fall asleep.

She could deal with ghosts. But for all her ability when handling the dead, she was remarkably powerless to help the living. Zoe was hurting, and Keira didn't even know what to do to ease her pain. Especially when her friend seemed so determined not to talk about it.

Keira had gotten into a fight with Gavin Kelsey, son of the town's only qualified doctor, in the general store where Zoe worked. It had been her first real glimpse of what Gavin was capable of. The teen had been taunting Zoe about her mother's tests. Keira tried to remember the details. Only one part stood out clear in her mind: Gavin had made a joke about a funeral.

She rolled over, her stomach turning cold. Gavin had very likely been flaunting a worst-case scenario to get a rise out of Zoe, but Keira didn't like the idea that it was on the table at all.

*If I'd known, I wouldn't have let Zoe come on this trip. This equals two full days away from Blighty. If her mother's sick—if they only got the results in the last couple of days—we don't even have phone reception this far out—*

*We should go back home as soon as possible. Which means beginning the hike back to Blighty at first light. Which means there won't be time to return to the cabin after packing up. Which means—*

She crawled out of her sleeping bag. Zoe mumbled something under her breath and squirmed farther under her coverings. Keira waited until she was certain her friend was dozing again and then moved to the tent's opening.

The forest's thick canopy blocked any moonlight that might have reached her, so Keira pulled her boots on half-blind.

*If I want to see the cabin again, it has to be now.*

She wasn't afraid of becoming lost. The farther from town she was, the better her sense of direction seemed to become, and the low electric-like static that hung in the air would lead her to Gerald's home without fail.

But a visceral layer of metallic fear coated her tongue when she thought of the cabin. She didn't want to face it alone.

*It's better this way.* Communing with the dead had always felt like it should be a private event. And although she knew Zoe and Mason would want to help her, there was very little they could actually do in the moment. Especially if the visions turned dark. Instead, she needed them at the camp to help ground her into reality once the work was done. They didn't seem to realize how much of an impact their presence had, but having them there helped Keira more than they would ever know.

She dragged her coat over stiff, shaking limbs and retrieved a flashlight from their pile of equipment. The forest was too dark to see more than small patches, so Keira reached one hand ahead of herself and moved into the woods blindly.

She waited until she was well away from camp before turning the flashlight on. Small forest critters rustled the underbrush as they darted away from the light. Keira squared her shoulders and drew deep, slow breaths as she began the hike back to Gerald Barge's cabin.

# CHAPTER 25

SHE STOOD, SWAYING, ON the edge of the clearing. The light from her flashlight roved over bleak shapes—the edge of the pit she'd fallen into. The moss-coated stones marking the cabin's entrance. The collapsed tree, tilting at a steep angle, half-rotted, strips of bark and crumbled wood hanging from it.

The cold air stung her skin. Keira took a step closer, then hesitated, trying to collect her bearings. There was no reason to believe Gerald would have a second pit or any other traps, but she couldn't afford to make another mistake of that caliber.

Keira measured every footfall as she paced toward the old building. Her flashlight's beam flashed over dead leaves and exposed ground.

Her path carried her near the pit. She didn't want to look inside, but she felt compelled to regardless. She came to a halt at its edge, her breathing ragged and painfully fast as she extended the flashlight and gazed into the abyss.

Still empty. The blanket of decaying leaves in its base created a kaleidoscope effect where she imagined, if she looked long enough, she might begin to see faces staring back out at her.

*When I fell in, I imagined the pit was full of bodies. What was that?*

The answer came quickly enough. *It was an imprint from a death.* Someone had been thrown into the pit before they'd completely died, and when Keira touched the same earth they had, she'd experienced their last moments of life.

Keira doubled over, forearms braced on her knees, as she fought the urge to be sick. The headache was back. Her eyes stung and her throat felt raw, as though she'd been screaming for hours.

It would be so easy to turn around. She could be back at the camp within twenty minutes, crawling inside the tent and getting close to the two souls who made her feel safest.

Not yet, though. She still had a job to do.

She fixed her gaze on the stone doorway, one of the few remnants of the building's original structure. Her legs were sluggish as they dragged her toward it. The flashlight played over the weathered stone, highlighting its cracks and worn-down edges. The ground was tainted, and the emotional stains grew heavier with every step. Even breathing became painful. Keira stretched out one hand as she neared the entrance, dreading what might happen when she touched the stone, knowing it would be unavoidable.

The rough surface seemed unnaturally cold under her fingers.

It held something like an electric charge—prickles flowed along her nerve endings, making her muscles twitch, then her mind abruptly flashed white.

She couldn't see much, but she could hear a voice screaming for help, vocal cords strained raw. The words were distorted by time, like an old recording that had worn down from being played too often. There was despair in the voice, though. They knew how deep into the forest they were. They knew no one would answer them.

Then a flash of vision. Hands grasped the stone entrance as a woman tried to pull herself to freedom. The soft *whick* of an ax cleaving air. The hard *thump* as it hit home. The screams cut out.

Keira staggered away from the entrance, shaking and gasping. For a second, she'd felt the ax embed itself into her back, right below a shoulder blade. She raised her arm, expecting a flood of pain, but felt nothing except a dull twinge from the injury left after Gavin's attack.

She pressed her hand over her face as she tried to reel her emotions back in. The flashlight, pointed at the ground, flickered. Keira had the wild idea that even it was being drained by the dark energy poisoning the land.

She'd come to the shack to retrieve the memories of the souls who had lost their lives at Gerald's hands, but age had blurred the images and the noises. She'd glimpsed a woman—dark hair and dark clothes—and heard the ax, but it had been buffered, as though she were kneeling on the edge of a riverbed and trying to watch a film that played underneath meters of swirling, clouded water.

But if Gerald had been even half as prolific as the reports said, this wouldn't be the only glimpse of the past contained in the building.

She took a moment to prepare herself, then stepped through the archway. A cold sweat coated her back as the electric charge redoubled. Every hair on her body stood on end. Shivers wracked her, making her grip on the light increasingly unstable. Without thinking, she reached for something to steady herself against and touched the other side of the archway.

A woman pressed her back to it, gloved hands covering her face. Blood ran from between her fingers. A man, tall and wild, raised something metallic. Keira wanted to look away, but she didn't even have the luxury of closing her eyes. The ax came down, aimed for the narrow gap between the woman's hands, then the vision cut out.

Keira doubled over, her stomach heaving, but dinner had been long enough ago that it didn't return easily. She dropped into a crouch, shivering and feverish, as she waited for her breathing to slow. Her pulse set a harsh tempo as it throbbed in her ears.

*I don't know how many of these I can handle.* She ran her tongue across the back of her teeth and tasted bile. *Or what I'm even looking for. Anything, I suppose. Anything that might help me beat him.*

The cold air was a small mercy; it dried the sweat dripping across her face, cooling her feverish skin. The cabin's walls had broken down over the years, leaving the interior exposed to the elements, and a slow wind wound around Keira. She tilted her head back to take advantage of it.

Her flashlight picked out the furniture in fragments. The tree that had fallen against the cabin cut through the room, partially supported by the remnants of the left-side wall. Its trunk was decaying in increments, and small, silvery insects fled when Keira's light touched them.

Underneath the tree was the crumpled remains of a hand-built table. She guessed that the piles of spongy wood on either side had once been chairs. Boxes, roughly made to resemble crude cabinets, outlined where a food preparation area might have once been. The cabin wouldn't have had access to water or electricity, but there was still the rusted carcass of a pail that Gerald might have used to collect rainwater in. The floors were made of boards, hand prepared, like most things in the shack. Something that looked vaguely like a raised planter had been constructed against the wall to Keira's right. It now grew an assortment of gifts from the forest: ferns, weeds, and grasses.

Keira's legs were unsteady, but they still supported her as she rose. She crossed to the low rectangular shape and, careful not to touch it, bent close to examine the organic material inside.

*A mattress. What remains of one, at least. This used to be his bed.*

It made sense. The trip from town took a full day. He would have needed somewhere to rest before returning home. Accounts from Gerald's friends had said he often spent weekends in the forest, allegedly hunting.

*Hunting. He must have felt so clever every time he used that excuse to explain his absence.*

Keira grimaced. She didn't want to know if anyone had died

in the bed, but she couldn't afford to ignore possible clues. She flexed aching fingers, then reached them in between the delicate ferns to touch the long-collapsed remains of the mattress.

Nothing happened. Keira released her held breath, then rocked back. She eyed the rest of the room, waiting to see if it gave up any secrets, then felt her blood turn cold as she picked up the discoloration of a deep stain in some of the floorboards.

The flooring had been laid across bare ground. As the soil shifted over decades, the floor had begun to bow and bubble, creating gaps between boards and causing some to spring up entirely. Some had worn down into nothing, but others had resisted the weather, including a set that retained what Keira was fairly sure were old bloodstains.

*No time to be squeamish now.* She reached for the marks before she could question her choice too closely. The images came rough and fast.

A middle-aged woman struggled with a man on the floor. Her fingers raked across his face. A small, silver pocketknife lay near her shoulder. The images bled away, then returned. He had his hands around her throat. The woman tried to pry him away with one hand while the other scrabbled across the floor. Twitching fingers fixed around the knife.

*Please*, Keira begged, even though she knew how this memory would inevitably play out. *Please, please!*

The image faded again, then returned, stronger and clearer than any of the others. The man, Gerald, had raised his fist. The woman plunged her knife into it. Gerald screamed, hand jolting back, still carrying the knife in its palm. The woman threw her fist into his stomach as she tried to force his weight off.

*Please.* Keira shook her head, desperate to leave the memory, but she was trapped as Gerald pulled the blade free from his hand. He brought it down. Into the woman's chest. Her throat. Her face. Then the images faded at last, leaving Keira alone again, shivering in the dark maw of the cabin, poised over the woman's long-dried pool of blood.

"Enough." She pressed her palms to her face. The skin was wet, but no longer from sweat alone. She couldn't tell when she'd started crying but now couldn't stop.

Something hurt deep inside, and it took a moment to recognize why: she didn't know the victims' names. The woman who had been stabbed to death had fought just as ferociously as Keira hoped she herself would if she ever encountered the same situation…but the woman had been lost to time. Even if she'd been reported missing, her body, left in the pit, might not have ever been identified. And there was something intensely unfair about that.

Keira was at her limit. Every minute spent in the cabin wore down her stamina, and every vision of the past felt like it was shredding her from the inside out. She had a frightening suspicion that if she spent too long there, she might never recover from the damage.

She began to rise, then stopped. This might be her only chance to understand Gerald. And it might be her last chance to save what was left of the graveyard's denizens. She'd made them a promise that she'd do everything in her power, and she was still standing, which meant she had more to give.

Keira grit her teeth and reached her hands across the floor, waiting for the images to overtake her as she searched for spots that still carried memories of death. She found them. A plump, sweet-faced woman, strangled by a length of rope. A woman in a thin, well-patched dress being held against Gerald's chest as he sliced a knife across her throat. Keira was sick in the room's corner, her head feeling like it was about to be split by the migraine, but she still returned to the killing ground for fresh images. A woman lay in the room's corner, bleeding out, while Gerald rummaged through her pockets for trinkets. He found a fob watch and, smiling as he admired it, carried it to the crates that made up the quasi-kitchen along the room's opposite wall.

The vision faded. Keira hunched over, sick again, only this time her dinner had already been lost and she had nothing else to bring up. She spat to clear her mouth as much as possible, then staggered up and approached the remains of the crates.

Her mind was fracturing in a way that made it hard to remember where she was or even her own name. The space behind her eyes pulsed in harsh beats as her consciousness tried to reconcile existing in two time spans. She could barely think. She only held on to a vague, irrational concept: she wanted to return the woman's stolen fob watch to her.

The crates were falling apart as rusted nails released their hold on crumbling boards. Keira tried to rest her hand on one, but only succeeded in pulling its side away. Its contents tumbled out.

She was grateful the contact hadn't resulted in another vision. She suspected that even one more would push her past the point of no return, until she lost the ability to return to the person she'd been before stepping into the cabin.

Keira laid the flashlight on the ground, pointed toward the crates, so she could use both hands to sort through the contents. There were old metal plates, age-stained cutlery, what remained of a brush to remove dirt from shoes, tattered scraps that might have once been clothes.

Keira shook her head in an effort to clear her mind. *It's not in the crates. Underneath.*

Her last glimpse from that final vision, before the woman's life left her and the images faded to black, was of Gerald pulling the second crate away from the wall. He wasn't putting something in it. He was uncovering the space hidden beneath.

Keira hauled the box away. The floorboards underneath hadn't been nailed down, and one jutted out of place, disturbed by the slowly settling earth. She wrenched it up, breaking it in the process.

There was a hollow in the ground below. And inside that hollow was a metal chest about the size of Keira's head. She lifted it out, her breathing painfully rough, her muscles shaking uncontrollably, and opened the lid.

# CHAPTER 26

KEIRA SPENT THE REMAINDER of the night sitting on a fallen tree close to Mason's tent, sifting through the box's contents by flashlight. She'd come close to finishing when Zoe, her eyes squinted and her bobbed hair poking in every conceivable direction, crawled out of the tent at dawn.

"There you are." Zoe pulled a face as she rubbed sleep out from the corners of her eyes. "Aren't you cold?"

"Not really," Keira said, hoping her chattering teeth weren't audible.

Zoe stretched both arms, then exhaled a puff of condensation as she began pulling her hiking shoes on. "When I woke up and saw you weren't in the tent, I worried you'd wandered off during the night."

"Technically, I did. But I wandered back, so no harm, right?" Keira lifted the box, letting the early light glint off the tarnished metal. "I found this in Gerald's cabin."

Zoe's tiredness melted away as curiosity lit up her eyes. "Treasure. Wait, no. Illuminati secrets. Wait, no, he killed people. It's trophies, right?"

"Got it on the third try." Keira lifted the small gold fob watch out of the box and tried not to let the sadness she felt show on her face. "He kept a memento from each of his victims."

"And they're helpful?"

Keira chewed over the question, then carefully laid the watch back inside the box. "I don't know. We should probably wait until Mason's up to go over it."

"Oy." Zoe reached behind herself to slap the tent's wall, making the fabric shiver. "Sun's up. Aren't you med students trained to only sleep twenty minutes a night?"

Rustling sounds came from the tent, then Mason, just as rumpled as Zoe and looking twice as tired, emerged. "It is impossible to care for others if you don't first care for yourself. Work is completed faster and with fewer mistakes when you're well rested. The university made it clear that it endorses healthy lifestyle choices." He blinked at them both, lips pulled into a thin line, before shuffling toward the cooker. "Unofficially, though? Yeah. Twenty minutes on a good night."

"The sheep are more malleable when they're exhausted," Zoe said, nodding. "Just so you know, our dearest friend availed herself of a midnight hike through the murder forest."

Mason made a faint grumbling noise as he switched the cooker on and set up a pot of water. "I wish I could say I was shocked, but…this is Keira. I'm mostly just resigned at this point."

Zoe leaned forward, fingers steepled under her chin as she fixed Keira with a questioning stare. "On a scale of one to ten, how much tetanus would you say is flowing through your blood right now?"

"I can't answer that, but I'm a ten on the scale of being ready to go home."

"Amen," Zoe said. "But not before I have something to eat. And not before you tell me what's in that box."

Mason, who'd been watching their water boil with bleary eyes, finally looked up. "You found that in the cabin?"

"Hidden under the floorboards, yeah. The contents are organized." Keira ran her fingertips over a series of wooden dividers. They had been used to keep the trinkets in categories. "I haven't completely figured out the system yet, but I suspect it's divided by year. There's…a lot."

"Well, go on," Zoe urged.

Keira hesitated. She'd wanted to return to town as quickly as possible—and not just because of the shade, but also for Zoe's sake. But Mason was preparing cups for hot tea, and besides, Keira wasn't sure she was physically capable of standing yet. She'd made it back to the camp, but the experience in the cabin had drained her more than she'd been prepared for. Her mind still felt scattered. Her limbs were weak. It was the kind of exhaustion that was so deep that she couldn't even sleep, which had led her to spend the last hours of the night hunched over the box, doggedly sorting through the contents.

She was ready for some outside help again. "The things Gerald chose to keep answer a lot of questions. But I can't see whether they answer the *main* question at all."

"What's keeping Gerald on earth," Mason said.

"Exactly."

"Start with the easy stuff." Zoe accepted her mug and cupped it between her pale hands. "What kind of questions *did* it answer?"

"Things I hadn't even thought to ask." Keira picked out a soft leather binder from the box and carefully undid the strap holding its contents together. "Like how he managed to lure his victims into the forest, and why they were all women."

Inside the envelope were letters. Some written by Gerald, some written by his victims. Keira hadn't yet read them all, but she'd scrutinized enough to recognize a pattern.

"He met his targets through newspaper postings. Back then, most papers hosted a section for unmarried men and women to write in looking for possible romantic partners."

"Ye Olde Match Dot Com," Zoe supplied.

"Pretty much. He replied to a lot of them and started a correspondence. They'd exchange letters for weeks or even months until he thought they were ready, and then he'd ask to meet, heavily implying that marriage was on the horizon. He said, before he could ask the most important question, he needed to introduce them to his sisters, who he was very close to, to be sure they approved."

Zoe frowned. "But he didn't *have* any sisters."

"Sneaky," Mason said. "They'd be more reluctant to meet him if he were alone. Believing other women were going to be present would have made Gerald seem safer. More trustworthy."

"Exactly. He'd write that he and his sisters were planning to travel into the forest, then ask his intended victim to meet them halfway."

Zoe nodded to herself. "By the time they arrived and found he was alone, they would have come too far to back out."

Keira put the letters back. "It answered one other question too: whether he'd had any male victims." The box was filled with all kinds of trinkets: hairclips, lockets, rings, all arranged carefully into different slots. It seemed Gerald had taken one item to remember each of his victims by. Occasionally photos—small ones, intended as personal keepsakes—were tied to different treasures. Gerald had likely asked his victims to send him one or to bring it to the meeting.

In among the attached photos was one loose portrait, not tethered to any item. Keira slipped it out. It was smaller than her palm and heavily creased around the edges, as though the bearer had carried it with them for years. A dot of discoloration at one corner showed where it had been stained by blood.

Two people had been captured in the photo. A woman in her late forties and a younger man who, based on their similarly dark hair, appeared to be her son.

The woman from the photo was familiar. Keira had watched as she fought for her life, ultimately stabbing her pocketknife into Gerald's hand.

Unlike the other photos, though, it hadn't been attached to the woman's memento. The pocketknife she'd used to attack Gerald had been wiped clean and stored in the box. The delicate decorations on the silver handle were designed to make it seem elegant, like any other pendant or necklace a woman might wear, and help disguise the bleak truth that it was a weapon being brought along to protect against a worst-case scenario.

Only one thing didn't make sense. The knife had been stored in one of the box's segments. The blood-tinted photo had been placed in another.

That mystery had irked Keira through most of the night. She'd tried to tell herself that Gerald had made a mistake, but the more she sorted through the box's contents, the more evidence she found of meticulous—almost pedantic—categorization. Everything was neat. Everything was where it belonged. Except for that photo.

Then she had tried to argue that the photo had jostled free from its position at some point—either while the box was hidden in the cabin, or, more likely, when Keira herself had carried it back to camp. But when the lid was closed, it created a tight seal. Keira had tested how much motion would be needed to shift the contents and found that even turning the box upside down wouldn't have been enough. The photo had deliberately been stored separately.

She hadn't found her answer until dawn's light broke through and helped illuminate the world. The photo was easier to see in daylight. The woman's face, lightly creased and serene, stared up at her from the image. Beside and slightly behind stood her son: tall, straight backed, a lopsided smile brightening his face. He wasn't familiar. But his coat was.

The long, brown, mended garment had been haunting her graveyard.

"I think I found the identity of my John Doe." Keira lifted the photograph. Underneath the image had been scribbled two names: Maria and Adrian Holcombe.

# CHAPTER 27

"AT FIRST I THOUGHT the photo had been miscategorized, but I was wrong." Keira, backpack strapped in place, fought to keep her pace and speak at the same time. The tremor that had spread through her body wanted to leak into her voice, but she was trying to keep it contained. "They were two separate mementos, for two separate murders, in two separate years."

"He came looking for his mother," Mason noted, his voice heavy. "She must have told him just enough about her secret admirer for Adrian to track Gerald down."

"And Adrian confronted him in the middle of the street," Zoe continued. She, along with Mason, walked ahead of Keira as they retraced the path that led to Blighty. "Gerald's house was near the murder site. Adrian must have arrived just before dawn, bumped into Gerald by accident, and started asking questions."

"And Gerald, realizing how close he was to being exposed,

retaliated." Keira kept her head down, so neither of her friends would see how heavily she was breathing if they happened to look back. "He killed Adrian, took any identifying material from his wallet, and left him in the street to be found hours later."

"Monster," Zoe muttered.

"This means I know what's holding my John Doe on earth," Keira said. "Revenge. His mother, widowed, went to meet a prospective new husband and never returned home. Adrian set out to find out what happened to her and, most likely, get justice for her. But he died before he could achieve that."

"So you get rid of Gerald, and you get rid of Mr. Empty Face," Zoe said.

"Theoretically. I hope."

Mason hitched his backpack slightly higher. "Adrian was killed just two months before Gerald himself died. If he'd waited just a little bit longer, he would have been able to expose Gerald's crimes."

"Or if he'd entered Blighty through a different route and bumped into literally anyone other than Gerald." The day was growing warmer, but the chills were still too present for Keira to remove her jacket. She swallowed thickly before continuing. "Or if he'd told someone in his own town where he was going and what for. He became a John Doe because he wasn't reported missing and no one recognized him. If they had, they might have been able to tie Gerald to the murder, even after Adrian's death."

"It's a comedy of errors, minus the comedy." Zoe blew a sharp breath to clear stray hair from her face. "Does this help you get rid of Gerald, though?"

Keira grimaced. "Nope."

"We can figure this out." Mason, steady as ever, spoke warmly as he led the group. "Let's start at the basics again. What motivated him to kill?"

Keira opened her mouth, but then closed it again. She had no answer.

The silence only lasted a moment, then Zoe said, "His mother."

"Yeah?" Mason looked over his shoulder. "You think he was trying to get revenge against her?"

"And punish other women like her. Keira, what was the average age of his victims?"

Keira tried to remember what had been written in the letters, but her mind kept drifting back to the faces she'd seen inside the cabin. "Mostly in their forties. Some in their thirties, some in their fifties."

"Yeah. He had a type. Middle-aged women. *Motherly* women."

"That could be biased by the kind of people who posted ads in the paper, though," Mason said. "Younger women might prefer to meet prospective love interests in society. Older ladies might be more pragmatic about it—they know what they're looking for, and if they can't find it within their town, they'll go searching for it."

"That's true." Zoe kicked a rock out of her path. "But remember, his mother left his family when he was twelve. The official story was that she became sick and passed away, but there were rumors of her living with another man in a different town."

Mason ran a hand over the lower half of his face. "Yeah, okay, I can see that. If she really did abandon him, he would have been old enough to resent her for it."

"Hence his choice in victims. It was a revenge fantasy. Or a power trip over a demographic of woman he'd begun to despise. He never married either; instead of confronting his emotions as he grew, he let irrational fear and resentment fester into something massively toxic."

"We might have our answer to what motivated him in life, then," Mason said. "But that's not exactly a reason to keep existing after death. It's not unfinished business. I could understand if he was afraid of what would happen to him in the afterlife, but he's not trying to hide either."

"He's not," Keira said. "Almost the opposite, actually."

"Exactly. So…what does he *want*?"

Keira shook her head bleakly. "To consume. That's really all I can see. He devours anything in his path. Sometimes he tries to lure victims by wailing, but since his hunting ground has grown, he's started stalking his prey instead."

"Is he only attacking female ghosts?" Zoe asked.

"No." Keira blinked and saw the spectral man, screaming, as he was torn apart. She grit her teeth. "He'll take anyone."

"Including you," Mason added. "And you're about twenty years too young to be his ideal."

"It's because I have more energy," Keira said. "Consuming the other ghosts gives him a small amount of power. If he can reach me, he'll be able to get so much more."

Mason made a small noise, something between anger and fear. His back was to her and Keira couldn't read his expression, but she could imagine it. She'd become familiar with the particular way his eyebrows tilted when he began to worry.

"Okay," Zoe said. "So the mother thing might have motivated him in life, but he's not so bothered by that anymore. He wants to consume stuff. But that doesn't line up with what we know about his life. He wasn't a hoarder or obsessed with wealth or trying to gain power. He mostly lived quietly. He had a modest house and a small farm, kept a lot of friends, and occasionally disappeared into the forest to indulge in his habit of being one of the most disgusting excuses for a human possible. That doesn't track with him being all-consuming after death."

"What are you thinking?" Keira asked.

"I bet this whole quest for more energy and a wider sphere of influence is all in service of some greater goal." Zoe snapped her fingers. "He's looking for something in particular, and he needs to be stronger to get it. If we can figure that out, we'll have figured out his tether."

It made sense. The shade hunted anything it could reach, but Keira hadn't been able to detect any trace of happiness or gratification when it caught a victim.

*He's seeking something, then. What, though? His house was razed to the ground decades ago. Is he trying to reach his cabin? Maybe he's looking for the trinkets? No. Ghosts stay during the short-term if they're lost, but the only reason they manage to remain present long-term is if they have unfinished business. Something they need to complete. Viewing trinkets one more time isn't a strong enough motivation for him to linger for a hundred years.*

"What else do we know about him?" Mason had slowed his pace so Keira was nearly abreast of him. "Don't worry about his past life any longer. Think about his shade form. Tell us every detail you can remember."

She ran her tongue across her lips as she thought. "He doesn't look human anymore. He's like smoke. His gravestone was cracked. Sometimes he can kind of…fade out, like the other spirits do, to avoid being seen. But he usually doesn't try to hide."

"Good." His voice was steady and warm, reassuring Keira that she had the answer somewhere in her grasp. She wished Mason had less faith in her. Both of her friends were looking at her, hopeful and expectant. She couldn't blame them. She was supposed to be the expert on the dead. They didn't know how lost she truly felt.

Her throat caught, but she pushed through it, recounting everything she remembered. "He can make noises, but he doesn't talk. He's growing stronger. He—"

Keira pulled up short. Her heart thundered, but this time it wasn't from the exhaustion or the stress, but from her first true taste of hope in a long time.

Both Mason and Zoe stopped as well, turning to face her. Keira couldn't stop a trace of shocked, relieved laughter from entering her voice.

"He's started carrying his bones inside of himself. Pulled out from the crack in his gravestone. All of his bones except—"

Zoe drew a sharp breath. "His skull."

"The one that was stolen when the mob dug his grave up." Mason crossed his arms as he stared into the trees. "Okay. Yeah. If my skull was missing, I'd want it back too."

"Do you think he'd accept a replica?" Zoe asked. "I can make a very convincing papier-mâché skull. I'd include some sweets inside, so he can have a fun surprise if he accidentally breaks it."

"Don't think I'm not enamored with the concept of the piñata skull, but I doubt that's going to be enough for him." Keira's legs ached, but she forced them to start walking again, setting a slightly faster pace.

"What about a more authentic replacement, then?" Mason let Keira take the lead, but followed close behind. "The ethics are dubious, but there are ways to buy bones, including skulls. Would he know if it was actually his?"

"Or if you want to avoid the dubious ethics," Zoe added, "just dig up one of the other graves and nab a skull from there. They won't mind."

Mason made a faint choking noise. "I'm becoming concerned about where you draw the line for *dubious ethics*, because grave robbing is a fair way over it for most people."

Keira ran her tongue across her teeth. Her gut instinct said yes, Gerald would be able to tell. But, then, would she be able to recognize her own skull if she had to? She tried to picture what it might look like and came up blank. Apparently a lifetime of use didn't guarantee familiarity when the object in question was hidden under layers of skin and hair.

"I don't know," she said at last. "He's not human any longer. He might accept anything that fits the vague descriptor of his unfinished business. But I feel as though he's more likely to have a sixth sense about it. Like an animal that can sense when a storm is coming. He wouldn't need to examine the skull; he'd just *know*."

"Well, damn." Zoe heaved a sigh. "That makes our job a heck of a lot harder. That skull was kicked into a field; the police said they searched for it, but there's still a good chance that it's half-buried under some corn right now. Or maybe someone *did* bring it home as a trinket but dropped it into the bin when they got bored. We're talking hundred-year-old corpse desecration here; the leads aren't exactly fresh."

Mason said, "We could ask around town in case anyone remembers a relative owning a skull, but I've never seen one, so it's probably a thin hope at best."

"Agreed," Zoe said. "I make it my business to know about the skeletons people keep in their closets, and I've yet to hear about a literal one."

Keira stopped walking. Mason bumped into her back, murmured an apology, and tried to step away, only to collide with Zoe in turn.

Keira's mind was racing. "Neither of you have been into Polly Kennard's home, have you?"

"The florist?" Zoe squinted her eyes. "Please don't try to tell me sweet Polly collects bones, because I'll take your word on the ghost-hunting stuff, but that's a step too far, even for me."

"Not Polly." Keira was breathless, but she lengthened her strides, desperate to reach town in time. "Harry Kennard owns a skull."

# CHAPTER 28

A VIOLENT-RED SUNSET STREAKED across the sky. Keira guessed they had less than an hour until night covered them. That would be barely enough time to get the skull and bring it back to Gerald…if they were lucky.

They struck out across Blighty Cemetery, weaving among the gravestones single file. Keira had led them through the last stretch of forest in a wide arc to avoid the shade, but he hadn't yet made an appearance. She didn't like that. She preferred it when he was visible, straining at the ends of his tether. Now, she didn't know how broad his circle of influence might be. How many spirits he might have slaughtered while she was gone. Whether even her cottage was safe.

"Leave the gear here." Keira dropped the backpack from her shoulders as she passed the low stone fence surrounding her dead garden. "We can pick it up later."

Heavy thuds and sighs came from behind her as her companions dropped their burdens, but Keira didn't slow down. She was exhausted, running on fumes after a night of no sleep and a full day of walking, but there was no chance for rest. It would be too dangerous to confront the shade after nightfall, and daylight was bleeding away fast. If she was going to do this, it had to be now.

Something dark shifted to Keira's right. She froze, staring into the trees, watching for motion. The forest was less than twenty feet away and already heavily shadowed. She could have sworn she saw something human-size standing among the trees.

It could have been a spirit. They often blinked in and out of sight. Even if it wasn't, the crushing tiredness was making reality blur, and her mind could have conjured a sense of movement where there was none.

*And if it's the other alternative—if the organization has caught up to me—well...they can wait.*

Her companions' breathing was ragged as they descended the driveway that led to Blighty's shops. The town settled early, and the roads were near empty. Keira glanced over her shoulder as they approached the strip of cobblestone that carried travelers to the town's center.

"Do we have a plan?" Mason asked. The florist's, the closest business to the church and graveyard, loomed ahead. Built in the town's old-world style, it had been constructed as two stories and was deeper than it was wide. The lowest level contained more flowers than Keira thought the town could consume in a year. The upper level was Polly and Harry's home.

Keira grimaced. "Uh, the plan currently stands at…talking to Harry?"

"I can keep Polly occupied," Mason said. "Just let me know how much time you need."

Zoe's expression lit up. "I see where this is going. Mason distracts Polly. You distract Harry. I run in and steal the skull while you're all yakking."

"Actually, I was hoping you'd help me with Harry. You know him better than I do. I'd really, really love to get this skull without committing any actual crimes."

"Roger. We'll keep the bone thievery as plan B."

They came to a halt on the florist's doorstep. The shop itself was dark; the buckets normally kept around the front had been moved inside, and the sunshiny *Open* sign had been flipped to a rainy-weather *Closed*. Someone was still inside the store, though. Footsteps moved through the building as that day's work was packed away.

Keira was hyperconscious of her appearance; she'd spent two days in a forest with no showers, and she looked it. She'd tried to brush her hair that morning, but grime and stray spiderwebs made it a futile effort. Her fingernails held a diverse sampling of forest floor. And her clothes needed more than a simple spin through the washing machine. There was no time to make herself more presentable, though. She tucked flyaway hairs behind her ears, then raised her chin and rapped firmly on the door.

It took a moment, but then the cloth shade over the door's window retracted, revealing Polly's round, well-creased face.

She peered at them over her pince-nez glasses, then her cheeks flushed pink with delight as she recognized them. The shade flapped back into place, then the door rattled and swung inward, its bell chiming in time with Polly's greeting. "Keira, what a lovely surprise!"

"Hey, Polly." Keira couldn't stop her own smile as the smaller woman beamed at her. "Sorry, I know it's late. I hope I'm not disturbing you."

"Of course not. You're welcome anytime." Polly glanced over Keira's shoulder and her smile slipped into pursed lips. "And I suppose your friends are welcome as well."

"Hi," Zoe called. "Sorry for trying to stage a protest outside your store that one time. I see you managed to scrub the spray paint off the bricks."

"Hmm." Polly's lips stayed tightly bunched until she turned back to Keira, then relaxed into a smile again. "Were you looking for more flowers? You know you're welcome to them anytime. I'll even make an exception to the clearly listed opening hours for you."

"Oh, no, thanks." Keira caught herself quickly. "I still have the bunch you gave me earlier. They're wonderful."

"That was all Harry." Polly's gray perm shone in the desk lamp's light as she tilted her head toward the stairs at the shop's rear. "He absolutely insisted, you know."

Keira would wager good money that Harry had nothing to do with it, but Polly had given her the transition she needed. "Do you think I could see him? To thank him in person?"

Polly looked as though she'd won the lottery. She slipped her arm through Keira's and pulled her toward the stairs. "He'll be *thrilled*."

Zoe and Mason hadn't been invited in, but Polly didn't seem to notice as they trailed behind. The florist spoke, her words running so quickly that Keira struggled to keep up. Polly bounced between talking about how her son would excel at sports if he ever tried them, to how he would almost definitely be good at chess as well, to how his band had decided to create a sense of scarcity for their last album by only producing two copies. They were still waiting to sell out. Keira let the words flow over her, nodding when it was appropriate and trying not to trip over her own feet as Polly practically dragged her up the narrow stairwell.

They stepped into the upstairs living area, and Keira squinted at the sudden brightness. Not only were the ceiling lights on, but so were at least six pastel lamps spread about the room. The space had been decorated in Polly's aesthetic: floral patterns on the plush couches, floral patterns in the wallpaper, and everything decorated in gentle pinks, yellows, oranges, and greens. It was cozy and cluttered, and wildly at odds with the sallow figure standing at the sink.

Harry Kennard looked like a product of another world. His black hair grew increasingly long, its sideswept bangs covering one eye and leaving the other, lined in black, to stare at them like a feral animal caught in headlights. The dark makeup contrasted against skin so pale that he could pass for a vampire, and all-black clothes didn't help the impression.

They'd interrupted him in the middle of constructing a jam sandwich, the butter knife held aloft as a glob of strawberries trailed down its blade. His wide, unblinking eye glanced from his mother to the three friends, then, apparently coming to the realization that he was about to be forced to entertain guests, Harry turned and wordlessly began loping toward his bedroom.

"No! No, you don't." Polly lunged, snatching his arm and pulling him back before he could vanish into the hallway. "Dear Miss Keira came to visit you. And you *will* be polite." She turned back to her guests, laughing breathlessly as she strained against her son's efforts to escape. "The trick is to stop him from getting into his room. He's really quite sociable otherwise."

"I only need a minute," Keira called. Harry slumped, defeated, and allowed himself to be dragged back into the living space, still carrying the jam-smeared knife.

Mason caught Keira's eye. She gave him a small nod. He stepped forward, his gentle, warm smile in place as he smoothly put himself between Polly and her son. "Ms. Kennard, I was hoping to ask about your daffodils—"

"Oh, you know you should call me Polly." She laughed, hand fluttering over her throat as Mason engaged her in botanical talk.

Only one part of the living space bore any trace of Harry Kennard. It was so out of place that Keira had noticed it the first time Polly had invited her up to the second floor. The entertainment unit held a TV, an assortment of decorative teacups, unlit candles, and bouquets of flowers—and, on its top, a bleached-white skull. It was old, growing crumbly, and imperfect enough that Keira could only believe it was real. The upper canine on its left-hand side was missing. Keira closed her eyes and struggled to bring up memories of what she'd seen in Gerald Barge's cabin. He'd cried out when his hand was stabbed. And, in his open mouth, Keira was certain she'd seen a dark gap in his teeth.

Zoe waited at her side. Keira found her hand and squeezed it, whispering, "It's his."

"Yes, it is mine." Harry had approached so silently that Keira hadn't noticed. He stood behind them, both his expression and his words perfectly impassive as he licked jam off the knife.

Keira took a sharp breath. She had to clench her hands to keep herself from reaching for the skull. "Where did you get it?"

"A friend."

Zoe squinted at him. "I didn't think you had friends."

Keira grimaced. They couldn't afford to antagonize Harry, not when they needed his help so desperately. But Harry made a small huffing sound that could only be interpreted as laughter.

"I don't," he said. "But I'll make an exception for Dane."

"Dane Crispin?" Keira asked, at the same time as Zoe said, "Ol' Crispy?"

They'd had a memorable encounter with the reclusive heir to the Crispin estate. And Keira had come very close to being riddled with bullets for it.

Zoe gawked, trapped somewhere between disbelief and awe. "But...*no one* is friends with Ol' Crispy."

"We share common interests." Harry finished licking jam off

the knife and tucked it into his pocket. "He likes dead things. I like dead things. And so on and so forth."

"So…he gave you this skull?" Keira nodded toward it. "Did he say where *he* got it from?"

"No."

"Probably inherited it," Zoe said. "The Crispins were a much bigger family back in Gerald's time. One of their kids must have collected the skull and brought it home. It would be easy to lose in that estate."

"Okay." Keira turned to face Harry, hands clasped in front of herself. On the other side of the room, Polly was laughing as she recounted some story, Mason grinning as he listened attentively. Keira took a sharp breath. "Harry, I need to ask a huge favor."

The one visible eye stared at her from under the bangs, unblinking, unemotional.

"I really need your skull," Keira continued. "I mean…not your skull…not the one you're using—you can keep that one, but—"

"This old thing," Zoe supplemented, nodding to the entertainment unit.

They waited for some kind of reaction, but none came. Harry was like a blank wall. He wouldn't even blink; except for the fact that he was still standing, Keira might have feared that he'd spontaneously descended into a coma. She cleared her throat. "I don't have much money, but I'll give you everything I *do* have."

He forced them to endure another moment of silence. It stretched and stretched until Keira was squirming from its pressure, then Harry tilted his head slightly, letting his bangs clear part of the second eye. "But…you live in a graveyard. You have so many of them already."

"Yeah." The conversation felt so ridiculous that Keira didn't know whether to laugh or cry. "But I need this one."

"Why?"

Keira opened her mouth, closed it, then tried again. Her mind was empty. She had no excuse, no plausible reason that she could give without sounding entirely irrational. He gave her no reprieve but kept staring, waiting for an answer she couldn't find.

Zoe leaned forward, smiling broadly as she threw an arm around Keira's shoulders. "We need it for an occult ritual."

"Oh?" Harry's eyebrows twitched up. He hesitated, then said, "Can I come?"

Zoe glanced at Keira. Keira's mind raced. Harry wouldn't be able to see the shade, and as long as she kept him at a distance, he wouldn't be hurt either. She'd intended to keep the plan to return Gerald's skull between herself, Zoe, and Mason, but if this was Harry's condition… "I mean, I guess? It won't look very impressive."

"They never are." Harry reached past Keira, his long, pale fingers lightly lifting the skull off the entertainment unit. "I'm just glad to be included."

Keira nearly choked on shocked laughter. "Okay. Okay! This, uh, this is happening!"

Harry held the skull ahead of himself, calmly staring into the cavities where the eyes belonged. "Will I get the skull back when you're done?"

"Um. Probably not."

"All possessions are ephemeral, I suppose." Harry sighed. "Even the nicest ones."

"Thank you, Harry. You don't know how much I appreciate this."

He didn't reply but gave a slow nod. Keira raised a hand to signal Mason. He touched Polly's arm as he moved back toward the doorway. "That's amazing. I had no idea jellyfish made such good pets. My friends need me to walk them home, but I hope we can catch up later so you can tell me more."

"Oh, of course!" Polly blinked, apparently having forgotten that there were other people present. "Keira, won't you stay a little longer? I'll put on the kettle—"

"Maybe another day." Keira crossed to the door. "Sorry, but I really need to get home while there's still light."

Polly frowned as Harry, carrying the skull, followed Keira. "Where are *you* going?"

"Occult rituals, Mother." Harry's voice, as always, was completely void of inflection. "I may not return. Or if I do, I will likely forever be changed."

"Well, all right then, have fun. Curfew's at ten. Do you want me to make you some hot chocolate for when you get back?"

Harry, already partway through the doorway, hesitated. "Yes."

The four of them thundered down the stairs, raced around the serving counter, and burst through the florist's front door and back onto the main street. Keira moved into a half run, glancing behind herself to check that the group was keeping up. Mason and Zoe were drained from the day but doggedly matched her pace. Harry, the delicate skull held with just his fingertips, loped behind them, dark hair ruffling in the rapidly cooling breeze, his wide eyes glinting in the failing light.

The sun had nearly set, and the splashes of vivid crimson across the horizon had deepened as shadows crept in. Keira's mouth was dry. Her head throbbed. Her whole body shook, and she knew if she let it, it would collapse from under her. But they had the skull.

She just hoped it would be enough.

# CHAPTER 29

THE MIST HAD STARTED to thicken as Blighty Cemetery, always colder than the surrounding land, descended into a chilled evening.

Keira opened her second sight as they moved between the weather-worn monuments. Only one flicker of light existed among the dead trees. The Victorian spirit, her back straight, her cane planted firmly in the ground ahead of herself, watched the group from a distance.

*Hold on*, Keira mouthed.

The woman tilted her head forward, and the few stray strands of hair that had come free from their arrangement floated about her head. Her empty eyes were narrow, creases spreading out from their edges. Her meaning was clear. *Hurry*.

Keira still couldn't see the shade. She silently prayed it would stay that way. A part of her wished she could just leave the skull at the forest's edge, but she doubted it would be so easy. The only way to truly ensure it was returned to Gerald would be to place it inside the cracked grave…and that meant crossing a battlefield with an invisible enemy.

"If you hear me yell, run." Keira spoke in a breathless stage whisper as she neared the forest's edge. "Don't wait, don't see if you can help, just get out. And don't stop moving until you're past the graveyard's boundary. Do you understand?"

No answers came. Keira stopped at the trees, pressing one hand into a nearby trunk to hold herself steady as she looked back at her group. "I need you all to promise, or I'll ask you to leave now."

Both Mason and Zoe glared at her, their faces etched with stubborn refusal.

"*Promise*," Keira hissed.

Harry glanced between the friends. "Okay?"

"Thanks, Harry," Keira managed.

"You can tell us to leave if you want," Mason said. He pulled a flashlight from his pocket and switched it on. "But I'm still coming with you."

"Good luck getting a restraining order at this hour," Zoe added.

Keira pressed her lips together in a weak effort to hide her smile. "You're the worst best friends I've ever had."

"Same to you." Zoe switched on her own flashlight and pointed it into the trees. "Lead the way, Ghost Lady."

Keira ducked to avoid overhanging branches as she pressed

into the forest. She couldn't hear anything over the crackling of fallen leaves and her own ragged breaths. The battling circles of light from Zoe's and Mason's flashlights bounced off bark and leaves in unpredictable patterns, leaving her disoriented. It wasn't hard to find her way, though. Just like the mill, just like the hospital, and just like Gerald's killing cabin, the ground had been stained with the wild energy of death. It guided her forward and repulsed her all at once.

Daylight had failed them. The forest seemed unnaturally quiet, as though every insect and bird had chosen to hide. Dead branches, so much like bony fingers, grasped at Keira's clothes and dragged across her cheeks.

And still there was no sign of Gerald.

*Does he know? Can he sense his skull coming closer?*

The unstable ground led her downward. The mist had been patchy at the forest's start but now thickened until the flashlights flooded her vision with swirling white. Keira tried to wet her lips but her tongue was already parched. They were approaching the gravesite.

"Steady," she whispered. "Keep your lights still."

Tendrils of fog swirled. Between them she could see the base of the hollow. The ground flattened out into a small clearing where nothing seemed to want to grow. Fallen leaves gathered there like snowdrifts, but they'd lost their warm-brown tones. Instead, they were soot black, like a flash fire had passed through the space. Keira recognized that color. It was the same one Gerald Barge himself wore.

He was close. She could feel it—a taste of sickness, a smear of fury, catching in the air and burning her lungs. Her second sight was open, but he was keeping himself concealed.

Zoe raised her flashlight. The beam cut through both mist and darkness and pierced between the rotting leaves. In the hollow's center was a dark slab of stone. A crack ran through it. Keira's breath caught. The gap had widened since she'd first seen it. Before, it had only been an inch wide. Now, it looked large enough for her to fit her fist through.

"Harry." Without taking her eyes off of the stone slab, Keira held a hand behind herself. "The skull."

Dry bone was placed into her palm. Keira pulled it around to her front and cradled it in both hands. The black pits where the eyes belonged stared up at her. The loose jaw rattled against the skull as she adjusted her hold. Cracks ran through the bones: natural divides in the skull's plates and one unnatural line that marked the place where it had hit hard ground when hurled into the field more than a hundred years before.

"Stay here. Keep your flashlights on the stone." Keira crept down the decline, planting each foot carefully, her jaw clenched so tightly that it reignited her headache. She had both hands wrapped around the skull. The bones felt painfully fragile. Her hands shook, and sweat beaded in her palms. She struggled to slow her breathing, or at least to calm her fingers enough that she wouldn't risk dropping the precious gift.

Her shadow, formed by the two concentrated beams of light, sliced across the stone slab ahead. Words, dulled by age, carved deeper layers into the shadows. *Gerald Barge, 1839–1892.* A simple memento for a monstrous man.

She was less than five feet from the stone. The ground under her trembled. Keira pressed the skull to her chest, clutching it to prevent it from slipping as the shudders subsided. He was here. And he knew what Keira had brought him.

"Gerald Barge." Her voice whistled across her parched tongue. "I am returning the lost part of you. But it comes with a condition. You must leave. Release your hold on this earth and never return."

She couldn't see him, but she could feel him, as close and as present as a heavy blanket dropping over her shoulders. The hairs on her arms stood on end. The energy buzzed in her ears and behind her eyes, infusing her, flooding her with raw, painful terror.

The skull glared up at her. Its awful maw seemed to grin, its blank eye sockets reading her, judging her. Keira crossed the last foot of land separating her from the slab and extended the skull. There was only one place to put it: over the jagged crack dividing the stone.

Keira had to stretch. The bones shuddered as they touched down. The cranium tilted slightly, falling askew from the jaw, giving it a broken leer.

Tremors passed through the ground again. The slab shivered in time, the bones setting up a clatter as they were disturbed. Then the slab shifted entirely, the crack widening into a stretching chasm, a plunging depth, a dark pit of nothingness. The skull dropped through, vanishing as suddenly as a light being switched out. Keira didn't hear it land.

The tremors subsided and, just like that, the forest was still again. Keira dropped to her knees. Her breathing was heavy but slowing. The two beams of light still flitted around her, alternately pointed at her back, the dark gap in the slab, and the trees above.

Then, from the top of the incline, Mason whispered, "Did it work?"

Keira blinked. A slight breeze had set up, sending pools of mist tumbling over her. In the distance, an owl hooted and then fell silent. Keira closed her eyes, reveling in the sense of dew forming on her too-hot skin and the slow ebb of the headache as she relaxed her second sight. A small, hesitant smile began to form. "I think so. I think…we're done."

Mason exhaled a long, shuddering breath, his flashlight dropping, while Zoe managed a weak laugh. "It's really over, huh?"

"It could have been worse," Harry said, his monotone surprisingly relaxing in the heavy forest. "Try getting some cloaks and candles next time. They help the atmosphere."

Keira let herself tumble backward, propped up on her elbows as she looked behind herself. Harry's baleful, pale face stood out against the deepening night as he stared down at her. "Thanks for the tip," Keira said, grinning. "I'll keep it in mind."

Mason crouched, extending his hand to help her up. "Ready to go home?"

"Oh, am I ever." She groaned as she shifted her weight back onto sore feet. "I don't know what I want more: to sleep or to shower. Do you think I could do them both at once?"

Something rattled behind her. Keira stopped, her hand just inches short of Mason's, to look back at the grave site. Zoe's flashlight still flitted over the pool of dead leaves and the dark slab of stone, and through the shimmering light, Keira was sure she saw something moving inside the grave.

"Keira?" Mason's smile fell. "Is it…*not* over?"

She held up a finger, asking for silence, as she squinted to see through the cracked slab. Something rolled over inside. Keira's heart plunged as the skull loomed in the dark gap, twisting to the side so one eye peered out at her.

The shade's inky-black form billowed out of the grave, pluming up like smoke, thick and noxious and furiously, uncontrollably powerful. Keira's voice caught as she scrambled back. White shapes rose with the inky form: bones swimming through the twisted figure, bobbing in and out of the flowing smoke. The skull swam up through the chest and swirled into the place where the shade's head belonged. For a second, it leered out of the wailing maw: a fissured, fractured plate of white inset with coiling rivers of black. The jaw stretched wide, into what might have been a grin or a scream, before sinking back under.

"What's wrong?" Zoe's voice had grown tight. "Is it the wrong skull?"

*No. It's his. And that's the problem*, Keira realized with a rush of growing horror. *We should never have returned it to him.* She made to speak, but her words rasped into silence. She swallowed around a painful lump in her throat and tried again. "Run. Run! *Run!*"

Gerald lunged forward. Disfigured hands reached for Keira. She kicked back, getting herself barely out of reach, and the shade's fingers plunged into the earth instead. A foul stench rose as the leaves shriveled, rotting in a matter of seconds.

He was enormous. The energy he'd feasted on had billowed him into twice the size he'd been during life. The bones clattered as they swirled, every movement setting them into motion again. Gerald's head stretched forward, his neck elongating, as a furious, wild howl rose from his jaws.

"*Run!*" Keira didn't have even a second to make sure her friends had listened. Gerald was closing in, cutting off her escape, looming above her until she had no choice except to shrink into the ground.

*I don't understand. We completed his unfinished business. That should have been enough.*

It had worked for other spirits. But as the shade's mouth stretched wide enough to engulf her head, Keira realized she'd misjudged him.

He hadn't lingered on earth because of regrets: he had none. He'd rotted his soul away during life, destroying it day by day. He'd delighted in being loved by a town that had no idea of his true nature. He'd reveled in causing suffering.

It had eaten at his humanity until nothing remained except for this twisted, malformed figure. He wanted for nothing... except to continue as he had in life. Consuming. Destroying.

Keira rolled, barely escaping the smoke-formed jaws that plunged toward her. They hit the ground. Hissing sounds rose, along with tiny wisps of soot as the leaves scorched and curled.

She'd tried to find and unravel his essence once before and had been burnt for it. Keira was in a far worse shape than she had been back then. She needed sleep. She needed food. She needed time for her body to stop shaking and her head to stop aching.

But she had to try again, and she had to try now. The shade was already swollen and powerful enough to cover the entire graveyard, perhaps even reach the town. There was nothing left to lose.

Keira's eyes burned. She dug her heels into the soft earth and did what little she could to prepare herself as the shade twisted back toward her, his elongated body swiveling until he was a column of swirling black and bone. She raised one hand into a fist, preparing to strike, bracing for the pain she knew would come with it. He rose up, stretching feet above her, then plunged down—a pillar of death, ready to absorb its next victim.

# CHAPTER 30

THE SHADE HIT HARD enough to force the air from Keira's lungs. She'd expected to feel the same scorching sensation she had when it had burned her wrist. Instead, all she felt was cold. Like being plunged into an ocean. Floating in the deepest ice-chilled ocean.

Keira let her eyes open. Flecks of smoke stung them. Her vision was filled with inky, swirling black. Bones flashed past, flung about like debris in a typhoon. And the cold was growing worse and worse, until it was all she could perceive, until even the aches paled in comparison to how crushingly cold she was.

*This is what it feels like to die*, she realized. Her energy, already so low, flowed out of her second by second. She couldn't breathe. Her heart missed a beat, and then another. *If I'm dying, I'm bringing him down with me.*

She stretched her hand into the darkness. The rush of spectral energy on every side was overwhelming. She fought with it, trying to hold on to her second sight just long enough to find the bundle of threads she knew had to exist somewhere inside the shade. The swirling mass of black soot battered at her senses, confusing and blinding. But there was a spark of something alive underneath. The threads, sickly black and tightly coiled, were straight ahead, shielded behind a wall of bone.

Keira plunged her hand forward and touched teeth. The shade had placed his skull around his essence, holding it inside what should have been his mouth. But the jaw wasn't attached to the cranium. Keira pushed harder, and her fingers broke through the fragile barrier.

She knew instantly when she found the threads. They were shockingly hot in an ocean of cold. As her fingers fastened around them, they cut her, like they had been formed out of broken glass, but she refused to let go. Teeth battered across her knuckles as the skull tried to shock her loose. A femur glanced off her shoulder, but she couldn't react. This was her last chance to make things right.

Keira pulled. The threads shifted an inch, then snagged on each other. They should have been sliding apart, the tangle falling away into nothing, but instead the knots only grew tighter.

*It doesn't want to go. It's not letting me undo its tether.*

She pulled harder, praying there might be some way to tear the thread. The smoky form stung her skin and filled her nose, suffocating her. The knot only grew harder and tighter under her fingers, unyielding, as the ferocious, battering gale stole her strength.

Her last scraps of energy were gone. She clung to the threads as her own consciousness faded and her eyes drifted shut.

Her heart was slowing, each thump weaker as the muscle strained against the exhaustion. She couldn't destroy the shade. Couldn't struggle away from it. She could only slump, stunned and numbingly cold, as the shade wrapped around her like a cloak.

Something solid and warm hit her from behind. Sparks of energy flowed from it, coursing through Keira's nerves and jolting her back to awareness.

A hand pressed against the exposed skin at the base of her neck. A human hand, filled with energy. And Keira was so empty that she was drawing on it, just like the shade had drawn from her.

Another hand touched her, this time fastening around the arm she'd left limp at her side. Then, a second later, a third, finding space on her shoulder.

Their energy pulsed. Keira opened herself to it, pulling on it, letting it send fire through her veins and light up her fading senses.

She still held the threads in her right hand. Keira opened her eyes, squinting through the storm of smoke, and saw the skull, twisting around her hand, cracked teeth grazing her skin. She tugged. The threads were immutable. They were a knot, a convoluted mess that she couldn't untangle even if she had an hour.

Instinct took over. Keira grit her teeth and, instead of pulling, *pushed*. She took the energy that had been lent to her and directed it along her arm, through her fingertips, and into the ball of burning thread.

The shade absorbed it. He billowed, stretching in every direction, crackles of blue light bursting through his form like lightning rippling through a storm cloud. Keira had only a second to question whether she was doing anything except expanding his power to unstoppable levels, but they'd come too far. She fed him more energy, then more, forcing it into him even when he tried to pull away. Her fingertips felt as though they were on fire, but she kept them clenched around the threads as the energy coursed into them.

The dark form cracked, splitting like an overfilled balloon. Billows of thick smoke spilled out from the seams. They twisted furiously as the creature tried to hold itself together, and crackling light lashed out as lines of energy, striking the ground and trees and leaving black smears in their wake.

He'd reached his peak. Keira clenched her teeth as she forced a final shot of energy into the writhing form. The shade surged upward, a column of black that shook the trees as it rocketed into the canopy and then plunged back down into itself as it collapsed. An immense shockwave of energy burst outward from the crumpling form, an explosion of energy that rattled Keira's bones and sent electricity through her core.

She fell back. For a moment, there was nothing—just her, lost in a void, tetherless. Then the world began to come back to her in fragments. First the aches—strained muscles, throbbing head, burning feet. Her vision returned slowly, blurred in the beginning but gradually clearing. The world was still black, but it was different this time. Now, staring toward the sky, Keira could see treetops interspersed with patches of stars.

She still held her fingers tightly pinched, but there were no threads left. No poison in the air. No shade. Gerald was gone.

Her hearing was the last of her senses to return. Slowly, almost as though it were nervous, a cricket started to chirp. It was followed by a second, then a disgruntled bird's chatter as the forest around them came back to life.

"Bloody hell," Zoe said from somewhere to Keira's left.

Keira tilted her head just far enough to see her friend. The flashlights had been dropped, and their lights did a poor job of illuminating the clearing, but she could see Zoe lying among the leaves, her face scrunched up.

"Did someone punch me?" Zoe's voice wavered. "Because it feels an awful lot like I just got punched about a hundred times."

"Sorry." Laughter rose inside Keira, and once it started, it wouldn't stop. "I told you ghost hunting would be boring."

Zoe's only response was "Augh."

On Keira's other side, Mason sat up, grimacing. "Ow."

"Sorry," Keira said again. "You should have run when I told you to. But also, thank you for staying."

"You looked like you needed it." He raised his hand, flexing the fingers curiously, and Keira wondered how much of the energy transfer he'd been able to feel.

Every muscle in her body complained as she sat up. The air was growing colder as the night deepened, and Keira shuddered.

It took her a moment to remember that there had been a fourth member of their party that night. "Where's Harry?"

Mason reached for his fallen flashlight and flashed it across the scene. They found Harry just behind Keira, lying facedown and half-buried in leaves that had been shaken from the trees above them.

"Oh no," Zoe murmured. "We killed the goth kid."

"I wish you had." Harry's voice was muffled through the leaf litter. He gingerly raised his head. "What happened?"

Keira pressed her lips tightly together. She could probably tell Harry the truth. No matter whether the shade had been visible to him, he would have felt the burst of energy. That would have been enough proof for a normal person, and Harry was already inclined to be interested in the darker sides of life.

On the other hand, she didn't know whether he'd keep her secret. She trusted Zoe and Mason; they had her back just as thoroughly as she had theirs. But she barely knew Harry or who he might be friends with or what damage her secret might do if it was leaked to the wrong person.

Zoe saved her. "Occult stuff," she said, flicking her dark hair away from her face. "You wouldn't understand it."

"You okay?" Mason asked as Harry shambled to his feet.

Harry's expression remained surprisingly placid, and except for the scraps of leaves clinging to his hair and clothes, he could have spent the last hour watching paint dry. He blinked at Keira, then at Zoe, then said, "Are we done?"

"Yeah," Keira said, glancing back at Gerald's grave. The

ground was still charged with a twisted kind of energy, but it no longer had any life. It had become nothing more than a stain now, something that animals might avoid, a place where plants would always grow sickly. Nothing more. "We're done."

"Good night, then." He turned and set off into the trees.

The three remaining friends watched him leave with a mix of incredulity and concern. Harry was nearly out of sight when Mason called, "You're going the wrong way!"

Harry only raised one hand in acknowledgment before vanishing between the trees.

"Leave him be," Zoe said, stretching her legs out ahead of herself and flexing her neck. "He spends ages walking through these forests. He'll be taking a shortcut home."

"Huh." Mason sat a moment, staring in the direction Harry had gone, before leaning closer to Keira. "What about you? Are you okay?"

"I'm good, yeah." As the words left her, she realized they were more true than she'd expected. She had some of her lost energy back. When she'd overloaded the shade and caused it to collapse, its dissipating force had spilled into the forest—and some of it had absorbed into her. She was still below her normal level, but she no longer felt inclined to collapse face-first into the dirt.

She flexed her hand. The fingertips were a sore, burnt red, but that would heal, she knew. Mason hissed between his teeth, taking her hand gently and examining it. "I'll get some burn cream on this when we get back to the cottage."

"Don't worry about it. I'm going to sleep for approximately a

million years, and I'll worry about patching things up afterward."
Keira glanced between the friends. "Did you see much?"

"The shade, you mean?" Mason still lingered over her hand,
frowning lightly as he examined the damaged skin. "No. You
looked sick, so I came down to help you, and…"

That had been the hand on the back of her neck. "I stole a
bunch of your energy. Sorry. Gerald had leeched almost everything out of me, and I had to draw on you to overload him."

"I definitely felt *that*. Will the, uh, borrowed energy come
back?"

"It should."

He nodded. "That's all good, then."

Zoe continued to stare down at the grave site, her face lightly
creased. "This is going to sound weird, but…a couple of times,
just really briefly, I thought I could see something. You know
how you sometimes catch motion off to the side?"

"Like peripheral vision stuff? Yeah."

"It was like that. Except I was looking right at it and still
couldn't see it properly, just this sort of…heat mirage kind of
movement."

Keira couldn't stop herself from smiling. "You might have a
touch of the gift."

Zoe's face twisted in disgust. "So we had a ghost so utterly
powerful that he could drain any human he came in contact
with, and the best I could manage was *maybe* wondering if I saw
a hint of something? That's tragically useless."

"It's better than what I managed at least," Mason said.

Zoe glanced down and one eyebrow rose. Keira followed her gaze and felt a trace of heat across her face. Mason had apparently forgotten he was holding her hand, and it had felt so natural that Keira had stopped noticing too.

She detangled herself and pushed to her feet, dusting down her clothes in a futile effort to clear away the day's accumulation of dirt. "I think it's time to follow Harry's example and get out of here."

"Ugh," Zoe said. "Only time he's ever set a good example."

"Hey, he helped a lot tonight. He's a decent guy." Keira took a deep breath, then scrambled out of the graveside hollow.

The skull had been a false end: Gerald had accepted it, but it hadn't been his goal like Keira had thought. Despite all of her assumptions about ghosts, it seemed that Gerald had existed simply for the sake of causing destruction. She prayed she wouldn't have to encounter too many other spirits of his caliber.

Harry had helped in another way, though. Mason and Zoe had lent Keira their strength, but a third hand had touched her. Harry, not understanding what was going on, had still tried to help. And Keira wasn't sure if they would have had enough collective charge to overload Gerald without the sallow man's contribution.

The mood had lightened dramatically, and even worn-down as they were, the three of them chatted and laughed on their hike back to the cemetery.

"Do you both want to stay at my place tonight?" Keira asked.

"On the downside, we'll have to share one shower. On the upside, you won't have to walk any farther to get home."

"I like that plan," Mason said. "We can have that sleepover we planned, only this time without interruptions from twisted ghosts and shady organizations. If we make it back in time, we might even be able to get pizza."

"Hold on." Zoe frowned. "Speaking of hot food, I swear I can smell, like, burning toast. Am I having a stroke?"

Mason lifted his head, frowning. "I don't think so. I can smell it too."

Keira tasted particles of ash on her tongue. Something *was* burning. And she doubted it was toast. She broke into a sprint to clear the last few meters of trees and stopped at the forest's edge.

Ahead, her graveyard floated in the mist: rows upon rows of disjointed, crumbling monuments fading in and out of sight as moonlight splashed across the thickening fog. In the distance she could barely make out the plants surrounding Adage's rectory. Beyond that, the church's steeple cut into the sky.

Her cottage was positioned partway along the graveyard, on its edge, pressed close to the trees. It was the easiest shape to spot. Bathed in sharp yellows and whites, its stone walls were alive with writhing shadows, a pillar of smoke rising across its roof. The building was surrounded by flames.

"This day can go to hell already," Keira said, and lurched into a ragged run toward her home.

# CHAPTER 31

KEIRA FLEW THROUGH THE graveyard, moving as fast as her muscles would allow her. A circle of fire surrounded the cottage and bathed the surrounding ground in harsh yellows. A man stood twenty paces away, half-hidden in the shadows of the graveyard as he clutched something to his chest. He moved toward her as she approached, but Keira couldn't spare even a closer look as she raced past. She made it as far as the opening in the low stone fence before an arm caught her around the waist and dragged her back.

"No!" Mason pulled her against his chest as she struggled to break free. "You can't do anything. Leave it."

Her mind flashed through everything she had inside the cabin: her clothes. The cuttings Mason had carefully prepared for her. The photo, the only thing she'd managed to bring from her past life.

And something more important than anything else: "Daisy!"

"She's fine. She's with me."

The voice came from behind them. Keira let Mason drag her away from the flames. Adage, the figure she'd seen outside the fire's light, stood with Zoe at his side. He held a bundle against his chest. It writhed, and its head broke free from the jacket it had been wrapped in. Daisy, her huge, liquid-amber eyes round and frenzied, hissed in the fire's direction.

"I'm so sorry, my dear." Adage's face was creased with distress, his glasses tucked into his pocket, and his eyes shimmering wet. "I didn't see it until it was already out of control. I found Daisy in among the graves, but I couldn't save anything else."

"It's okay." Keira closed the distance between them. She felt around the small black cat's face and checked its paws, searching for any signs of singed fur, but Daisy seemed mercifully unharmed. She only stared past Keira's shoulder, quivering, as she hissed at the growing flames.

Mason pressed Keira's arm. "I left my phone in my car, but it should still have charge. I'll call the firefighters. It might not be too late to save the cottage. Just don't try to go into it, okay?"

She made a faint noise. Mason disappeared in the direction of the parsonage.

Zoe stood with one arm around Adage's shoulders, holding him steady. Keira hadn't noticed before that he was shaking. She took his other side, pressing close to him, as she tried to keep the emotion out of her own voice. "This is okay. No one's hurt. That's all that matters."

"Thanks be," Adage replied softly. Daisy, still bundled in his arms, responded with a prolonged growl.

Zoe looked in the direction Mason had disappeared, frowning, then muttered something under her breath.

"Zo?" Keira asked.

"It won't work." She shook her head, her expression growing dark. "The firefighters won't be able to get through. There's no clear path."

"Oh," Adage murmured. "The trees. The fences. Fire avenues weren't a thing when the parsonage was established."

"Where's the nearest source of water?" Zoe asked.

"My home. I have a garden hose—"

"Will it stretch this far?"

"I have an extension for it."

"That'll do." Zoe turned to Keira. "I'll go with Adage. Keep watch on the fire. Don't get any closer to it."

Keira glanced at her cat, who had subsided into a constant rumbling growl. "Take Daze. Lock her in Adage's house. She'll be safe there at least."

"Got it." Zoe kept her hand on Adage's shoulder as they began jogging toward the pastor's home. Keira watched them until the licking firelight no longer highlighted their backs, then, with growing dread, turned back to her cottage. Someone had packed dead branches and kindling around the outside of her home. The flames licked across the stone and teased at the edges of the roof. Golden sparks rose toward the night sky as the heated smoke funneled them up. Even standing as far away as she was, Keira could feel the heat across her skin. The cottage wasn't completely ablaze—not yet—but she knew it was only a matter of minutes. And she was utterly powerless to prevent it.

Her heart ached more than she could have ever imagined to see her home burn. She'd only had it for a short time, but it was *hers*…and so little else was.

Everything she could call her own had been in that cottage. Including her only memories. She had no knowledge of her life before Blighty, except what she'd been able to glean from clues she'd found. As far as she could tell, her life before she'd arrived in the small, quaint town had been one of bare survival: fighting for food, fighting for shelter, never having anything that she couldn't wear on her back.

For the first time in her life, she'd had somewhere to settle. To love. To call her own. And now it was being taken from her, as though the universe was punishing her for the hubris of seeking joy.

There had to be some irony in that. She tried to smile, but the muscles in her face only ached from the effort.

Footsteps crackled in the dead grass behind. It seemed early for either Mason or Zoe and Adage to return, but Keira was so wholly focused on the building ahead that she didn't react until an unfamiliar voice spoke.

"I hope my message is clear enough *this* time."

Keira put her back to her burning home. Ahead, standing between the closest rows of grave markers, was a tall, well-dressed figure.

His spectacles glittered in the firelight. Sleek, platinum-blond hair had been combed neatly to the side, exposing streaks of white at his temples. Keira had only seen him once before, from across a street, but even that distant encounter had left an impression. "Oh, hey. Dr. Kelsey. You did this, huh?" Keira raised a hand toward her house, then let it flop back to her side. The grief was compounding with the exhaustion, and she knew she should probably be shocked—or at the very least angry—but she was struggling to muster any kind of appropriate response. "Mind if I ask why?"

He took a step closer, polished shoes scraping through weeds. When he lifted his chin, his eyes disappeared behind the slim disks of reflected light. "That should be clear already."

"Please don't make me play the guessing game. Was my home an eyesore? You hate cemeteries? Just tell me already."

His thin lips peeled back with scorn. "Don't be smart. I know you received my note."

"Note?" Keira squinted, then drew in a sharp breath. "Right. The note on the door. Yeah. Forgot about that. Go on."

He watched her, incredulous, his fingers curling and uncurling at his side before he managed, "Are you simple?"

"Nothing about my life is simple. That's the whole problem here."

They stared at each other across an expanse of dead grass and flowing embers. The fire's heat flowed across Keira's back. Any mist that made it past Dr. Kelsey's long coat evaporated, but farther into the graveyard, it coalesced into an ocean of white.

The night would have been beautiful under better circumstances. Keira sighed.

If she'd had even slightly less occupying her mind, she might have anticipated there would be trouble from the doctor. She'd made an enemy out of his son, Gavin. And she'd inadvertently discovered that Gavin had blood on his hands. Crouched in a stream, a knife held to Gavin's throat, she'd promised him that she would truly kill him if he came near her or her friends again. But apparently Gavin wasn't used to the concept of accepting defeat.

"Look, I'm pretty sure I get the gist of this all. I know what your son did, and now he's panicking. Maybe *you* know what Gavin did too, and you've come to shut me up before I can say too much. But truthfully? You're not the worst thing I've dealt with this week." She shrugged. "You're not even top five."

The color had faded from his already-pale face, and Keira chose to take that as her answer. He knew what had happened on Blighty's bridge winters past. He was aware that his son had killed a man. And he was prepared to do anything—absolutely anything—to keep the family skeletons safely buried.

She reasoned that she should probably be more careful around him. He was well respected in Blighty and could turn popular opinion against her. If it even got that far. He'd set her home on fire to send a message; he was very likely prepared for more drastic action before the night was out.

But she just couldn't muster the energy to care. She'd wrecked herself mentally and emotionally to protect the town from

Gerald, only to find her home had been lost while she was facing the specter. A part of her hoped Dr. Kelsey would turn the confrontation physical. She bet it would feel really, really good to land a punch or two into his smug face.

His back straightened as his lips pulled down in barely controlled anger. One hand grazed the edge of his coat, pushing it away from his side, exposing the handle of a small, silver pistol. "I'll repeat myself as plainly as I can. You're not wanted in Blighty. You'll leave tonight if you want to keep what's most valuable to you."

"My...toaster? I'm pretty sure you already set it on fire—"

"Your *life*."

"Right, that makes sense." She scratched the back of her neck as Dr. Kelsey's hand twitched toward the pistol. "It's just that the toaster cost, like, forty dollars, and I only got it the other day, so I'm still kind of upset about it. I'm staying by the way."

"Pardon?"

She lifted her hands in a halfhearted shrug. "This is my home now. Shoot me if you want; it won't change that fact."

The doctor looked as though he genuinely believed she'd lost her mind. Something moved between the graves at his back, though. Keira switched her attention from the doctor and opened the aching muscle behind her eyes. She was rewarded with a spirit.

The elderly Victorian woman stalked through the grave markers, her cane stabbing the earth with each step. Faint wisps of hair flowed behind her as she passed Dr. Kelsey and came to a halt.

*He's gone,* Keira mouthed.

A small, reserved smile flitted across the woman's creased lips. Keira had a suspicion that she'd already known and had perhaps known since the moment Gerald's form tore itself apart.

Dr. Kelsey was speaking again, but Keira tuned him out. She only had eyes for the Victorian woman, who leaned on her cane. She reached one gloved hand toward the graves and then raised it—a wordless beckon. At the motion, a sea of forms appeared.

Keira took in a sharp breath, her heart overflowing. The graveyard was alive. Spirits looked toward her from every corner. Some burned as bright as lamps in the night; others were no more than wisps. Every one of them smiled. Keira skipped her gaze across the crowd as she counted familiar faces. Tony Lobell, still fully nude. Marianne Cobb, the worker woman. The children.

She'd lost too many spirits. But so many more had survived.

The Victorian woman stood at the formation's head. She left her cane planted in the ground as she held both hands at her sides, then slowly, smoothly, lifted them toward the sky.

Every spirit mimicked the motion. Spectral forms shimmered as they raised hands, hundreds of them, toward the stars above. The mist thickened dramatically, drowning Keira in it, spilling outward from the graveyard until even the fire's heat couldn't compete.

Dr. Kelsey had stopped talking. He stared at the ground around his feet, pale eyebrows pulled together as he watched thick clouds of fog flow past him. "What—"

Thunder crackled above them. Keira looked up in time to see

the last stars vanish behind walls of gathering clouds. She drew a sharp breath as she realized what the spirits were doing.

They drew energy from their environments. It was a slow process; the weaker spirits, like the hollow-faced man, would need days or weeks to gather enough to appear, even briefly. But now they were giving back, releasing the energy they'd stored while in hiding. Sending it into the air to condense into rain clouds.

Keira let her eyes fall closed as the first heavy drop hit her flushed skin. More came quickly. It only took seconds for the clear night to transform into a torrential downpour, as heavy and unyielding as the night Keira had first arrived in Blighty.

She could hear Dr. Kelsey's breathing: quick, panicked, uncertain. He turned, one hand still holding the pistol's butt, searching the graveyard behind them but failing to see anything. He swung back toward Keira, his pale-blue eyes wild. "What are you doing?"

"Nothing," Keira said, and laughed. The air behind her was growing cooler. Even with the accelerants that Dr. Kelsey must have used to start the blaze, she doubted the fire could last long when the rain was so heavy that she struggled to breathe through it.

She held her hands out to the downpour. Her clothes were drenched and plastered to her skin. Her hair was saturated. When she opened her mouth, she tasted the sharp tang of smoke on the water.

"How are you doing this?" Dr. Kelsey's voice was sharp, but it shook at the edge.

Keira let her eyes open. He'd removed the pistol from its holster. His fingers trembled as he raised it.

A flicker of movement appeared at his side. Tony Lobell seemed to be overflowing with delight as he clasped Dr. Kelsey's hand in both of his own. The doctor made a short, sharp noise as the pistol fell to the ground. Keira glimpsed a trace of frost across the metal before the rain washed it away.

"Stop it," the doctor said, and the words came out as something between a command and a plea.

Keira couldn't have stopped smiling even if she'd wanted to. "No. This is my home now."

He was already backing away, the pistol forgotten. Keira didn't bother watching him go. Her focus had returned to the Victorian woman, who approached her, close enough that a rolling chill made its way through Keira's soaked clothes.

"Thank you," Keira said.

The woman bowed her head in an elegant nod.

Keira swallowed around the rain that dripped over her lips. "I'm sorry. I never learned your name."

The woman shook her head. *Not important.* She strode past and, at the last second, raised a gloved hand to touch Keira's face. The contact was blisteringly cold, and Keira shivered, but in the next second, she was alone again, left to touch her stinging cheek in quiet wonder.

One by one, the remaining ghosts dispersed—fading if they were weak or returning to their graves if they were ready to enjoy their freedom from the shade. Tony Lobell waved. Keira waved back as he faded. In only a few moments, she was alone again in front of the smoking remnants of the fire.

She'd lost so much, but she felt as though she'd gained far more in return. Even if the toaster *had* cost forty dollars.

"What the actual hell?" Zoe's sharp voice cut through the pounding rain. She ran toward Keira, dragging a hastily extended garden hose with her, while Adage followed, his arms filled by an enormous watering can.

"Hey," Keira said. She lightly indicated toward the cottage, her face aching from a smile that refused to die. "Fire's out."

# CHAPTER 32

THE DELUGE GRADUALLY SLOWED into a gentle fall of spitting rain that would likely fade entirely by midnight. Keira pitied anyone in Blighty who had trusted the weather forecast enough to hang out washing, but the rain had done its job: the piles of kindling stacked around the cottage had become nothing but charred, wet wood that sent up slowly snaking tendrils of smoke.

Mason had returned, and he, Zoe, and Adage carefully explored the stone building. Keira watched from a distance as they navigated the sooty building with scarves and jackets pulled over their faces to protect from the residue in the air.

Keira didn't feel any pressing need to look more closely at her home. She already knew what the outcome would be. No matter how bad the damage, she would repair it. Even if Dr. Kelsey had managed to raze the cottage to the ground, she would have rebuilt it one stone at a time.

But not just yet. Assessing the damage and forming a plan would begin in the morning, once she'd had enough sleep. But there was one final task on her to-do list that she still wanted to complete that evening.

A few dozen paces from the cottage, near the forest's edge, the nameless gravestone flickered in her flashlight's light. Keira stopped beside it and rested her hand on the smooth stone. "Hey," she called, her voice soft. "Are you here?"

Biting wind snagged at her damp clothing, and although it dragged thick waves of mist around her, she couldn't see the faceless ghost.

Keira took a slow breath, then released it. "I think I understand why you stayed now. You didn't want closure for your own death, but for the loss of someone very dear to you."

She pulled the photo out from where she'd tucked it into her pocket. Even in the depths of night and with erratic lighting, she could make out the two smiling faces looking out at her.

"She was your mother, wasn't she? She'd been widowed for years before she met someone who she thought she might love. She traveled to meet him. And she never came home."

Gerald had been careful to ensure the letters couldn't be traced back to him. He'd never given out his address and always asked to meet along the path through the forest. And he'd even taken precautions against his victims speaking about him too frequently. *I want to be sure this is love before we involve our families. Please, at least until we meet, keep this a secret.*

Adrian Holcombe had achieved the remarkable, then, in tracking his mother's killer as far as Blighty.

Cold air grazed Keira's back, a degree or two below the ambient atmosphere. She turned. The faceless specter stood on his grave, staring into the distance. Deep shadows hung across the hollow in his head.

Keira moved to his side, arms wrapped around herself as she spoke through numb lips. "I'm so sorry, Adrian. Your mother was killed by a man named Gerald Barge. The same man who killed you when you confronted him."

The hollow-faced man showed no reaction, but Keira knew he must have heard her. She shuffled her feet to keep blood moving through them. "Gerald died two months afterward. A stroke. And now he's gone for good. He tried to cling to this earth—he even attacked the spirits in this graveyard—but he's gone."

Adrian's hair moved languidly in a breeze Keira couldn't feel. His long, tattered coat flapped around his ankles. Keira lowered her eyes so she wouldn't have to stare into the empty maw where his face belonged anymore.

"I haven't had time to find out if your mother's body was ever identified, but if it wasn't, I can make sure it is now. I have a box of evidence from Gerald Barge's cabin. It's full of letters, photos, and trinkets. Tomorrow morning, I'll leave it outside the constable's house with a note explaining. Gerald divided his box into years, so the police should be able to identify nearly everyone. Graves will finally be given names. Including your mother's." Keira gently rested her fingertips on the worn, leaning stone at her side. "And yours."

The spirit's jacket swirled in a fresh gust of wind. He continued to face the distance, unresponsive.

Keira inhaled, preparing to bid the spirit farewell. She'd averted her eyes from his face, and her gaze had fallen on his right hand. It hung limply at his side, the fingers slightly curled, the fingernails still bearing traces of dirt from his time of death.

And the palm...

Keira took a step back, abruptly dizzy. The hand bore a scar. Small and crescent-shaped, it was painfully familiar. It marked the place where Maria had stabbed Gerald Barge.

Keira had watched the blade plunge through the skin. Her mind had replayed the image a half dozen times on her sleep-deprived walk back to town. The mark was so distinct that it was hard to imagine an identical injury happening by accident.

She lifted her eyes to where the face belonged. It was hollow, carved away from the hairline to the chin, removing every identifiable trace from his life. Adrian Holcombe had been murdered just two months before Gerald died of natural causes. No one at the time had realized, but Adrian's body would have been stored in the same morgue as his killer's. It would have been preserved and kept there for some time as the police conducted their investigation and allowed visitors who might have been able to identify the body.

And allegedly, the mortician at the time had been unstable. Dressing the bodies in costume, posing them, making up conversations between them. He might have been interrupted and had to re-dress the bodies and push them back into their designated storage spaces in a rush.

Adrian and Gerald had approximately the same body shape: tall and slim. Their ages were different, and anyone close to Gerald would have been able to identify him at a glance, but the funerals must have both been closed-casket affairs.

Keira tried to draw a breath, but her throat had closed over.

The bodies had been switched and no one had realized. The burials had gone ahead as scheduled, a week apart. And years later, the grave marked as Gerald's had been exhumed, his corpse desecrated, and his body reburied inside the forest, all while the real Gerald Barge lingered less than a hundred meters away.

It would be impossible to prove. The mortician and anyone else who could have given testimony had passed half a century before. She could only trust what was before her eyes.

Keira turned toward the forest, where she'd confronted the spirit she'd believed to be Gerald Barge at his gravesite.

*All this time I was trying to find out his unfinished business. If the shade was truly Adrian Holcombe, it could only be one thing: revenge. He consumed spirits to grow stronger. He attacked me to take my energy. All so that he could expand his circle of influence in search of his mother's killer. A hundred years after death, and he still refused to give up.*

The shade had been voracious and monstrous. It was easy to imagine its creator had been equally a monster during life. She'd believed Gerald's nature had twisted him, unraveling him into that darker form.

In some ways, she supposed she'd still been right.

Keira looked back at the faceless man at her side. He was, and always had been, unresponsive. He existed because he simply seemed to have no choice in the matter.

His monstrous nature had rotted his soul from the inside out. But it hadn't made him stronger. It had left him empty. Hollowed out. He wore another man's clothes because that was what he had been buried in. He had no face because he couldn't remember what it was supposed to look like. He'd lingered after death, but he barely existed any longer.

Perhaps he'd barely existed during life. Especially in his final few years.

"Goodbye, Gerald." Keira stretched her hand into his body. The shade had been full of ice and fight and fury. Touching Gerald, all she felt was cold. His essence hung in the center of his chest, and he made no motion to guard it as Keira found the edge of a tangled thread. She tugged. The hollow-faced man shimmered, then his form spilled away, like smoke released from a container. He was gone within seconds.

Keira inhaled deeply as she sat beside the abandoned grave. A sense of peace, of relief, filled her in a way that had been missing when she'd defeated the shade.

Adrian had needed to be destroyed. His quest for revenge had turned him into a mindless hunter, and that instinct to destroy had stayed with him even long after his prey had perished. She'd had no choice, but she still felt a touch of grief for him. The smiling face in the photograph had looked like it belonged to a good person. Only tragedy and circumstance had led him to end up in that state.

She felt no such grief for the real Gerald Barge. Only relief to know that he was gone finally. She tilted her face toward the sky. Fine spits of rain glanced off her cheeks. She sat for a long time, letting her thoughts consume her and carry her where they would, like a boat adrift on the sea.

Through the haze of thoughts, one clear concept reached her: Gerald Barge had worn Adrian's clothes in death because that was what had been given to him later, but they weren't what he had died in. Which meant spirits were capable of having at least *some* control over how they looked in death. Which meant…

"Tony Lobell," Keira muttered. "You're doing it *deliberately*."

She wasn't sure how long she sat there but only came back to herself when Mason called her name.

"Hey," she said as he sat at her side. The dead grass did very little to protect them from the mud, but Keira figured they were already so dirty that it barely mattered. Behind them, flashlights still moved through the cottage as Zoe and Adage continued their reconnaissance.

Mason moved close enough that his shoulder nearly touched hers. His gentle, green eyes scanned her face. "Are you okay?"

"Yeah. Very much so."

Mason nodded toward the nameless gravestone. "I see you're trying to tie up loose threads. Have you had any success?"

"Mm." Keira opened her mouth, then simply shook her head. She'd explain the truth later. Once she'd had some sleep. "Long story short, yes. Both Adrian and Gerald are gone."

"That's some good news. I brought something for you." Mason held something out to her. Keira took the small, creased photo and felt emotion rise until it stuck in her throat.

"I found it in the doorway. It must have blown there during the fire."

The corner had turned dark and started to curl, but the rest of the image remained clear. It was the picture of the three unknown persons Keira had brought with her to Blighty. She tucked the photo down the side of her boot, between her sock and her skin. It was one of the only parts of her that was still dry, and the photo would be protected there until she could find somewhere safer. "Thank you."

"As an aside, Zoe says she needs to speak to you once we're, you know, not dead on our feet. Apparently, she sent a sketch of your logo to some acquaintances. A reply came back while we were hiking through the forest. She thinks we might have some avenues to explore."

"Thank mercy for Zoe. If it were left up to me, I'd be lost."

"Mm." Mason's eyes were soft with concern. "It's not going away, is it? You'll never be truly safe until you at least know who—or what—those people are."

"I'll be fine. I'm pretty sure I have a gun now." Keira cast a glance toward the edge of the gravestones, where a hint of Dr. Kelsey's silver pistol glittered. She doubted he would be coming back for it.

"You have…" Mason choked on his words. "Where did you get *a gun*? How…" He breathed deeply, then let it out. "No, I'm going to put that one aside for another time. Today's already been too much."

"Amen to that." Keira tilted her head back and felt the soft touch of rain across her skin. "I still can't believe my house was set on fire."

"The cottage survived better than I'd hoped." Mason stretched his long legs ahead of himself as he matched Keira in staring toward the fog-disguised forest. "The outside is pretty badly singed and a couple of the windows are gone, but the flames didn't make it inside. The roof will need some patching, but once that's done, it should still be livable."

"Good." Keira felt herself smile. "It's a bit burnt at the edges, but it's still my home."

"Until the repairs are complete, you can stay at my house. The spare room's always been yours, even though you've rejected it a half dozen times. There's room for Daisy too. It'll be nice to have some company."

"It would," Keira mused. She tilted her head to read Mason's features. His smile was gentle and still held hints of concern for her. His wet hair hung close to the warm, green eyes. Saturated like it was, it almost looked black. Keira had the impulse to push it back, out of his face, but pressed her hands together in her lap to keep them still. "Can I ask a favor?"

"Of course. Anything."

"Can I borrow your tent?"

His smile turned incredulous. "Oh, please don't—"

Keira laughed as she looked across the undulating grave markers. Angels clasped hands under their chins as rainwater flowed over their eyes. The ground rose and sank as the coffins beneath decayed and the earth settled. The stones burst from the earth like teeth, broken in some places, tilting at others. Through the fog, faint spectral shapes glittered as they moved between the markers.

"Yeah," Keira said, this time with more certainty. "I think I'd really like to stay here. It's home."

# ABOUT THE AUTHOR

Darcy Coates is the *USA Today* bestselling author of *Hunted*, *The Haunting of Ashburn House*, *Craven Manor*, and more than a dozen other horror and suspense titles.

She lives on the Central Coast of Australia with her family, cats, and a garden full of herbs and vegetables.

Darcy loves forests, especially old-growth forests where the trees dwarf anyone who steps between them. Wherever she lives, she tries to have a mountain range close by.

# THE HAUNTING OF LEIGH HARKER

## SOMETIMES THE DEAD REACH BACK.

Leigh Harker's quiet suburban home was her sanctuary for more than a decade, until things abruptly changed. Curtains open by themselves. Radios turn off and on. And a dark figure looms in the shadows of her bedroom door at night, watching her, waiting for her to finally let down her guard enough to fall asleep. Pushed to her limits but unwilling to abandon her home, Leigh struggles to find answers. But each step forces her toward something more terrifying than she ever imagined.

A poisonous shadow seeps from the locked door beneath the stairs. The handle rattles through the night and fingernails scratch at the wood. Her home harbors dangerous secrets, and now that Leigh is trapped within its walls, she fears she may never escape.

# FROM BELOW

## HUNDREDS OF FEET BENEATH THE OCEAN'S SURFACE, A GRAVEYARD AWAITS.

Years ago, the SS Arcadia vanished without a trace during a routine voyage. Now its wreck has finally been discovered more than three hundred miles from its intended course…a silent graveyard deep beneath the ocean's surface. Cove and her dive team have been granted permission to examine the wreck, film everything, and, if possible, uncover how and why the supposedly unsinkable ship vanished.

But the Arcadia has not yet had its fill of death, and something dark and hungry watches from below. With limited oxygen and the ship slowly closing in around them, Cove and her team will have to fight their way free of the unspeakable horror now desperate to claim them. Because once they're trapped beneath the ocean's waves, there's no going back.

For more info about Sourcebooks's books and authors, visit:
**sourcebooks.com**

# THE FOLCROFT GHOSTS

## EVERY FAMILY HAS ITS SECRETS.

When their mother is hospitalized, Tara and Kyle are sent to stay with their only remaining relatives. Their elderly grandparents seem friendly at first, and the rambling house is full of fun nooks and crannies to explore. But strange things keep happening. Something is being hidden away, kept safely out of sight…and the children can't shake the feeling that it's watching them.

When a violent storm cuts off their only contact with the outside world, Tara and Kyle must find a way to protect themselves from their increasingly erratic grandparents…and from the ghosts that haunt the Folcrofts' house. But can they ever hope to escape the unforgivable secret that has ensnared their family for generations?

# VOICES IN THE SNOW

## NO ONE ESCAPES THE STILLNESS.

Clare remembers the cold. She remembers dark shapes in the snow and a terror she can't explain. And then…nothing. When she wakes in a stranger's home, he tells her she was in an accident. Clare wants to leave, but a vicious snowstorm has blanketed the world in white, and there's nothing she can do but wait.

They should be alone, but Clare's convinced something else is creeping about the surrounding woods, watching. Waiting. Between the claustrophobic storm and the inescapable sense of being hunted, Clare is on edge…and increasingly certain of one thing: her car crash wasn't an accident. Something is waiting for her to step outside the fragile safety of the house… something monstrous, something unfeeling. Something desperately hungry.